WHAT SHE WANTED

Gabe was teasing her—in an old, familiar way that Jonni didn't find offensive. She was conscious of his hands on her waist. She could feel the outline of each finger through the material of her blouse as if he was touching her bare skin. His touch was warm and oddly stimulating. Her forearms were resting on his, her hands feeling the muscled flesh beneath his sleeves.

Jonni's heartbeat didn't draw her hand out of his grasp. She knew she should have. Her heartbeat began to quicken as his gaze slid to her mouth. He was going to kiss her, and she realized that she wanted him to.

from "The Mating Season"

Wearing White

JANET
DAILEY

ZEBRA BOOKS
Kensington Publishing Corp.
www.kensingtonbooks.com

ZEBRA BOOKS are published by

Kensington Publishing Corp.
850 Third Avenue
New York, NY 10022

First Printing: July 2007
10 9 8 7 6 5 4 3 2 1

Printed in the United States of America

CONTENTS

A TRADITION OF PRIDE

Chapter One

Ransom MacQuade paused on the porch of the brick cottage. Overhead, the morning sun was bright in a cloudless sky. A cool northwest breeze rustled through the pines, carrying a chilling January nip to the air. He allowed his corded jacket of wheat tan to swing open, indifferent to the temperature.

His narrowed brown eyes took in the long, straight rows of pecan trees in the rolling field across the road from the cottage. They were wooden skeletons without their summer foliage, stretching in seemingly endless lines.

The firm line of his mouth curved upward at the corners in satisfaction, carving masculine dimples in his lean cheeks. All of this was virtually his. He was in complete charge of the entire operation of Alexander land.

Nothing less would have induced him to leave Texas to move to southern Mississippi. Rans had made that clear to Martin Alexander before he accepted the position. The man had given his word that

Rans would be in total control and Rans welcomed the challenge of it. After nearly two full months, Rans was willing to concede that Martin Alexander was a man of his word.

A quick glance at his watch reminded him of the time. Smooth, effortless strides carried him down the steps to the pickup truck parked next to the cottage. The breeze rumpled the wayward thickness of his tobacco-brown hair. His fingers raked it carelessly into a semblance of order as he climbed into the cab of the forest green and white truck.

It was only a short drive to the main house. Normally Rans would have walked through the stand of pines between his cottage and the Alexander home, but after going over last year's production report in detail with Martin Alexander, he was driving to the cattle barns. It was more practical to leave from the main house.

The Alexander home was an imposing structure, although not the typically palatial Southern plantation. The Spanish influence was evident in its austere design and the liberal usage of lacy grillwork. The grandness of age was understated. Many times Rans had seen it in the early evening hours, the windows ablaze with welcoming light. It was first a home and second a house.

At the front door, Rans let the brass knocker fall three times. He wasn't on such familiar terms with his employer that he felt comfortable walking into his home unannounced. So he waited, a thumb hooked in his belt loop while he absently studied the white enameled door and the flanking windows that ran the length of it, protected by intricate iron scrollwork.

The door opened and his gaze shifted to meet a pair of jet dark eyes on the same level with his own. Considering Rans's height of six foot one, that wasn't something that happened often.

"Good morning, MacQuade." There was a flash of white teeth as the man smiled and opened the door wider. "You must be here to see Martin. Come on in."

"Good morning, Trevor." Rans returned the greeting diffidently as he stepped into the entrance hall. "Martin's expecting me."

"Yes, I know." Trevor Cochran smiled again. "He's on the phone right now. Why don't you go into the living room and make yourself comfortable? He won't be long. Would you like some coffee, tea or anything while you're waiting?"

"No."

"I'll let Martin know you're here." With a condescending nod, the tall, dark-haired man moved off in the direction of the study.

Rans's gaze lingered on the man's back before he turned toward the open double doors to the living room. A muscle twitched briefly along his hard jaw. He knew the cause of his impatience was Trevor Cochran.

When Rans had arrived the last of November to take charge, he had been surprised to discover that Martin Alexander had a young and intelligent son-in-law, Trevor Cochran. He was the husband of Martin's only child, the heir apparent of the vast Alexander holdings. Presumably Martin should have been grooming his son-in-law to take over the reins. Instead he had offered Rans a long-term contract giving him total charge of the farm.

Mentally Rans had braced himself for the hostility he had expected Martin's decision to bring. Yet Trevor Cochran hadn't seemed at all bothered by the turn of events. Although Trevor had an active role in the company and lived with his wife in the same house with his father-in-law, he seemed satisfied that someone else was solely responsible for the operation.

Even while he recognized Trevor's lack of ambition, Rans couldn't understand it. He didn't know how anyone could be a part of an operation this size and not rush out to aggressively meet the challenge of running it smoothly and successfully.

There was another factor to be recognized, too. Despite Trevor Cochran's muscular physique, he didn't have much endurance or backbone. He was neither able nor willing to meet the physical demands of the position. His prowess, Rans decided, was probably limited to the bedroom. Trevor's dark good looks had undoubtedly appealed to Martin's daughter—some women were satisfied with a man who was no more than decorative.

Pushing the draperies of green brocade aside, Rans gazed out the window at the expanse of well-kept lawn shaded by towering pines. Footsteps sounded on the tiled floor of the hallway, followed by a second, lighter pair. He released the draperies and turned expectantly.

"Sally." It was Trevor Cochran's voice, and Rans sighed impatiently at the delay in meeting with Martin Alexander. "Has my wife been down this morning? She wasn't at the breakfast table."

"Lara—Mrs. Cochran," the housekeeper corrected

herself quickly, "had breakfast in her room about an hour ago."

"Oh."

Rans said nothing but he smiled with cynical amusement. He thought separate bedrooms had gone out with hooped skirts. However, it did explain some of the gossip he'd heard on his arrival—that Trevor Cochran spent more time with other women than he did with his wife.

"But she hasn't been down?" Trevor Cochran repeated from the hall. "Are you sure?"

"Were you looking for me, Trevor?" A second female voice drifted into the living room from the large hall. It was very cool and composed, yet soft and faintly husky.

A fiery color caught Rans's eye. Instantly his gaze focused on the large, ornate mirror in the living room. From his angle it reflected the scene in the hallway, showing the lower half of the staircase where Lara Alexander Cochran had paused.

She was strikingly beautiful. There was no other way to describe her. As Rans openly studied her reflection in the mirror, he felt the stirring of his pulse. She was wearing a tweed suit of ocher gold and brown, while revealing a shapely pair of legs.

Despite its practicality, the material of her suit seemed to cling to the curve of her thighs and hips. The molding lines of the jacket suggested the slenderness of her waist and the shape of her rounded breasts, which Rans knew would fill his large hands.

If her disturbingly feminine curves didn't attract a man's attention, then Rans knew the striking combination of shimmering red gold hair and green eyes would. To top it off, Lara Cochran had a face like an angel—a vision of perfection from the delicate wings of her brow to a classically straight nose and a mouth with a sensually full lower lip.

The housekeeper discreetly left the Cochrans alone in the hallway, but Rans felt no such compunction to halt his hidden observation.

"Yes, I was looking for you," Trevor replied to her question. "I knocked at your door, but you didn't answer."

Knocked at her door, huh? Again Ran's mouth twitched in dry amusement. This marriage was taking on the overtones of a Victorian novel.

"I was probably taking a bath and didn't hear you." Lara shrugged eloquently and descended the last few steps. "I was just on my way out. What did you want?"

Her marble features were completely devoid of expression as she tilted her head upward to gaze at her husband's face. Rans's eyes narrowed on her reflection.

The key word was "marble." The smooth, classic beauty of her face seemed to be carved out of that hard, white stone, with any imperfection polished away, leaving a hard veneer devoid of any animation. It was probably the reason Rans appreciated her loveliness without feeling a surge of lust. She was a cold work of art.

"I arranged my schedule at the office so that I could take today off," Trevor was saying, giving his wife a winning smile guaranteed to set a female heart fluttering. Yet Lara Cochran seemed unmoved by his attempt to charm her. "It's been so long since we've had a day to ourselves that I thought we might drive to the Gulf coast."

Glistening copper-colored lips curved into a smile of insincere apology. "I'm on my way to Lumberton, Trevor."

"What's in Lumberton?" His smooth forehead was drawn into a frown.

"Angie Connors," was the composed response. "Her husband flew down to Longleaf to do some quail hunting and she came along."

"Oh, right," he thoughtfully repeated the name. "Angie's the brunette who was matron of honor at our wedding, wasn't she? The two of you went to college together."

"That's right." Lara Cochran turned away as she answered. By her actions, Rans MacQuade guessed that she was looking at herself in the oval hall mirror. "It's been over two years since we've had a chance to get together, and she'll be leaving the day after tomorrow."

Rans watched the long, slender fingers smooth the liquid-fire hair away from her face, although he could not remember ever seeing a strand out of place. And always she wore it pulled back in a coil or a bun to emphasize the classic beauty of her features. He had never seen it falling loose around her shoulders where the breeze could play with it or a man could run his fingers through the red-gold tresses.

"I never did have a chance to get to know her. I'll come along with you," Trevor stated. "It's only right that I become better acquainted with your best friend."

"No." The refusal, was instant yet firm. "You would only be bored, Trevor. Besides, I'm sure Daddy would much prefer that you are at the office today, regardless of whether you can arrange to be away or not."

Trevor's expression darkened. "Lara—" He seemed

about to argue the point, when a hallway door opened and closed out of range of Rans's limited view.

"Trevor, did you say Rans had arrived?"

At the sound of Martin Alexander's voice, Rans glanced away from the mirror, letting his gaze focus indifferently on the blackened hearth of the fireplace.

"He's in the living room. I'll get him," Trevor replied tightly.

"Good morning, Dad." Lara Cochran's warm greeting to her father echoed above Trevor's quiet summons as he paused in the open doorway of the living room. Rans took his time moving toward the hall.

"Good morning, pet." Martin Alexander returned his daughter's greeting with definite affection. "I missed you at breakfast this morning."

"I indulged myself and had it in bed." The laughing words were uttered as Rans stepped into the hall. Yet her green eyes were aloof when they swung to him. "Good morning, Mr. MacQuade."

"Mrs. Cochran." Briefly he inclined his head to acknowledge her greeting before turning to his employer. "Hello, Martin."

"Since you two are obviously heading for the study to talk business"—Lara removed a set of car keys from her brown purse—"I might as well make my exit now. I've already told Sally I won't be home for lunch."

"Take care," her father smiled. "And say hello to Angie for me."

"I'll walk you to the car, honey." Trevor slipped his hand under her elbow.

With almost practiced ease, she slipped free of his touch. "That isn't necessary," Lara answered coolly. "We can say our goodbyes here."

Rans noted the tightening of Trevor's jaw. As if aware of his audience, Trevor smiled automatically and graciously accepted her wish.

"Very well." His dark head bent to kiss her. At the very last second, Lara moved her head slightly so that his mouth brushed the smoothness of her cheek instead of her lips.

"I'll see you at dinner." She smiled at her husband without warmth or emotion and moved to the front door with unaffected grace.

One corner of Rans's mouth lifted sardonically as he turned to follow Martin to the study. His sympathy was directed to Trevor. He had married a cold witch with red hair. Why was it, Rans wondered idly to himself, that the truly beautiful women could be so unattractive in terms of personality? And poor Martin. Imagine having that hollow shell of a woman as a daughter. Perhaps being her father blinded him to all but her exquisite loveliness.

Lara was ten miles south of the farm and Hattiesburg before her inner tension began to ease and she could relax. The highway was a tree-lined avenue of pines. The peaceful scenery released her mind from its self-imprisonment and let it wander.

Sunlight flashed on the diamond solitaire of her wedding ring. A small sigh of relief escaped her lips that Trevor had been unable to force his company on her today—not that he often tried anymore.

Her fingers tightened around the steering wheel as she remembered Trevor's announcement that he was free to spend the day with her, as if she was supposed to be so grateful that she should have fallen to her knees. If the prospect wasn't so revolting, it would have been laughable.

The thought brought back the image of the cynical look that had been in Ransom MacQuade's eyes. Lara knew what he had been thinking—that she was a cold, unfeeling bitch, pampered and spoiled by her father. Men always stuck together and he would be likely to come to that conclusion.

A shiver of apprehension danced down her spine—the same sensation she had experienced the first time she had met MacQuade. Her father had brought him to dinner one evening a day or two after the Texan had taken over the management of Alexander land.

Compared to her husband, Ransom MacQuade was not a handsome man. His features were too boldly chiseled. Yet his virility and vitality made him compellingly attractive, forces equally as potent as Trevor's considerable charm and looks.

His hair was not jet black like Trevor's, but in varying shades of brown, like tobacco. His eyes were the same brown, seemingly lazy in their regard yet never missing anything. Although the same height as Trevor, Ransom MacQuade was the larger of the two. Lara had an idea of just how powerful the muscles beneath his shirt were and knew there wasn't an ounce of spare flesh on him.

After nearly two months, she still hadn't decided what there was about him that she didn't trust, that made her feel so apprehensive whenever he was around. Maybe it was simply because he was a man.

Her father certainly thought highly of him, although her father tended to think highly of most people.

Martin Alexander was a born optimist. Not that Lara questioned Ransom MacQuade's credentials. When her father had requested her opinion of him after their first meeting, she hadn't cast any doubts on his ability nor did she endorse her father's choice. But she had offered her opinion of his personality.

"I think his decisiveness borders on arrogance," she had replied.

That comment got a pretty big laugh from her father. Then he'd launched into MacQuade's qualifications, his extensive breeding experience with Santa Gertrudis cattle, the mainstay of the Alexander farm, coupled with an excellent knowledge of pecan orchards. So in the face of her father's hearty approval, Lara had not voiced any more intuitive comments that warned her against Ransom MacQuade.

The car slowed. Lara glanced around her in surprise. She was on a county road that turned into the lane leading to Longleaf Plantation. She was so lost in thought she hadn't even been aware of where she was. But one part of her mind must have functioning, since she had made all the right turns to get here. With a shake of her head, she tried to banish all her unwanted thoughts and concentrate on seeing Angie again.

Tall pine trees towered over the landscape to shade the vast lawn. The evergreens were of the longleaf variety that had given the private hunting lodge its name. The sun glistened on the mirror-smooth surface of a small lake. A graveled driveway curved lazily through the sylvan setting, ending at the rustic elegance of the rough-hewn cypress buildings of Longleaf.

A full smile spread across Lara's face at the sight

of the petite brunette leaning against the porch railing, dressed in a bulky blue sweater that looked several sizes too large and slim-fitting jeans. At the honk of the car's horn, Angie Connors raced down the steps, waving excitedly and reaching the car as it stopped in front of the main lodge.

Lara was barely out of the car when she was wrapped in an exuberant hug. "Just look at you!" Angie exclaimed, her dark eyes dancing with happiness. "My, but don't you look chic!"

Laughing, Lara brushed away the comment. A tight lump entered her throat as she gazed at her best friend whom she hadn't seen in so long. On the surface, Angie hadn't changed. She had the same bouncy curls, styled to show off her petite femininity and add a spice of impish mischief.

"You haven't changed a bit," Lara sighed, but she couldn't stop herself from wondering if, like herself, Angie had changed on the inside.

"In two years was I supposed to grow fangs?" she teased, then bit into her lower lip. "It's so good to see you again," Angie added in a choked voice filled with emotion. "This is so much better than e-mailing each other. We have so much to catch up on. Tell me about Trevor. How is he?"

Lara turned away, reaching into the car to get her purse. "He's fine," she answered noncommittally.

"Is he still the handsome devil who whisked you off on your honeymoon before the wedding reception had barely begun?" Angie laughed.

"The same." But Lara's answering laugh was decidedly brittle. "And Bob, how's he?"

A puzzled light fleetingly entered Angie's dark eyes

before she was sidetracked by Lara's question. "The mighty hunter is fine. The hunting party should be back any time and you can see for yourself. It's nearly lunchtime and Bob has an alarm clock in his tummy that goes off at breakfast, lunch and dinner time." As if on cue, the first of the hunting jeeps rumbled into sight. "See what I mean?" Angie laughed as she spied her husband in the front seat with the guide.

The straggling arrival of the various hunting parties from different areas of the plantation kept the excitement of the morning's quail hunt running until lunchtime. Angie and Lara, the only two women, listened politely to one after another of the dozen hunters to relate their adventures.

Through lunch, the two friends had exchanged only superficial comments about their lives. The conversation was dominated by the men, not that Lara objected. She kept seeing that radiant glow in Angie's expression every time she looked at her husband. It twisted her heart with a bitter sadness.

Sitting on the black leather sofa in the main lounge, Lara gazed into the flames licking at the logs in the massive fireplace. Her pensive mood separated her from the hunters preparing to leave for the afternoon shoot.

It was a cozy yet spacious room. The unfinished cypress wood in the open-beamed ceiling also paneled the walls. The large, small-paned windows let the outdoors come in. But Lara was indifferent to the room's natural charm.

"Well, Lara, are you going to tell me what happened?"

Angie's voice caught her off guard. She glanced up

in surprise. The room was empty and the hunters were gone. Angie was leaning forward in a large cushioned chair, her expressive face calm and serious.

Lara shook her head. "I don't know what you're talking about." She smiled and tried to look blank.

"Yes, you do," her friend answered patiently. "And I want to know what's happened to change you."

"I haven't changed," Lara protested. There was suddenly nothing for her nervous hands to do and she folded them in her lap.

"Of course not," Angie agreed flippantly. "Which is why you're staring into the fire like it would go out if you didn't keep your eyes on it."

Lara shrugged. "You never know. A spark could burn a hole in the rug or something."

"And you've become defensive. The openness I remember is gone. Each time I ask anything that remotely resembles a personal question, you withdraw. There isn't any other way to describe it. Oh, you answer me," Angie laughed without humor, "but it's always a standard response that tells nothing. I've done all the talking, with my-Bob-this and my-Bob-that. You've barely mentioned Trevor's name. What's wrong?"

Lara stared at her twisting fingers. "It's the classic syndrome in every marriage." Her voice was hard and deliberately uncaring. "Didn't you recognize it? It's commonly known as 'the honeymoon is over.'"

"Nothing is as simple as that." The dark curls bounced in a definite negative shake. "At your wedding, you were happier than I had ever seen you. Something has to have happened to make that change."

Lara wearily rubbed her forehead. A pain had

begun to throb in her temples. "Maybe I was happy then. I don't remember anymore," she sighed. "I was a stupid new bride, lost in a fantasy world of romance complete with a tall, dark and handsome Prince Charming."

"That does describe Trevor . . ." Angie hesitated. "Doesn't he love you?"

"Of course." Lara gave her a wry smile. "I'm Lara Alexander. He also loves Julie, Ann, Connie—speak a girl's name and he loves her. But I'm Lara Alexander so he married me."

"Are you sure? I mean, about the other women?"

"Oh, yes." She took a deep breath, pressing her lips tightly together. She hadn't expected to feel pain about that again, but it wasn't really pain. It was pride. "I am very sure about the other women."

A hand closed over the clasped fingers in Lara's lap. Her green eyes met the look of sympathy in Angie's dark eyes. But Lara's own expression remained blank from long practice.

"How did you find out?" Angie whispered.

"Not quite three months after the wedding, Trevor called the house one afternoon to tell me he was going to be working late on some reports Daddy wanted. Me, in my rose-colored glasses and with grains of rice still in my hair, decided to surprise him. I packed a dinner and wrapped a bottle of champagne in a cooler and went tripping along to the office. I expected to find him poring over papers on his desk. Instead he was on the couch with his blond assistant."

"Lara, I'm sorry." The offer of sympathy was issued tautly. "What did he say? Did he explain?"

"There wasn't a great deal to explain, was there?"

Lara countered dryly. "I left the office immediately and Trevor came rushing home full of explanations. We had an enormous fight. I went around for days silently weeping and wailing and beating my chest trying to figure out what I had done wrong. Then I wanted revenge and I flirted outrageously with any man I met, trying to pay Trevor back and make him jealous."

"Didn't he promise to stop?" Angie frowned.

Lara nodded mutely. "And for a while I believed him." Her impassive green eyes slid to the sad expression on her friend's face. "You would be surprised at the depths you sink to when you stop trusting your husband. I went through his personal papers and found rent receipts for an apartment in Hattiesburg. It was his private little love nest. I couldn't be sure he still used it after his promise, so I followed him one day when he made a trip into town, supposedly to meet an attorney friend. The meeting turned out to be a rendezvous and the attorney had a striking resemblance to the blond assistant Trevor said he would fire."

She leaned her head back on the leather sofa and turned her head from side to side, trying to ease the tension in her neck. Angie looked like she was trying to think of something to say, with no success.

"For all I know the apartment is still in use, although I believe the girl has changed several times. Trevor is always discreet. He has to maintain his respectable standing in the community."

"How did your father react to this? I can't imagine him tolerating this treatment of you." It was Angie's turn to clasp her hands together.

"Angie"—Lara laughed hollowly—"my father is a holdover from Victorian times. One of the first things I did when I learned Trevor was cheating on me was to run to Daddy and cry out my woes. His words of comfort consisted of a lengthy explanation that just because a man steps out on his wife doesn't mean he no longer loves her. He actually said something about how I should be grateful that Trevor didn't expect me to endure all of his manly passion."

"You're kidding." Angie stared at her in open-mouthed disbelief. "Surely when your father saw what it was doing to you, he had more to suggest than grin and bear it."

"His antiquated notion was the old standby that I should have a child." Lara rose to her feet, walked aimlessly to the sliding glass windows and stared through the small panes. "I couldn't bring myself to tell him that Trevor and I hadn't slept together since I had found him with his assistant. The thought of having sex with him made me ill."

A stillness permeated the room. The fire crackled in the hearth while outside the laughing babble could be heard as the waters of Black Creek rushed over the rocks. A rocking chair on the porch overlooking the creek was stirred into movement by the breeze.

"Lara, what are you going to do?" Angie broke the silence at last. "You shouldn't put up with it and your father's word isn't law or anything. Sounds like you ought to file for divorce."

Lara turned away from the peaceful outdoor scene. None of her composure had been the least bit affected by any of the incidents and emotions she had just related. Time had reinforced her armor to the point that it was nearly impenetrable.

"Do you remember meeting my Aunt Beatrice

from Gulfport at the wedding?" Lara asked. At Angie's bewildered nod, she continued. "The morning of the wedding she took me aside, taking my mother's place and giving me all the advice and instruction a bride needs. One of the things she stressed most fervently was the fact that in all the history of the Alexander family, there had never been a divorce. It's a tradition that everyone is very proud of, including my father. In essence, she said that even if love dies, a couple should stay together."

"Family tradition is all very well, but that's carrying it too far!" Angie protested vigorously. "You can't ruin your life because of someone else's outmoded beliefs!"

"I agree." Lara sat up straight again. "But I don't see any point in getting a divorce. True, I'd be rid of Trevor, but in everything but name, I'm rid of him now. He's just a man living under the same roof that I do. I don't love him anymore, nor do I hate him. I simply don't care about him, period."

Angie raised her hands in a helplessly beseeching plea for Lara to reconsider what she was saying. "But . . . you'll meet another man someday and want to marry him and have his children."

"No." Pity flashed in her green eyes, knowing her friend was seeing life through the rose-colored glasses she herself had once worn. "I know I must sound hard and cynical to you, but I don't care to have any man in my life . . . ever."

"You can't mean that," Angie sighed. "It's not natural."

"I've been celibate for nearly two years. It's really not so difficult." Lara glanced at her left hand, watching the play of light on her diamond. "This wedding ring insulates me. If it was off, I would be fair game, and I would just as soon not have any men around. So Trevor can have whatever status and money he feels is a part of the Alexander family—and his girlfriends—and I'll have the solitary life I want."

"Do you expect me to believe that you've stopped feeling, Lara?" Angie asked quietly.

"Feeling toward a man the way you mean? Yes, I have stopped feeling. Marital bliss doesn't last," was her reply.

"Sometimes it does," her friend murmured, her dark eyes rounded with deep sadness.

Lara smiled confidently. "We'll see."

Chapter Two

Lara carefully poured the brandied syrup over the salad of assorted fruits and nuts in the stemmed serving glasses and set the emptied cup in the sink. A pecan pie was cooling on the counter, the flaky golden crust complementing the toast-brown pecan halves.

"As far as I'm concerned, Sally," she smiled, "you can skip the meal and serve the pie. It looks delicious."

"And fattening," was the reply. "Not that you'll ever have to worry."

"Is there anything else I can help you with?" Lara wiped her hands on a towel and glanced around the kitchen.

The housekeeper paused near the oven door. "You can carry the wineglasses into the dining room. They were covered with water spots again. You're going to have to talk to your father about that dishwasher. It's next to worthless if I have to keep redoing everything I put in it."

"I will," Lara promised, picking up the wineglasses. "Anything else?"

"No." Sally opened the oven door and peered in side. "Don't let your father linger over his whiskey. I don't want to overcook this quail."

"All I'll have to do is tell him that you're serving his favorite and he'll probably be at the table before the quail is done." Lara pushed the free-swinging kitchen door open with her elbow, taking care not to knock the crystal glasses in her hand. "I don't know what Dad would do if Henry didn't go hunting every couple of weeks."

"Henry didn't bring us the quail," Sally corrected, her words checking Lara's exit from the kitchen. "He's down with arthritis again."

"I didn't know." She tipped her head curiously to the side and the red-gold coil atop her head shimmered with fire from the overhead light. "Who did give us the quail?"

"Mr. MacQuade."

"Oh," Lara murmured and pushed on through the doorway. As the door swung back, she wondered idly if Ransom MacQuade had known of her father's taste for quail and brought them to edge up higher in his book. She supposed he had. It never hurt to keep scoring points with the boss.

There was a knock at the door as Lara set the wineglasses around the three place settings at the table. From the kitchen, she heard the housekeeper's grumble and smiled inwardly. "I'll answer it, Sally," she called, touching fingertips to her hair, making sure there were no escaping tendrils.

Her heels clicked loudly on the tiled floor of the hallway. Before Lara reached the front door, there was another knock and she wondered who the impatient visitor could be, arriving at the dinner hour. She swung the door open.

The polite smile of greeting froze at the sight of Ransom MacQuade. Her green eyes focused in shock on the bouquet of red roses he held in his hands. She searched his face bewilderedly for an explanation.

"Good evening, Mrs. Cochran." His glittering brown eyes lazily surveyed her from top to bottom. "That's a homey touch," he mocked. "May I come in?"

For an instant, Lara didn't understand his comment until she realized she had not taken off the gingham apron that protected her apricot dress. A hand nervously smoothed the front of it as she swung the door open wider to admit him.

"Of course. Please come in. You can call me Lara, by the way." Her voice was totally composed, offering no sign that she had been flustered even for a second.

"Okay. Call me Rans, then."

She nodded. "You'll have to forgive my appearance. Dinner is nearly ready to be served."

Her gaze slid briefly across his wide shoulders, noting the flawless cut of his nicely-made suit and the cream-colored shirt, opened at the throat.

"I guess my timing is perfect." The suggestion of dimples appeared in his angular cheeks.

The wing of one eyebrow lifted slightly at his comment. Was he inviting himself to dinner, Lara wondered. Remembering the amount of food that had been prepared, she knew it would be straining even Sally's capabilities to stretch the servings to four people. Rather than tell him he couldn't stay, Lara chose to ignore his comment.

The roses were offered to her. "These are for you, I believe," Rans said dryly.

She hesitated for a split second before reluctantly accepting them. "Thanks. Very kind of you, but not necessary." Lara fingered the small card attached to the bouquet. Why on earth was he giving her flowers?

"They aren't from me." Laughter danced behind his hooded look. "A florist delivery man was at the door when I came. He had several other stops to make so he asked me to give them to you."

At the first sensation of warmth touching her cheeks, Lara turned away from his speculative gaze. The trouble with having red hair was that she tended to blush too easily. It had been ages since she had committed an embarrassing blunder like this. It was a novelty to discover she was still capable of blushing.

Curiosity led her to remove the card from its small envelope. The familiar handwriting satisfied Lara before she even read the message. The words were simple: "For my wife. Happy Valentine's Day, honey. Trevor."

Her mouth twitched cynically at the corners. She had so completely blocked out all romantic notions from her mind that when she had glanced at the calendar this morning and noticed the date was February fourteenth, it hadn't meant anything to her. Trevor, inveterate Romeo that he was, would never overlook any romantic occasions.

"From a secret admirer?" Rans's husky voice questioned from behind her.

Lara slipped the card back in its envelope, an indifferently cool smile curving her lips as she turned slightly toward him. Her complexion again was the smooth color of marble.

"A Valentine gift from my husband," she responded. "I hope I didn't embarrass you by thinking the roses were from you."

"Not at all." Rans shrugged, his roving gaze moving over the fiery crown of her coiled hair. "I wouldn't have chosen red roses, anyway. They clash with your hair." His attention shifted to the artistically draped folds that formed the neckline of her dress. "The shade of your dress would have been more suitable."

His observation was so impersonally offered that it was impossible for Lara to take offense at his remark. She had the impression that although Rans MacQuade might find her attractive, he was definitely not interested in her. There was faint arrogance in his dismissal of her as a desirable woman, but Lara experienced only relief at the knowledge.

"But red roses are a symbol of love." Trevor had descended the stairs unseen to pause on the landing before making his presence known. The charcoal-gray suit and matching vest he wore perfectly complemented his dark good looks. He flashed a smile at Lara and traversed the last few steps. "I'm glad they were delivered before I had to leave."

Leave? Lara hadn't been aware that he was going anywhere, but she was disinclined to admit it in front of Rans MacQuade. She touched a delicate red petal.

"The roses are beautiful, Trevor. Thank you." It was spoken without the warmth of sincerity.

Long strides carried Trevor to her side. His hand cupped the flower of the petal she had just touched and his head bent to sniff its fragrance.

"It was the least I could do since the monthly club dinner was scheduled for this evening." He gazed deeply into her cool green eyes. Lara was unmoved by his supposed adoration. If she felt anything, it was amusement that his male ego was still determined to win back her affection. He couldn't seem to stand it when a woman was indifferent to him. "It's my way of saying I'm sorry I can't be with you tonight."

"I understand," Lara nodded.

"I have to leave or I'll be late." Trevor brushed a kiss across her cheek.

"Does Sally know you won't be here for dinner?" Lara inquired as an afterthought.

"I reminded her this morning. I'll probably have a drink with the others when the meeting is over. If I'm late getting home, don't wait up for me," was his parting remark as he moved toward the door.

As if she would, Lara thought. Watching Trevor leave, her gaze accidentally focused on Rans MacQuade's rugged profile, also observing her husband's departure. The knowing gleam in his brown eyes told Lara that he too was guessing that Trevor's drink with the others referred to the female sex and not the male club members. Trevor, she thought cynically, do you really think you are fooling anyone but yourself?

The incident had answered another question that had been forming. The third place setting at the table, Rans MacQuade's unexpected appearance and Sally's previous knowledge that Trevor wouldn't be dining at home this evening—obviously Rans's offering of the quail had elicited an invitation to dinner.

As if feeling her gaze, Rans turned to meet it. The knowing gleam left the velvet brown of his eyes, which held a thoughtful, measuring look, silently trying to judge if Lara had guessed that Trevor's evening would end in some other woman's arms. Pride elevated her chin a fraction of an inch, but her bland expression revealed nothing.

"My father is in his study. You'll have time for a drink before dinner if you'd care to join him," Lara suggested coolly.

"Thank you, I will." He inclined his head slightly.

With the bouquet of roses in her hand, Lara started toward the kitchen to find a vase to put the flowers in. She heard the firm strides that carried Rans MacQuade to the study door.

The few times that Rans had been to dinner before, Trevor had been present. Trevor was an expert at table conversation. His charm and wit always maintained a steady flow of talk among the people seated around the table.

Lara's father, on the other hand, tended to be either garrulous or silent. Unfortunately it turned out to be one of his silent nights, which left Lara with the burden of carrying the conversation. Generally she didn't find it difficult. She simply asked the necessary questions to get a man talking about himself and the problem was solved.

This time she wasn't so successful. Rans MacQuade was not cooperating. He answered her questions without elaborating, as if he sensed her lack of genuine interest in his replies. His reticence was becoming irritating.

"I know much of your time is taken up with your work, but tell me, Rans"—Lara concealed her impatience at playing the role of an interviewer that had been thrust upon her—"how do you spend your free time? Obviously you hunt since you provided tonight's quail. You must have other hobbies you enjoy, too."

"Fishing, swimming, reading, watching TV—the usual pursuits." Before Lara could seize on one of the subjects, his gaze moved over her. "And how do you amuse yourself?"

Lara guessed immediately what he was doing. Rans McQuade was reversing their roles, asking her the questions. The faintly mocking tone of his voice made no attempt to disguise his own lack of interest in her answers.

"The free time I do have, I usually spend horseback riding or reading. Like you, much of my time is taken up with work," she answered with cutting politeness.

"Really?" A dark eyebrow arched with disbelief.

The action scraped at her nerves. "This is a large house," Lara responded in a coldly defensive tone. "It requires constant attention. Sally couldn't begin to cope with all of the housework and the cooking, too."

Wry amusement danced wickedly in his eyes. "I find it difficult to visualize you scrubbing floors, Lara."

The comments were becoming too personal. Ignoring his remark, Lara adeptly changed the focus of attention. She smiled at her father seated at the head of the table, his dark auburn hair salted with gray.

"A good portion of my time is spent deciphering and typing daddy's notes. Now that Trevor has taken over much of the office paperwork and you, Rans, have taken over the management of the farm, Daddy's finally begun to fulfill an ambition that he's had for years. I don't know if you are aware of it or not, but daddy is writing a definitive book on growing pecans."

"I'm trying, pet, I'm trying," her father corrected modestly. "I believe I mentioned it to you, didn't I, Rans?"

"You said you were doing some writing, but you didn't indicate the subject matter."

"I decided some years ago that it was time there was a book on the market that dealt with all facets of the pecan industry. There's not all that much available online, and besides, I'm old-fashioned. I don't want to put what I know on a website, I want to write a book." Lara could see her father warming to his favorite subject and leaned back in her chair. "A thoroughly researched book that will deal with grafting and planting, diseases, methods of disease controls, harvesting, marketing and the advantages and disadvantages of the known varieties—most of it from the research and knowledge I have obtained over the years."

"That's a challenging and demanding project," Rans observed.

"I'm trying to do one phase at a time," Martin Alexander explained earnestly. "Right now I'm accumulating information on the various varieties. You're more familiar with the Texas varieties. Perhaps you could give me some assistance on them."

"I'd be happy to."

A catlike smile of contentment came to Lara's mouth. Within moments the conversation consisted of an in-depth discussion on the various merits of different varieties over others. Information and opinions were freely exchanged throughout the rest of the meal.

Once Lara accidentally encountered Rans's gaze. The knowing gleam in his eyes told her that he was aware she had directed the conversation to safer channels. It was disconcerting to learn that he had seen through her so easily.

Coffee was served with the dessert. When they had finished, Lara rose from her chair, knowing if it was up to her father, the two men would linger indefinitely at the table.

"Daddy, why don't you take Mr. MacQuade into your study and offer him brandy?" she suggested.

"Excellent idea," her father agreed enthusiastically. "Will you join us, Lara?"

"No, thank you." A polite but firm smile of refusal on her lips. "I'll help Sally clear the table."

When the dishes were finished, Lara avoided the study, choosing the solitude of the living room. She wasn't really expected to join her father. He really was incredibly old-fashioned and he thought women should gather in one area to talk and leave the men to their important discussions. It was a decidedly archaic notion that women were incapable of intelligent conversation, but for the most part, Lara didn't care. She had reverted to the childhood practice of entertaining herself.

With a crossword puzzle in hand, she switched the television set on. The movie being televised was a sugary romance. Lara watched half of it before impatiently turning it off. She couldn't accept, even as fiction, a love story where bells rang and rockets soared and the couple supposedly lived happily ever after. Her experience had made her too much of a cynic. The mystery novel in her bedroom offered more enjoyable entertainment.

As she entered the hallway, a door opened and closed in the direction of her father's study. Lara glanced over her shoulder and paused politely at the sight of Rans MacQuade.

"Are you leaving?" She watched the tall, muscular frame approaching. A shiver of apprehension danced along her arms.

"Yes, I don't want to overstay my welcome," he answered in a low, courteous voice.

"I know how much Father enjoyed discussing his book with you, so I'm sure you couldn't do that," Lara murmured with cool good manners.

His brown gaze flicked from her to the staircase, her obvious destination. "Are you calling it a night?"

"I was going to my room to read for a while." She stifffened, uncertain why he had asked. A smile played at the edges of his mouth as if he was amused by the No Trespassing sign he saw in her green eyes.

"Then I'm glad to have this opportunity to thank you for an excellent dinner," Rans offered.

"We should thank you for the quail." This polite conversation was beginning to grate on Lara's nerves. She wished he would say goodnight and leave.

"Would it be possible for me to leave through the courtyard?" He glanced over his broad shoulder at the exit door on the opposite end of the hallway. "It's a closer walk to my cottage from there."

"You walked here?" A delicately arched brow lifted slightly. It was nearly a mile from the main house to the cottage through the pine woods.

"Yes." The wicked light in his eyes held a flash of pride. "I enjoy the fresh air and exercise."

Lara chose not to comment further, but it was rare in this era of SUVs and gigantic personal trucks for anyone to walk even a short distance. Instead she turned away.

"The gate is locked. I'll get the key," Lara said.

"I don't mean to inconvenience you."

"It's no trouble," she assured him coolly.

The hall closet was concealed beneath the staircase. Pushing the latch hidden in the panel, Lara opened the door and reached for the ring of keys hanging in a far corner.

After a second's hesitation, she removed a tightly woven, black wool shawl from its hook. The night air would be cool even in February. She turned as she draped the shawl over the shimmering red gold of her hair and around her shoulders, encountering the bemused look on Rans MacQuade's chiseled face.

The tilt of her head was defiantly regal, the keys jangling in her hand. "Is something wrong, Rans?" Ice chilled her voice.

"Seeing you like that reminds me of the chatelaine of a castle." He seemed to lazily draw himself up another inch taller and half-turn toward the opposite end of the hallway. "Shall we go?"

With an unconscious sweep of her skirt, Lara preceded him down the hallway to the far door leading into the miniature courtyard. The Spanish-style house was built in the shape of a blunted U, forming a small courtyard enclosed on three sides by the house. The fourth side was a towering brick wall to ensure privacy. The only access, except through the house, was a sturdy wrought-iron gate in an arched opening of the wall. It was kept locked at all times.

The front lawn of the house was bare of any flowering shrubbery or landscaped foliage. Loblolly and longleaf pine trees shaded the green grass, punctuated by two wild magnolias. The courtyard, however, was rampant with leafy foliage that soon would be bursting into bloom. It was a cool and colorful retreat when the summer sun blazed overhead.

At night, without the benefit of light from the courtyard lanterns, it was a dark, shadowy place. The pale moonlight illuminated only the small, circular fountain in the center. Lara disliked the aura of intimacy the night created by seemingly shutting off the rest of the world. Alone she enjoyed the quiet solitude, but not with Rans MacQuade at her side.

"You have a very beautiful home, Mrs. Cochran," he observed, slowing his step to gaze about him.

"Thank you." Lara was forced by politeness to check her desire to hurry him on his way and slow her stride to his strolling pace.

"It isn't often that a girl marries and doesn't have to leave home."

Warily she glanced at him. Had she detected an edgy undertone in his comment? The shadows concealed his expression and she couldn't be sure.

"As large as the house is, neither Trevor nor I thought it was practical to set up another residence," Lara found herself defending their decision. "And Daddy didn't look forward to rambling around the house alone."

"I wouldn't have thought a newly married couple would consider things in the terms of practicality."

Although she couldn't see his face, she could feel his speculative gaze studying her. It was an uncomfortable sensation, like being under a microscope.

"I think you're mistaken, Rans. Every married couple has to find a place to live. Our choice was here."

They were near the center fountain. Moonlight streamed down, touching her creamy white complexion with its silvery glow. The black shawl framed her oval face in a medieval fashion, highlighting her delicate bone structure and the royal carriage of her head.

"I know your father is happy with the choice." His tone became impersonal, losing its inquisitive note. "When I first came here, I was curious why a man as young and fit as your father would need a manager for the farm. He's entirely capable of running it himself. Now that I've learned about his plans for a book, I understand why he doesn't want to. But don't you find it boring?"

"Even if I did, that's neither here nor there."

Rans nodded. "Okay. I guess you're content with being a housewife, keeping the home fires burning for your husband."

Her frosty green gaze moved to his face in time to catch his mocking look. If he had meant the remark as a joke, she didn't think it was funny.

"My life is fulfilling," was the only reply Lara gave. She knew their dislike of each other was mutual.

The black grillwork of the gate was in front of them. Lara paused while inserting the key into the padlock. It turned grudgingly, then finally clicked. Loosely grasping one of the iron bars, she started to swing the gate open. It unexpectedly didn't budge and her hand slipped free of the bar as her impetus carried her a stumbling step backward.

A pair of large hands closed around her waist to steady Lara for the instant necessary to regain her balance. Then the firm support was removed and Rans MacQuade stepped around her. There was a protesting screech of the hinges before the gate could be pulled open by him.

"It needs oiling," he said, swinging it experimentally a few times. "I'll send someone up in the morning to see to it."

"Thank you." Lara accepted his offer with cool indifference.

He stepped through the gateway, closing it behind him. "Good night, Mrs. Cochran."

"Good night."

While she snapped the lock securely closed, Lara watched the long, lazy strides that carried him into the cobwebby shadows of the pine trees. She paused, trying to analyze that moment when his large hands had nearly spanned her slender waist. She could still feel their warm imprint. His steadying touch had been automatic and impersonal.

Her own reaction had been just as bland. She had felt nothing then, and now there was only the lingering impression of his grip. An absent smile quirked the corners of her mouth as Lara turned away from the gate.

She must remember to mention the incident in her next letter to Angie. After their visit nearly a month ago, this provided proof of her assertion that she was indifferent to a man's touch. The warmth of his hands had neither aroused her nor repulsed her. Angie had not been convinced of Lara's indifference to a man's attention. Lara's reaction—or rather, non-reaction—to Rans should help change her thinking.

A breeze whispered through the pines, dancing into the courtyard to tease at the shawl around her head. Lara clutched the shawl tighter around her throat and hurried toward the house before the night's chill penetrated her slight covering.

Chapter Three

The blaze-faced bay snorted and tossed his head, sidestepping spiritedly amid the straight rows of pecan trees. The barren branches almost formed an arch above the horse and rider. Green, thick grass muffled the horse's high-stepping strides.

Lara soothingly stroked the silken curve of his neck before lifting the hand to her hair. The gallop had loosened a few red-gold tendrils from the French braid. She tucked them back in place.

"Nothing like a gallop to chase away the tensions, is there, Pasha?" She laughed throatily in satisfaction as she patted the hunter's neck again. "And the weather is perfect. It feels like spring is here already, and it's only the end of February."

The sky was a brilliant blue with not a cloud or jet trail in sight. The temperature, too, was that of a balmy spring morning. The ribbed knit of her black turtleneck sweater was ample coverage, even here where it was cooler. The horse had carried Lara deep into the pecan orchard.

Reining the horse at a right angle, she turned him toward the distant fence and the connecting gate to the next field. Her gaze studied the outstretched branches. Although the dogwood trees growing wild in the pines had begun to show signs of budding, the pecan trees remained dormant. They generally waited until around the first official day of spring to begin budding. Yet always it was an event for Lara when the first shoot was seen.

As she neared the adjoining field, the decreasing rows of trees enabled her to catch a glimpse of the fence. A telltale patch of brown black contrasted with the green rye grass in this orchard, pasture land for the cattle, until the autumn harvest when the nuts began falling from the trees. The furrows of brown in the next field answered the question that Lara had been wondering about since she had started out.

Touching the riding crop to the hunter's flanks, she urged him into a rocking canter. Plowing had started in the next orchard to prepare the field for the hay crop to be planted. All the orchards served dual purposes, first to grow pecans, and second as grazing land or cropland.

Where there were freshly furrowed rows of dirt on Alexander land, Cato could not be far away. With a quick smile, Lara corrected the silent thought—Cato and his mules couldn't be far away. It was one of the traditions that hadn't been cast aside. No matter how many tractors and modern farm machinery there were in the sheds, the plowing was always done by Cato and his mules.

As a child Lara had not questioned the custom, spending many hours tagging along beside the tall, spare man as he walked behind his mules, always talking to them as if they could understand every word he said. Officially the mules were Alexander property. Unofficially they belonged to Cato. For sixty-seven of his eighty-two years, he had taken care of the mules and walked behind them as they plowed the fields.

Despite his advanced years, his body wasn't encumbered by age. He could still walk as long and as far as he had when he was thirty. With a smile, Lara remembered that last fall Cato had planted a strawberry bed for his ninety-eight-year old mother, grumbling that the cranky old hen would probably live to see it bear fruit.

Not until Lara was sixteen did she question the wisdom of letting Cato plow the fields when tractors would be so much faster. The occasion had been brought about by the discovery that the seemingly ageless man was in fact seventy-four. She had argued with her father that surely something else could be found for Cato to do. To this day, she could vividly recall her father's response.

"Cato doesn't know anything else, pet," her father had explained patiently. "His mules are his life, and his work is his pride. After the loyalty he has shown us, surely we can return it by letting him keep his job for as long as he's capable of holding it."

"But he's worked all these years. Why don't you give him a pension and let him retire? He's certainly earned that right, too," Lara had pointed out.

"To take away Cato's mules and his pride?" He had shaken his head. "I might as well give him a gun to shoot himself with, because he wouldn't have anything else to live for."

The white boards of the fence gate appeared in front of Lara. Without dismounting, she unlatched the gate and rode through, closing it behind her. The bay's hooves ground deeply into the freshly turned soil.

A frown creased Lara's forehead. It was not the jangle of harness she heard on the other side of the knoll, but the steady hum of a tractor motor. She couldn't believe it, and turned the bay hunter down one of the straight furrows; urging him into a slow canter with a click of her tongue and a touch of the riding crop.

As she crested the small ridge, there was the tractor and plow moving steadily through the row of trees. She recognized the driver and called, meaning to find out why Cato wasn't there, but he couldn't hear her over the din of the motor.

The uneven ground made the going too difficult for the bay and Lara reined him over to the unplowed section. When they had passed the tractor, she cut across, halting the horse directly in its path and forcing the tractor to stop. The bay didn't like the noisy machine and tossed its head in vigorous protest when Lara guided him alongside of it.

"Where's Cato?" she shouted to the driver.

The man cupped a hand to his ear, a curious frown on his face as his mouth formed the word "What?" Her mouth thinned into an exasperated line. Quickly she signaled to John Porter to cut the engine. It sputtered and died, the cessation of noise intensifying the peaceful silence of the orchard.

He smiled at her. "What's the trouble, Miss Lara?"

"Where's Cato, John?" Lara repeated her earlier question. "Why are you doing the plowing instead of him?"

"MacQuade's orders." The man shrugged, turning his head away from her to spit out his chaw of tobacco.

"Didn't you explain to him that Cato has always done the plowing here?"

"I tried." The dubious shake of the man's head indicated it hadn't made much difference. "But he didn't seem to care how things were done before he came."

Temper flared and Lara controlled it with effort. "Then I'll explain it to him," she said determinedly. "In the meantime, John, you can drive the tractor back to the sheds. Cato will be doing the plowing here."

A look of uncertainty flashed across the man's face. "MacQuade told me to plow the field," he argued hesitantly. "Your father made it real clear when MacQuade took over that he was the boss and none of us would be expected to take orders from anyone else, not even your father. It could mean my job, and my wife's going to have a baby in a couple of months. I can't risk MacQuade using me as an example to the others that he's in charge. You understand, don't you?"

"Yes." The admission was clipped out with irritation while her mind raced to find an alternate solution to achieve the same ends. "Give me the ignition key, John." She breathed in deeply. "Tell MacQuade that I stopped you and took the key. He would hardly expect you to fight with the boss's daughter to try to get it back. This way he'll see that I'm solely responsible and not blame you."

"Well," he murmured uneasily, "if you think it will work."

Lara dismounted as John Porter removed the key from the ignition and swung down from the tractor. Reluctantly he handed it to her.

"MacQuade isn't going to be happy about this." He shook his head. "You know that?"

"I can handle Ransom MacQuade," Lara asserted confidently.

There was an upward flick of his eyebrows as if John Porter wasn't too sure that Lara knew what she was talking about. He glanced at the tractor and plow.

"I suppose I oughta start back," he sighed.

"I'll walk with you." Lara fell into step beside him, leading the horse by the reins. "I might as well find MacQuade and get this mess straightened out about Cato."

The man offered no encouraging comment as they followed the brown-red furrows toward the road fence. Reaching into his shirt pocket, he took out a pouch of chewing tobacco, put a pinch between his cheek and gum, then returned the pouch to his pocket.

"Would he be at the sheds?" Her inquiry broke the uneasy silence.

"At the sheds or checking one of the fields. They're plantin' some new seedlings in that acreage that was cleared last winter. He might be there."

Lara pressed her lips tightly together. Just thinking how carelessly Rans MacQuade had cast aside one of the valued traditions of Alexander land made her blood run hot. She cautioned herself to deal with confrontation coolly and calmly, but it was going to be difficult not to allow her personal dislike of the man to get in the way. Of course, he wasn't the type to take kindly to being ordered around by a woman. To be successful she would have to be diplomatic.

They were nearly at the fence when a pickup truck rolled into view on the graveled road, a cloud of dust following it. The pickup slowed, tires crunching on the gravel, and turned into the orchard entrance, stopping short of the gate.

John Porter darted Lara a grim look. "You aren't going to have to go looking for MacQuade."

Mentally Lara braced herself for the meeting, wishing she had been allowed a little more time to formulate what she was going to say. The truck door on the driver's side was opened, then slammed shut. Sunlight glinted on the golden highlights of Rans MacQuade's brown hair as he walked around the cab through the gate.

His gaze flicked briefly to Lara then centered on John Porter. "Did the tractor break down?"

In the outdoors he seemed taller and leaner and more rugged-looking than Lara had remembered him being the few times she had seen him at the house. He was definitely a man that the workers would look up to with decided respect. She understood why John Porter was reluctant to deliberately disobey him—which didn't alter her decision at all.

"Not exactly." John Porter shuffled nervously as he tried to answer the question put to him. He paused and spat a stream of yellow tobacco juice onto the plowed ground. "You see . . ."

He glanced expectantly at Lara. The action brought a thoughtful narrowing of Rans MacQuade's brown eyes, but they didn't waver from the man's face.

Lara came to John's rescue. "I believe there's been a misunderstanding, Rans." At that point she was pinned by the hard, piercing gaze. Her fingers closed tightly around the tractor keys. "I think I understand how it happened. You haven't been here long enough to be familiar with all of the ways we do things."

"Does this have something to do with the man Cato and his mules?" Rans inquired in an ominously low voice.

"Yes." A stiff smile curved her mouth. "It's a tradition that he always plows Alexander ground. My father has stated many times that it's one that will continue for as long as Cato lives. To deprive him of his job would be the same thing as taking away his dignity and self-respect. Hardly the way to reward him after all his years of loyal service."

Rans MacQuade breathed in deeply and glanced away, irritation in the compressed line of his mouth. "Where's the tractor?" The question was addressed to Porter.

"About a third of the way down this row." The man gestured over his shoulder.

"I want you to go back to the tractor and—" Rans began.

"I don't have the key," John interrupted and quickly avoided the sharp gaze that was directed at him.

"John was reluctant to stop plowing since you had ordered him to do it," Lara explained evenly. "So I took the ignition key away from him."

His jaw tightened as Rans MacQuade turned back to study her coldly. "May I have the key, Mrs. Cochran?"

There was a flash of triumph in her green eyes. Lara concealed it with a sweep of her gold-tipped lashes. She hadn't expected him to give in so quickly. Admittedly, emphasizing tradition and her father's wish to honor this particular one had probably resulted in her success. She extended the hand with the tractor key to him.

"I knew once it was explained to you, you would understand," she offered graciously.

Her comment brought a sardonic twist to the set line of his mouth. He took the keys and turned to John, holding them out to him.

"Here," Rans said shortly. "Enough time's been wasted. Get back on that tractor and get this orchard plowed."

Like Lara, John stared at him in stunned disbelief. With a surge of white-hot anger, Lara realized her explanation had meant nothing. She had been a fool to think she could reason with anyone as arrogantly confident as Ransom MacQuade. She had let herself be tricked into returning the key.

The riding crop hung from a strap around her wrist. During the instant when John was too surprised to reach for the keys, her fingers closed around the leather whip. Driven by her flaming temper, Lara struck out with the short whip, lashing it across the back of the outstretched hand that held the keys.

Immediately they dropped from his fingers, falling onto the plowed sod. A hissing curse accompanied the abrupt spin by Rans in her direction, the chiseled features harsh with anger, Lara's breath was coming in uneven spurts, but her expression was completely composed, with a barely challenging lift of her chin.

The air crackled with high-voltage tension. Her gaze slid to the angry red welt across the back of his hand, the fingers doubled to form a fist. She was aware of John glancing hesitantly from one to the other.

Rans had not forgotten his presence, either. "I left the keys in the truck, John." The smoldering glare of his eyes didn't leave Lara's face. "Drive it back to the sheds and report to Clive."

Lara didn't make the mistake of interpreting his order as an admission that he was going to allow Cato to plow the fields. Rans was getting rid of John so he wouldn't witness the argument that was to come. Lara had no doubt that his self-control would disappear when John left. Burning anger raged through her veins. She was in no way intimidated by him.

John spat again on the ground, glancing at her out of the corner of his eyes. He was torn between two loyalties. He had known Lara for years and was reluctant to leave her alone with Rans MacQuade. At the same time, he didn't want to risk losing his job since the welfare of his growing family depended on the money he brought home.

With an almost imperceptible nod of her head, Lara indicated that John should go. She was capable of fighting her own battles, even with an opponent as formidable as Rans MacQuade. Rans caught the exchange and his expression darkened as John walked toward the pickup truck parked at the gate.

The bay horse snorted nervously. Reacting to the turbulent tension in the air, he tossed his head and tugged at the reins in Lara's hand. The heavy silence continued until the pickup truck door was opened and shut and the motor growled. Lara didn't give Rans an opportunity to take the initiative.

"I don't believe you heard me correctly, MacQuade.

Cato always does whatever plowing needs to be done on Alexander land. It is a longstanding tradition that not even you are going to stop."

"Let's get this straight, Mrs. Cochran." His cold voice would have made an icicle shiver. "I am the one in charge now. It makes no difference to me what your father thinks should be done in this case. I have no intention of wasting precious time while an eighty-two-year-old man strolls up and down a field behind some overweight mules. My concern is getting the land ready for planting in the fastest and most efficient way possible."

"Efficiency isn't everything!" she flared. "Look around you. Time means something different here. The land, the trees, the animals—this place is a lot like it was a hundred years ago and we like to keep it that way. We take care of our people, Rand. The efficient use of time is meaningless if it means sacrificing the principles of human dignity." Green fires flashed in her eyes as she paused to catch her breath. "And you obviously have never spent any time with Cato to dismiss him so contemptuously. I assure you he doesn't stroll. That man works harder than just about anybody. His mules are always kept in condition. That's not fat but muscles you see."

"It doesn't change anything. My decision stands," Rans stated with unrelenting hardness.

A finely drawn brow arched upward. "It will stand only until my father hears about it," Lara declared haughtily. "And once the rest of the hands discover that the Alexander family doesn't support you in this, you'll have difficulty finding anyone to do the plowing. We have always taken great pride in the loyalty of the people who work for us."

"I wouldn't be too sure about your father, if I were you." A self-satisfied glint appeared in his narrowed eyes. "I already discussed the matter with him and he left the final decision to me."

"That's a lie!" she gasped in sudden, trembling outrage. "My father would never condone this! He would never betray Cato's trust!"

One corner of his mouth quirked. "It's not betrayal," Rans said. "The man will receive a good pension. He'll be set for the rest of his life."

"Is that all?" Lara asked sarcastically. "Don't you want to throw in a gold watch, too?" A muscle twitched along Rans's jaw as his lips thinned into a straight line. "Have you told Cato of your decision, or do you intend to let the grapevine inform him that he's out of a job because he's too old?"

"I haven't had the opportunity," he replied coldly.

"Oh, you've been busy, I'm sure," she responded. "Too busy to do the dirty work. Let Cato think my father is to blame. What does it matter to you?"

"I have been busy. Some fool forgot to latch one of the bullpen gates and two of our prize bulls got into a fight. I'm still not sure we aren't going to lose one of them. Plus one of the cows died giving birth to a calf, and I've spent the last three nights trying to keep the calf alive. Since the decision was mine, I chose not to delegate the responsibility of informing Cato to anyone else. When I do talk to him, I'll make it clear that the decision was mine."

The bay pranced nervously behind Lara, who was now trembling with the fierceness of her anger. "I am going to fight you on this, Rans MacQuade. I don't accept that your decision is the final one. You'll regret it if you try to carry it out. No one who works here is going to approve of what you're doing. Believe me, I won't be fighting you alone."

He looked at her levelly and when he spoke, his voice was calm. But what he said was infuriating. "Mrs. Cochran, you can rant and rave and throw all the temper tantrums you want, but if you ever try to usurp my authority with the workers, you'll find that you have tackled more than you can handle!" The fire glittering in his eyes warned that it was not an idle threat.

"I doubt that," Lara jeered.

"Do you?" A thick eyebrow arched arrogantly. "Pick up the tractor keys and hand them to me."

It was undeniably an order. Mutinously Lara stood her ground, her red-gold head thrown back in open defiance, daring him to try to make her, Martin Alexander's daughter, obey.

"I said pick up the keys," he snapped.

His fingers wrapped around her wrist, jerking her forward. The bay reared, pulling the reins free from the same hand he held. Lara's reaction was instinctive. The riding whip arced toward that arrogant face.

The whip didn't reach its target, checked in midswing as he seized her other wrist. Brown eyes glinted with mockery at her futile attempt. Rigidly Lara stood in front of him, moving her wrists only slightly to test the firmness of his hold while she smoldered with rage.

"Let me go!" she hissed.

A hard smile broke the strong line of his mouth, his grip tightening. "So you can use that riding crop? Not a chance." Harsh laughter sounded in his throat. "If anyone uses it, I will . . . on your backside. Something your father should have done years ago."

Lara tossed her head back, green eyes glinting with confident challenge. "You wouldn't dare."

The strength of his grip was slightly increased, his fingers pressing into the delicate bones of her wrist, forcing Lara to lean forward.

"Wouldn't I?" Rans murmured softly.

In that split second, Lara realized that there was very little this arrogant, dominating man wouldn't dare. And she just might have goaded him into proving it. There was no way she was going to suffer that kind of humiliation at his hands.

With a quick downward twist of her wrists, she tried to surprise him and pull free, without success, but that was only the beginning of the struggle. Kicking and twisting and clawing the air around his face even as he held on to her wrists, Lara fought to get loose. He seemed amused by her vigorous efforts.

Two of the pins fell out of her hair. Tousled waves of shimmering red gold brushed her cheek, half down and half up. Her heart was racing madly, the exertion of her struggles coloring her cheeks. Green eyes blazed with the light of battle, refusing to submit to superior strength.

Lara stiffened her arms, straining her wrists against the overlapping of fingers and thumbs. With a quick twist, Rans curved them behind her back, imprisoning her against the solid wall of his chest.

Her hips were right against the hard muscle of his thighs. Breathing heavily, her energy nearly spent, Lara kicked weakly at his shins with the toes of her riding boots. After a serics of harmless, glancing blows, a toe found its target, drawing a stifled curse near her ear.

Rans controlled himself otherwise but he managed to arch her more firmly against him. "Aren't you the hellcat," he muttered savagely.

He had that right. Reacting to the unwanted closeness, Lara jerked her head back and up. Her parted lips accidentally came in contact with his mouth. Instantly she became totally incapable of any movement. The scent of him enveloped her in an invisible, musky cloud. She was suddenly conscious of his shirt buttons biting into her breasts.

The same stillness gripped Rans. Neither moved. No longer blinded by her temper, Lara couldn't ignore her vulnerability to a male assault. Frightened, her rounded eyes gazed helplessly into the brown depths of his, veiled by thick, spiky lashes. Her pulse quickened, drumming loudly in her ears. His attention seemed to be focused on the flaming disarray of her hair, then his gaze moved with unnerving slowness to look into her eyes.

For ticking seconds they were locked together, lips touching without kissing. There was no one to hear her if she screamed. She was at his mercy and Lara doubted if he possessed any. But she wouldn't beg for it, not from him or any man.

When the intensity of their contact reached a fever pitch, his grip shifted on her wrists, releasing one as he spun her away with the other. Before Lara could draw a shaky breath of relief, pressure was applied to the still captured wrist, bending her down toward the ground.

"Pick up the key," Rans growled thickly.

She had completely forgotten the cause of the argument only moments before and stared at the ground blankly. The plowed earth bore imprints of their scuffle and the key was nowhere to be seen.

"I can't see it." Her voice trembled with emotion.

Rans pushed Lara to her knees, then joined her, raking the dirt with his fingers and uncovering the key. He picked it up himself and pulled her to her feet, his eyes glittering with a dark light. Reluctant curiosity flickered across her face as she wondered why he hadn't made her pick up the key.

"I couldn't have the chatelaine of the castle getting dirt beneath her fingernails, could I?" His mouth crooked as he answered her unspoken question. There was no change in his expression when he let go of her wrist. "Unless you want to walk home, I suggest you go catch your horse."

Lara glared at him, massaging her numbed wrist and hand. He glared right back, then strode away, down the swath of turned soil in the direction of the tractor.

Tears burned the back of her eyes and she blinked furiously to check the impulse to cry. With the back of her hand she rubbed her mouth, trying to rid her lips of the warm sensation of the nearness of his. It didn't work. They still trembled achingly in remembrance, as did the rest of her flesh where his body had been imprinted on it.

Wrenching her gaze away from the sight of his powerful body, Lara searched the orchard for the bay hunter. She glimpsed a flash of a dark, sleek coat through the branches of the trees some distance away.

The horse appeared to be grazing, his impulse to escape checked by the temptation of green grass.

Tapping the riding crop against her tan breeches, Lara forced her legs to carry her to the horse. Luckily Pasha was easy to catch. The sound of the tractor motor reminded Lara of Cato and she was filled with new purpose.

Once she caught the hunter, she would take the shortcut home through the tangled growth of pines. She was going to corner her father about his supposed endorsement of Rans MacQuade's plan to pension off Cato. She hadn't given up the fight by any means.

CHAPTER FOUR

When Lara arrived at the house, it was to discover that her father wasn't home. Two or three mornings a week, depending on the workload, her father went into the office. This turned out to be one of those mornings. Sally informed her that he would be back for lunch, but Lara didn't want to wait that long before talking to him.

Her attempt to contact him at the office was thwarted by the receptionist's announcement that he had taken a prospective buyer to look over the young bulls that were for sale. Lara restlessly prowled the house, pouncing on Martin Alexander the instant he walked through the door shortly before noon.

"Well, hello, pet," he greeted her in mild, but pleased surprise when she met him at the door.

Lara dispensed with the formality of a greeting and went straight to the point. "Is it true you told MacQuade he could pension off Cato?"

Her father paused, taken aback by the fire in the eyes of his usually calm and composed daughter. "I wouldn't put it quite that way," he frowned. "Rans discussed the possibility with me about a month ago. I made it clear that my wish was to keep him, but the decision ultimately rested with him since he is in charge."

"He chose not to consider your wishes," Lara retorted acidly. "As of this morning, Cato was forcibly retired."

"You must be mistaken." Confusion drew his sandy brows together.

"I'm not. MacQuade told me himself. Daddy—"

"But that's impossible," he interrupted. "I drove by the Desirable orchard not ten minutes ago and Cato was plowing with his mules."

"You must have been seeing things."

"Then I was hearing things, too," Martin Alexander chuckled softly, "because I stopped to ask how his mother was. He said she was just fine and that he would be stopping by in a day or two to drop off a couple of jars of his mother's fig preserves. There was no mention of retirement. You must have misunderstood Rans."

Stunned, Lara could say nothing. She knew positively that she hadn't misunderstood Rans. He had been very definite that Cato was through. She stared at her father, bewildered by his statement. "I don't believe you," she murmured.

"Go see for yourself," he shrugged. "I imagine he's having lunch under one of the trees."

"I will," she stated flatly, opening the front door he had just closed.

"Hey, what about your lunch?"

"Tell Sally I'll have something cold when I get back," Lara replied as she closed the door.

The garage, housing her blue Mustang, was at the back of the house near the stable. Lara hurriedly followed the brick sidewalk around to the rear. Within minutes she was speeding out of the house lane behind the wheel of her car.

When she arrived at the orchard, there was definite evidence that more ground had been plowed. No sound of a motorized vehicle could be heard, which meant nothing at lunch hour. Parking the car in the orchard turn-in, Lara climbed quickly out and pushed open the gate.

Following the most recent swath of plowed soil, she walked swiftly down the row of trees, her gaze scanning the area ahead of her. She spied the mules first, standing together beneath a tree. Cato's spare frame was seated beside them, leaning against the trunk. His keen eyes saw her immediately and he lifted a weathered hand in greeting.

"Hello, Lara." He waited to continue until she was closer. "It's been a long time since you've come to walk beside old Cato." He clicked his tongue reprovingly. "Now where's your hat? You know your skin turns as red as your hair if you get too much sun."

His words evoked fond memories that brought a smile to her lips. He had told her that time and time again—it was a running, but friendly, argument between them. Lara knelt beside him, curling her legs beneath her to sit cross-legged as she had done so many times before.

"Actually, I didn't come to walk with you." She didn't know how she was going to explain why she came.

"Well, then, something's troubling you. I can tell."

Cato nodded sagely. "Your eyes always turn that dark shade of green, like the pines on a cloudy day."

"I never could fool you, could I?" Lara smiled wistfully, then glanced at the grass, plucking a blade and twirling it in her fingers. "Cato"—she hesitated—"did Mr. MacQuade, the new man daddy hired to run the farm—did he stop to see you this morning?"

"Hee, hee, hee!" A high-pitched chuckle rolled from a snaggle-toothed grin. "So that's it. Yep, he stopped to see old Cato."

"And?" Lara prompted as the old man shook his head as if remembering the meeting, the grin still splitting his weathered face.

"I was chopping logs, when he came, for my firewood customers," he said. "I knew why he'd come, a new man and all. He was going to tell Cato he was too old to work any more."

Lara flinched at the perceptive words. "I'm sorry, Cato."

"Don't you be sorry for me," he scolded sharply. "I've lived long and hard and seen me some good times and I don't mind growing old. Not that there's a damned thing I could do about it if I did mind." The gentle smile returned, the one of a man who knows inner peace. "Well, as I was saying I knew why he'd come, but I didn't want to hear the words, not right off. So I told him I couldn't talk until I finished the chopping. He took a look at the big pile of logs I had laying there and said he'd give me a hand."

Lara remembered Cato's woodpile. It always seemed to be about the same size, but maybe that was because it was constantly being replenished. Cato wouldn't give up his wood-burning stove.

"I always keeping a sharp ax handy in case the one I'm using gets dull, so I won't have to stop to sharpen it. I pointed it out to him and told him he was welcome to help if he was up to it."

He paused to laugh again, his dark eyes full of glee. Lara felt her own tension lessening. She couldn't help smiling with him.

"So we chopped and we chopped and we chopped until finally that pile was all gone," Cato continued. "He was a-sweating by then. When he buried the ax in a chuck of wood, I looked at him and said, 'We ain't done. I still got that other pile to do.' It wasn't as big as the first, but I think it looked bigger to him. That's when he smiled and shook his head and said to me, 'Cato, you've proved your point. I came here today to tell you that you were too old, but right now I feel older than you.' Then he told me I'd better get my mules hitched up and out to the field."

"He really said that," Lara breathed. "Oh, Cato, I'm so glad. Neither Daddy nor I wanted you to retire and I hope you didn't get your feelings hurt by what happened."

"Hurt?" He straightened, drawing his head back to give her a hard look. "This is a proud day. I wouldn't want to keep my job on any man's sufferance. I earned my right to work here today and that new man knows it or I wouldn't be here."

"You're right, of course," she agreed with a happy smile.

"Ransom MacQuade's going to be good. It's a pity you didn't marry someone like him instead of that skirt-chasing fool," Cato said bluntly.

The smile vanished from her face. Hastily she got

to her feet, averting her head to hide the rush of color to her cheeks. She should have realized that the old man would have heard some of the gossip. There was no escaping it.

"I'd better be getting back to the house." She changed the subject hurriedly with a lie. "They're holding lunch for me."

"I'm too old to mind my own business, if that's what you're saying," he chuckled, "but I gotta get back to work now. You stop by to see me again, Lara. And bring a hat for your head."

"I will, Cato," she promised as he closed his lunch bucket and agilely rose to his feet. "Goodbye."

He lifted a hand in acknowledgment, then turned to his mules. As Lara walked away, she could hear him talking to them in a low, musical tone. A smile played on her lips. She found it amusing that Cato had got the best of Rans MacQuade. She had thought no one could change Rans's mind, but she was glad that he had. And she was glad about the way it happened.

Lara was still smiling when she reached her car. At the sound of an approaching vehicle, she glanced up with absent curiosity. Her hand remained poised on the door handle at the sight of the familiar green and white pickup. It stopped opposite her car.

A tanned arm was crooked over the open window on the driver's side. The rugged face of Rans MacQuade looked impassively at her. His thick, tobacco-brown hair had been ruffled by the wind. The truck's motor was still running. The sight of him brought back the all too recent memory of their morning confrontation. Her skin tingled where she had been pressed against him.

"For the record," he said flatly, "you didn't change my mind. Cato did."

"I don't particularly care what changed your mind," Lara began, but her retort was drowned out as he put the truck in gear and drove away, leaving a choking cloud of dust behind.

The first week of March brought an explosion of spring color to the countryside. The snow-white blossoms of the flowering dogwood competed with the mauve shade of the redbud trees, their colors heightened by the contrasting backdrop of the thick pine forests of central and southern Mississippi.

In the courtyard the roses were blooming in red and pink profusion, their fragrance filling the air. The delicate flowers of the honeysuckle vines that clung to the brick walls were a vibrant yellow, their sweet scent vying with the rose fragrance. Azaleas and camellias were budding to join in the annual rebirth of spring.

The riotous display in the small courtyard was illuminated by lanterns scattered in strategic locations throughout the garden area. Light blazed from every window of the house. The tiled floor of the entrance hall was waxed to a high-gloss shine. The woodwork throughout the house gleamed with fresh polish.

Lara paused beside a hallway table to adjust a floral arrangement in a vase. Her empire gown was a shade of pastel pink that brought out the marble creaminess of her complexion and highlighted the fiery color of her hair piled in old-world ringlets atop her head. At the sound of footsteps, she turned toward the staircase.

"Lara, would you fix my tie?" Trevor turned at the

landing and came down the last set of steps, his hands fumbling with the black bow. "I can't seem to get it right."

"Of course," she agreed blandly. Trevor looked darkly elegant in his black suit and a vest of silver brocade. Now Lara could see how easily her head had been turned by his handsome looks, not the man.

While she expertly started tying the bow, she could feel his dark eyes possessively studying her. The diamond in her wedding ring flashed brilliantly on her fingers, but Lara was no longer blinded by what it was supposed to represent.

"You are beautiful, Lara," Trevor murmured huskily. "You are an absolute vision tonight."

"Thank you," she replied politely.

"We don't really have to be here for this pilgrimage tour. Let's sneak off somewhere, just the two of us." His hands settled around her waist in suggestive familiarity.

Impatiently she pushed them away. "Stop it, Trevor."

"You are my wife, Lara. Have you forgotten that?"

"I haven't. Have you?" Her gaze flicked coldly to his face.

"You know you're always on my mind." He caressed her with his voice and eyes.

"Really? Do you mean that between the blonde and the brunette you think of your wife?"

"Why must you keep bringing up the past?" He frowned. "That, uh, fling I had with my assistant has been over for a long time."

"Has it?" Lara smiled cynically. "Or have you merely replaced her with someone else?"

His dark, nearly black eyes narrowed harshly. "If I have, can you honestly blame me?" Trevor challenged. "I have normal physical needs, obviously unlike you. You were the one who shut me out, Lara. It isn't my fault that I have to go outside my marriage to seek satisfaction."

"That's a pat explanation." Lara knotted the bow. "Unfortunately it doesn't hold true for your first affair with the blonde. At least, I presume it was the first," she added tautly.

"I was a fool. I admit it." His arms slid around her waist before she could stop them. His hands locked together at the small of her back and he drew her against him. "You are still the most beautiful woman in my life. All I'm asking is another chance to make you the happiest." Trevor bent his dark head to nuzzle her ear, ignoring the rigidity of her body. "Once you enjoyed having me make love to you. I can make you feel good again. Let me show you tonight. We can slip away to some intimate little spot, drink some champagne and dance. We did that on the first night of our honeymoon, remember? And I carried you all the way up to our hotel room."

Lara remembered. But that girl in his arms had been someone else. She closed her eyes. Every nerve in her body now seemed to be dead at his touch.

"Let me go, Trevor," she said at last. "Save your romantic words and kisses for someone who's interested. I'm not."

"I can't accept that," Trevor murmured against the corner of her unresponsive mouth. "In time you'll change your mind and admit that you want me."

"You're wrong, Trevor. Now let me go," Lara commanded in a low voice.

"Okay, you two lovebirds, break it up." Her father's affectionately chiding voice joined them in the entry hall. "The tour will be here any time now."

Knowing Lara would not openly resist him in her father's presence, Trevor took advantage of the embrace to claim her lips in a possessive kiss before releasing her. Lara accepted it with cold tolerance, straightening the edges of his bow tie, then walked calmly away, the soft material of her long gown swishing around her ankles.

"The house looks as beautiful as you do, Lara," Martin Alexander declared.

"She is beautiful, like a goddess," Trevor agreed, his dark eyes glowing as he looked at her.

Her lips curved with the semblance of a smile at the compliment she knew was insincere. At the first sound of activity in the driveway outside, Lara turned toward the front door.

"I believe the tour is arriving now." Trevor was immediately at her side when she opened the door to admit the group. His hand rested on her waist, acting out the part of a romantic and happy couple.

It was going to be a long and trying evening, Lara thought silently, if Trevor was going to take advantage of the touring guests to make his unwanted advances. There was very little she could do about it as she welcomed the guests to their home.

As usual, the group consisted mainly of couples. There was a trio of elderly women, who were obviously friends, and a representative of the Hattiesburg Historical Society. Lara was mildly surprised to see a young, attractive brunette in the group. She supposed she was the daughter of one of the couples.

The woman was staring at Trevor, something that didn't surprise Lara. It would have surprised her more if the brunette hadn't taken notice of him. Her dark gaze shifted to Lara, envy flashing across her face. Lara smiled faintly and looked away. If the woman only knew, she thought wryly, how totally false her impression was. She would probably be shocked.

Quietly Lara remained at Trevor's side, listening to her father as the group gathered around him and he explained the details and the dimensions of the house and some of its early history. He was proud of his home and enjoyed showing it to visitors. He had just invited the group to follow him into the living room when there was a knock at the door.

Lara used the interruption as an excuse to separate herself from Trevor. "You go ahead with the others. I'll answer the door."

She almost expected him to protest, but he smiled an acceptance and followed the group into the living room. With a little sigh of relief and a flicker of curiosity as to the identity of the late caller, she walked to the door and opened it.

Rans MacQuade was framed by the opening, vitally masculine in a crisp white shirt, opened at the throat, and dark trousers. She had seen him just a few times since the incident with Cato, and only at a distance. Her fingers curled into the palm of her hand, her head tilting to a faintly haughty angle.

He seemed to notice her instinctive and proud reaction with some amusement. His gaze moved insolently over the perfection of her features, traveling down her slender neck to the hollow of her throat. It didn't stop there, but continued over the bareness of her skin, halting for an instant on the brooch, her grandmother's, that modestly concealed the shadowy cleft between her breasts, then swept over the clinging material of her gown.

Her skin burned as if he had physically touched her. Lara's green eyes flashed her dislike of his insulting inspection when his gaze returned to her face.

From the living room came the chattering of several voices. Lara guessed that her father had invited the group to ask questions. Rans MacQuade heard them, too, and glanced in the general direction of the living room, hidden from his view by the house walls.

"I'm sorry. I wasn't aware you were entertaining this evening," he apologized smoothly.

"Not entertaining, exactly," Lara corrected in a coolly distant tone. "This is the night of the candlelight tour in connection with the annual pilgrimage. Was it something important you wanted?"

"No." Rans shook his head, a glint of curiosity in his eyes. He raised his left hand slightly to indicate the thick folder he was carrying. "I promised Martin last week that I would gather the notes and literature I had on the Texas varieties of pecans, I finished about an hour ago and decided to bring them over."

"If you'd like, you can leave them in his study," Lara suggested, opening the door wider to admit him into the house. "I'm sure he'll want to go over them with you another evening when you are both free."

"I'll contact him tomorrow." Rans stepped into the hallway, his gaze idly sweeping into the living room where guests were trailing into the adjoining area.

"Did you say it was a tour? I'm sorry," he offered with a trace of curious confusion, "but I wasn't aware that your home was open to the public."

"It isn't, with the exception of Pilgrimage Week."

Lara escorted him down the hallway toward the study. She was strangely reluctant to let him linger in the house longer than it was necessary to deliver the papers he had brought.

"Oh. Is that a local tradition?"

"Not just around here, if that's what you mean. Various cities throughout the state and the South have what is referred to as a pilgrimage scheduled at various times. It's sponsored by the Hattiesburg Historical Society, which arranges for private homes that are historically significant to be open to the public once a year. Most of the tours are in the afternoon, but certain homes are viewed in the evening on what is referred to as a candlelight tour," Lara explained.

"Historically significant?" He looked at her inquiringly.

"In our case, it's more the unusual architecture of the house than famous personages or events. Generally the architecture of southern plantation homes is Greek Revival or Colonial. Many homes are full of valuable antiques. Our appeal is mainly the Spanish influence and the picturesque courtyard within the house walls."

"Doesn't it bother you to have a group of strangers parading through your home?" He closed the door, his gaze on her face.

"It's only once a year," she smiled like a tour guide herself, "not an everyday occurrence. Besides, my father enjoys it." Lara glanced pointedly at the large mahogany desk in front of filled bookshelves. A large chair covered in wine-colored leather was behind it. "You can put the papers on his desk."

The tall windows in the study were actually parted glass doors opening into the courtyard, as in every room on the lower floor except the living room and side parlor. Heavy, velvet draperies in a matching wine color flanked the doors. The draperies were open, providing a view of the softly lighted courtyard.

As Rans passed the windowed doors to put the papers on the desk, he glanced out. "I had hoped to use the courtyard gate again, but your tour group is out there."

"They'll be coming inside in a few minutes to see the parlor and the study before Daddy takes them upstairs."

"They actually go through your private rooms, too?" he mocked.

"No, only the two guest rooms and Daddy's sitting room," she answered stiffly, glancing through the window to see the visitors begin filing toward the door leading into the entrance hall. "They're coming back into the house now."

"Is the gate locked?"

"Yes, it is." Lara was angry with herself for forgetting that. "Excuse me, I'll get the key."

She slipped quickly into the hallway. The tour group was slowly congregating inside the rear area of the hall, waiting for the stragglers still gazing around the garden. In the buzz of conversation, Lara's quiet trip to the closet and back to the study went unnoticed.

Rans was leaning a hip against the side of the desk, his arms folded in front of him when she returned. He straightened with lazy nonchalance as she closed the door and walked swiftly toward the glass-paned doors.

"I should apologize for keeping you from the tour," he said.

"It's quite all right. Daddy usually takes over, anyway." Lara shrugged his polite remark aside.

The door latch turned silently in her hand. She started to walk through the opening when she heard a woman's voice in the courtyard. She hesitated for a fraction of a second, not wanting to encounter the tour group, then decided it didn't matter whether she did or not. A step later, she froze at the sound of Trevor's voice.

"Baby, you took such a chance coming here like this," he whispered. "What were you thinking?"

The voice was close to the study, but wherever Trevor was, he and the girl must have been concealed in the shadows, because Lara could see nothing.

"I had to see you. It's been so long," the girl murmured with an aching throb in her voice. "I couldn't help it. I had to come."

"I know," Trevor responded. "I've been wanting to see you, too, but someone from the tour is going to notice you aren't with them and come looking for you."

Lara's stomach lurched as she realized the girl had to be the pretty brunette she had noticed earlier. Her hand spread its fingers across her stomach to check its sickening turn.

"Not for a few minutes," the brunette protested. "Damn it, Trevor, you never told me your wife was so beautiful. I wanted to die when I saw the two of you together. I wish I could take the ring from her finger and tell the world that you belong to me, but I guess you don't. Not yet." Her jealousy and envy vibrated in her words.

"Lara is beautiful, yes," Trevor agreed, "but so is a statue. To me, she will never be as beautiful as you are. I swear it's the truth, Melinda, love. All evening, until I saw you walk through that door, I kept trying to find some way, some excuse, not to take part in this tour so that I could slip away and be with you tonight."

Remembering his ardent pleas to spend a romantic evening with her, Lara sunk her teeth into her lip to choke the gasp that rose in her throat at his audacious lie. Trevor had certainly found another fool.

"It must have been knowing how much you wanted to be with me that brought me here tonight," the girl murmured. "Oh, Trev, hold me. Hold me for just a little while."

A silence followed, faintly broken by the rustle of clothing. Lara knew they were embracing. A nauseous chill raced over her skin. Her husband was in the courtyard of their home, kissing and caressing another woman. Lara pivoted back into the study, not wanting to hear any more sounds or words of the disgusting scene.

She spun into the hard wall of Rans MacQuade's chest. In her shock, it hadn't occurred to Lara that he had also overheard what she had. The discovery paralyzed her for a humiliating second, long enough for Rans to reach around her and close the study door to the courtyard.

"You look pale," was all he said at first. She didn't answer. "Surely you weren't surprised by what you heard. You've known all along about your husband's other women."

Her pallor disappeared immediately in a flood of warmth. The words formed on her tongue to deny his statement, but it seemed pointless to deny the truth. "I guess I thought he would be considerate enough not to meet them in my home. Stupid of me," Lara retorted, lifting her chin scornfully.

He matched her cynical look with one of his own. "Guess he takes his loving where he can get it. He's no worse than a lot of other men."

She fought the urge to slap him by telling herself that Trevor would deserve it more. And she wasn't about to discuss the bitter facts of her marriage with Rans. There was no point in insisting that she was once passionate. Trevor's male ego would never allow him to be faithful. He constantly had to prove his manhood. He couldn't ignore the challenge of a pretty face, regardless of his love life at home. Lara didn't have to explain that either.

"I don't recall asking for personal advice from you, MacQuade," she said icily. "Would you please leave through the front door?"

The corners of his mouth twitched in dry amusement, carving brief grooves in his lean cheeks.

"I'll see myself out." His brown eyes glinted wickedly. "Good night, Mrs. Cochran."

The brunette had returned to the tour group when Lara rejoined it. The girl looked flushed and radiant and faintly triumphant as she met Lara's glance. Trevor had evidently reinforced his ardent words with action.

Chapter Five

Almost a week had passed since the pilgrimage night. Lara might have been able to block it from her mind if it wasn't for the knowledge that Rans MacQuade had witnessed her humiliation. She knew there would be something different in his eyes the next time she met him, something that mocked her and questioned her womanhood.

The knowledge was an irritant to her pride. Thus far, circumstances had not created a meeting. When they did, she wondered if she could contain her temper and treat him with the arrogant disdain he deserved.

Her finger turned the page of the book in her hand. Impatiently Lara flipped it back. Her eyes had skimmed the printed page, but none of the contents had registered. What was the use? Lara closed the book with a snap, rising restlessly to her feet and walking to the front window in the living room.

"Don't you like the book?" Trevor asked, glancing

up from his own. "I read it last week and found it very absorbing."

Lara stared out the window at the dark landscape. This was one of Trevor's duty evenings that he spent at home with her to maintain his image of a devoted spouse—for her father's benefit, she supposed. She doubted if her father guessed how totally empty their marriage had become.

"When do you find time to read, Trevor?" she remarked.

He either didn't hear or ignored the cutting barb in her question. "Oh, now and then. I speed through. Novels that used to take me days to read now take only hours, sometimes minutes depending on their length. You should try it."

"No, thank you." Lara sighed, choosing to reply directly to his suggestion and not get into a fight. "I don't care to read that fast. In a well-written book you would miss the passages where an author weaves the words together to create a spell. You might absorb the gist of it, but you would lose the magic. And when a book is good, I like to prolong reaching the end as long as possible."

"Is that why you've stopped reading—to prolong the end?" Trevor teased.

A wry expression flashed across her face. She should have known he wouldn't understand what she meant. Lara wondered if he read because it was the expected thing for an educated man to do as opposed to reading for the enjoyment of it.

Glancing over her shoulder, Lara indifferently noted the way the blue shade of Trevor's shirt accented the blue-black highlights in his hair.

"I couldn't concentrate," Lara replied with a restless shrug. "I'm not in the mood to read, I guess."

A speculative gleam entered his dark eyes as he watched her. Thoughtfully Trevor closed his book. "Was there something you would rather do?" he asked with studied casualness.

Lara shook her head. "No."

Nonchalantly Trevor got to his feet, and strolled toward the window where she stood. "It's a beautiful evening for a drive through the country."

She walked away from him. "I'm not in the mood."

"Poor Lara." He followed her, a smile of amusement flashing across his mouth. "You really don't know what's bothering you, do you?"

Folding her arms in front of her, she jerkily rubbed her elbows and her bare upper arms. "Nothing's bothering me. I'm simply not in the mood to read."

"Something's causing your agitation," Trevor murmured huskily. "And I think I know what it is."

"I don't know what you're talking about," Lara declared sharply, not liking his sly innuendoes.

"You're human. Don't you ever want to be caressed and loved? No matter how hard you try to suppress it, inwardly you're reaching out for something to satisfy you. Not that you would ever admit it."

Involuntarily Lara listened to his softly spoken words. The stirrings of dissatisfaction within her, the vague feelings that she was incomplete, indicated that Trevor might just be right about their cause, even if he was a cheating bastard. Lara firmly told herself that even if it was true, she could control them. She ruled her flesh, not the other way around.

"Is that what you think?" Lara laughed hollowly. "How nice of you to tell me." She turned away.

Trevor's hand shot out, turning Lara to face him and taking hold of her shoulders. "I'm right. I know I am," he said.

His gaze moved suggestively over her feminine figure while his hands began to languidly caress her shoulder blades. Lara didn't move as he came closer, his hands moving down her spine. He aroused only indifference, but his male ego was confident of his ability to make her respond.

"Lara," he whispered, and let his lips trail along her neck to her earlobe. "You are more beautiful than any woman I know. I want to be with you tonight."

The hypocrisy of his words produced a reaction that his caress had not. Violently she twisted away from his exploring mouth. Her expression was a cold mask of utter rejection. His words too closely echoed the things he had said to the brunette.

"Don't touch me!" Lara hissed. "I can't stand to have your hands on me!"

Trevor stared at her in disbelief, an angry frown gathering together his dark brows. He couldn't believe she honestly found his caress repulsive.

As Lara's cold green eyes started to move their attention away from Trevor's face, they saw the tall figure standing in the entry hall outside the living room doors. It was Rans MacQuade. How long had he been there? And how much had he overheard? All of it, Lara decided bitterly, judging from the sardonic expression in the brown eyes that held her gaze.

What was he doing in the house? How did he get in without being heard? He appeared to be coming from her father's study. Perhaps he'd arrived shortly after dinner when she had been in the kitchen helping Sally with the dinner dishes.

If that was true, then Rans had been on his way out of the house when he had seen Lara with Trevor in the living room. Her lips tightened. He had probably heard the nature of their conversation and paused to see if Lara was going to follow his unwarranted advice and passionately welcome Trevor's advances.

He had seen her reaction. He didn't even have the grace to look sorry or guilty that he had been eavesdropping. Angrily Lara spun away from his eyes, turning away from Trevor at the same time.

"What is wrong with you, Lara?" Trevor said finally, exhaling a heavy sigh of anger and confusion.

She glanced over her shoulder, her gaze first seeking the figure in the hall. There was no one there. In the next second she heard the front door softly closing.

Her gaze flicked to Trevor. "Nothing is wrong with me. I've simply stopped believing lies, that's all. Excuse me, I'm going to my room," Lara concluded.

Trevor didn't question her answer or her decision to leave. It was as if he sensed that she had seen through him and didn't want to be confronted with it.

In the days that followed, Trevor didn't press his attentions on her, virtually ignoring her when they were alone. Lara decided he was trying a new ploy, hoping to gain her interest by showing none in her. He could play all the games he wanted to play, but he played them alone.

Rans MacQuade came to the house several times,

conferring with her father. Outside of a few courteous exchanges, usually in the company of her father, Lara hadn't had to field any of his personal remarks about her life and herself.

His visits had sparked a surge of writing by her father, who thought nothing of claiming Lara's time with requests to type up his copious notes. She brought her laptop into his study to get through it all, wishing that he would get a computer of his own. Hidebound traditionalist that Martin Alexander was, he seemed to prefer having his daughter do it.

She printed out the documents using the regular computer and printer in her small study upstairs, almost surprised by how professional the end result was. Of course, a stranger to his methods would have found his notes impossible to follow since there were constant arrows, asterisks and amendments that had to be deciphered and inserted in the right places. Her father was in the downstairs study this evening, going over what she had typed and printed out today and no doubt filling up another legal pad for more to be done tomorrow. Lara turned the hair dryer onto her face, letting the hot air blow over her skin.

The night air was so heavy with humidity that she felt as sticky as she had before she had taken a shower and washed her hair. It could have been summer outside instead of spring. She ran testing fingers through her shiny hair. There was only a trace of dampness at the back of her head.

Turning off the dryer, she set it back in its box and put it away. Lara paused at the open window overlooking the pine woods at the rear of the house. A faint breeze gently stirred the needles, hardly a breath of it entering the room. A moth beat its wings against the screen, seeking the light from her bedside lamp.

With so much typing to do for her father, Lara had barely been out of the house in the last few days except to take care of her horse. Usually she took time for a morning ride on the bay hunter, Pasha, but the horse had sprained a muscle in his left front leg the last time Lara had ridden him.

There had been little swelling in the leg. Cato had looked at it and given Lara some foul-smelling liniment to put on it, decreeing that the hunter would be all right in a week or so. Cato was almost as knowledgeable as a veterinarian when it came to horses.

With a sigh, Lara decided it was much too hot to even attempt to sleep. Untying the sash of her robe, she walked to the closet and took out a pair of Levi's and a white cotton blouse. She would walk to the stable and check on Pasha. Perhaps the night air would be cooler.

She opened the lingerie drawer of her dresser and closed it again without removing anything. When she had changed into the Levi's and blouse, she turned to the mirror, winding her freshly washed hair atop her head. It was as slippery as silk, sliding through the pins that tried to hold it in place. Giving up, Lara secured it at the back of her neck with a tortoiseshell clasp.

Trevor was out that evening and, as she'd thought, her father was in his study working. There was no sign of Sally as Lara slipped out the front door. Few lights shone from the windows of the house, making it look dark and empty.

Stuffing her hands in the pockets of her Levi's, she strolled along the brick sidewalk. The dense shadows from the pines made her feel very much alone. Only a few stars glittered through the treetops that blocked out all but the moon's halo. It wasn't much cooler but the air was fresh.

The bay whickered curiously as Lara opened the stable door and switched on the light. The building was small, with stalls for three horses plus a tack and feed room, but Pasha was the only one. Her father had owned a horse at one time, although he had never been much of a horseman. When age had claimed his mount, he hadn't bothered to get another.

The horse stretched his blazed face toward her, nuzzling her shirt buttons as Lara rubbed his forelock. She crooned softly to him, meaningless words that were meant to soothe. A large mound of loose hay lay at the bottom of the ladder to the loft. She scooped up an armful and put it in the manger.

Leaning on the stall door, Lara studied the horse as he turned his attention to the hay. He was still favoring his front leg slightly, not putting all of his weight on it. Another application of liniment would help, she decided, and walked to the tack room and took the brown bottle from the medicine cabinet.

"Whew!" She made a face as she uncorked the bottle, telling herself she was going to have to take another bath when she got through putting the stuff on Pasha.

As Lara reached to unlatch the lower half of the stall door, the stable door opened. She turned with a start to see Rans MacQuade standing there. For a split second he paused, his gaze raking the length of her body.

"What do you want?" Lara demanded, frostily meeting his look.

"I noticed the light was on and stopped to see if anything was wrong," he replied evenly.

"Not a thing," she retorted, but he stepped into the stable anyway and closed the door. His presence dominated the concrete corridor, making the space seem smaller than it actually was. "I said nothing was wrong."

"What's the matter with your horse?" Rans was completely ignoring her answer.

As he walked toward her, Lara was nearly overwhelmed by an impulse to retreat. It was crazy. There was no reason to be intimidated by him.

"Nothing." She steadfastly held her ground, forced to tilt her head back slightly to look directly into his face when he stopped in front of her.

He held her look for an instant, then glanced at the bottle in her hand. Her knuckles were turning white from gripping it so tightly, a sure indication of the wary tension that claimed her.

"What's the bottle for then?" Rans asked.

A flash of anger raced through her veins, but Lara checked it to reply. "Pasha has a slight sprain, but I assure you it is nothing serious. I thought I'd put some liniment on it."

"I'll do it for you." His hand closed around the bottle, his fingers touching hers.

Lara's first instinct was to jerk her hand away from the burning contact and let him have the bottle, but she wouldn't give in to such a display of weakness.

"No, thank you. I'm quite capable of taking care of my own horse," she refused, not relinquishing her viselike hold on the bottle.

"I'm sure you are, but the odor coming from this bottle hardly smells like perfume," Rans drawled lazily. "I wouldn't want the lady of the castle to have to have two baths in one night."

Her head jerked back as betraying warmth rushed to her cheeks. "What do you mean?" she demanded stiffly, wondering how he could possibly know she had stepped from the shower barely an hour ago.

Dark, spiky lashes veiled the wicked gleam in his velvet brown eyes as they roamed with insolent thoroughness over her shining hair and face, moving down to her cotton blouse. The material clung to her sticky skin, outlining the rounded fullness of her bare breasts. Flames licked her skin where he had undressed her with his eyes. Her breath came in agitated spurts of barely controlled temper.

He knew she was outraged by his action. It sparkled like a jewel fire in her eyes. Her reaction amused him, as if he had done it deliberately to get a rise from her.

"You smell like scented soap, Lara. That's only a guess. But I think I'm right."

Lara tore her hand away from the bottle, her arms held rigidly straight at her side. "Put the liniment on if you like," she snapped. "Then please get out of here."

The line of his mouth quirked as she stepped away from the stall gate to let him enter. The bay's ears pricked at the stranger. For once in his well-mannered life, Lara wished her horse would decide to bite. It wasn't to be.

The caressing deepness of Rans MacQuade's voice seemed to assure the horse that the man meant him no harm, and the bay submitted readily to the stroking firmness of the hand on his sleek neck.

"The left front?" Rans inquired, running a hand along the horse's withers and across his chest.

"Yes," was Lara's clipped answer.

Ducking under the horse's neck, Rans moved to the left side, squatting to run an exploring hand over the injured leg. The bay shifted uneasily as he probed the sore area.

"Hold his head for me, will you?" It wasn't a request.

Hating the necessity to obey, she reluctantly took hold of the halter, crooning softly to settle Pasha down. "Cato has already examined him," she said when Rans continued testing the extent of the injury.

He poured some of the liniment on the leg, and the powerful odor filled the air. "Uh-huh. I know this is a homemade remedy," he muttered, turning his head away.

Lara concealed a smile, knowing how vilely strong the liniment was from her own experience. For several minutes Rans rubbed it in while she held the bay's head. Finally he straightened, patting the horse on the haunches as he walked around him to the stall door.

"That ought to do it," he remarked absently. "Where's the top to this?"

Lara pointed to the cork balanced on a wide manger board. He stuffed it in the bottle top and glanced inquiringly at her.

"Where does it go?"

"In the medicine chest in the tack room. I'll put it away," she answered.

He handed it to her without voicing any objection. Lara took it, carefully avoiding any accidental contact with his hand. As she started toward the tack room on the opposite side of the corridor, Rans followed, going to the stable door, she assumed. It was in the same direction.

When he followed her into the tack room, she realized he wasn't leaving. The medicine chest was just inside the door. Lara stopped in front of it, tilting her head to a challenging angle as she turned to confront Rans.

The words to dismiss him formed on her lips, but he walked by her, going straight to the work sink on the far wall. Pressing her lips tightly together, Lara faced the medicine cabinet, listening to the sound of rushing water from the tap as he washed the liniment from his hands.

"I noticed the light on in the study when I walked by the courtyard." Rans turned off the faucets. "Is your father working tonight?"

"He's hardly stopped in the last few days." Lara set the liniment bottle on the shelf and closed the cabinet.

"That means a lot of typing for you," he remarked, drying his hands on a towel and hanging it over its rack.

"Yes, it does." She removed the curry rake and brush from their hooks and walked into the corridor. Grooming the hunter would be an excuse to remain in the stable when Rans left. Impatiently Lara waited in the corridor while he took his sweet time about joining her.

"Do you resent it?" He stopped in the doorway, leaning a hand against its frame and studying her face.

She did her damnedest to keep it expressionless. Why didn't he take the hint that she wanted him to leave—quickly? It occurred to her that he probably had taken the hint and was lingering just to irritate her. He was succeeding.

"Resent what?" Lara couldn't help but look at his face, roughly chiseled and—she had to admit it—handsome.

Tobacco-brown hair waved with thick carelessness on his forehead. His white shirt was opened at the throat, accenting the sun-browned skin and revealing the curling golden brown hairs on his chest. Muscles rippled beneath his shirt. His masculinity seemed to wrap around her with suffocating intensity.

"The book demands a lot of your father's time. It doesn't leave him much to spend with you," Rans replied.

She snorted. "I'm a big girl now, MacQuade. I no longer need to be entertained by my daddy."

"Or by your husband," he suggested dryly.

Breathing in sharply, Lara throttled her temper and allowed a sugar-coated smile to curve her lips. "That's correct. Not that it's any of your business."

"No, I guess not. So where is your husband tonight?"

His casual tone didn't fool her. "He's part of a foursome that plays golf every Wednesday after work. They have dinner and drinks at the club afterward. A weekly 'boys' night out,'" she answered coolly.

"Do you believe that?" The grooves deepened around his mouth.

"Does it matter?" Lara challenged.

"Not to me." The wide shoulders lifted in an indifferent shrug. "I was wondering if it mattered to you."

"Not in the slightest." She studied the polished enamel on her fingernails, wishing they didn't itch with the desire to scratch that arrogantly mocking expression from his face.

"You must not mind sleeping in a cold bed." His voice laughed at her as he slowly straightened up.

Lara tipped her head back, the overhead light flaming over her hair at the new angle. Boldly she met his look, not intimidated by his superior height as he towered before her.

"Well, well. Interesting choice of subject. While we're on it, what's your bed like?" There was freezing scorn in her voice.

A wickedly seductive look shone in his brown eyes. "Would you like to find out?"

"I knew you were going to say that," she laughed abruptly. "Men are so convinced that they are great lovers most of them never realize that they don't even come close."

"And your husband failed in that regard," Rans ventured.

"Miserably," Lara answered evenly.

He shrugged. "The solution is simple. Get a divorce instead of prolonging the cold war."

Pride drew her up another inch. "The Alexanders don't get divorces," she informed him.

"Another long-standing tradition," he said quietly. "And so they lived miserably ever after." He eyed her.

"So if an Alexander makes a wrong decision, he or she has to live with it forever, huh?"

"I'm not interested in getting married again, ever. Once is enough for me," Lara declared loftily, the tip of her nose tilting slightly upward in disdain.

"So you stay. He has affairs and eventually you will too," Rans concluded.

"Trevor does the fooling around. He's good at it. Lots of experience." Bitterness suffused her tone.

"While you pretend you don't feel a thing. Desire and passion must scare you half to death. But you're so beautiful, Lara. What a waste."

His thoughtful gaze held hers, blinding her to the movement of his hand as it reached up to touch the smoothness of her cheek at his last comment. Quickly she pushed his hand away as if his fingertips had burned her skin.

"Don't touch me!"

"Sorry. I forgot," Rans chuckled in amusement. "You don't want a man's hands on you, do you?"

Lara remembered a little too late that he had witnessed the scene between her and Trevor.

"Are you afraid you might like it, Mrs. Cochran?"

"Never!" Lara hissed.

The sun lines at the corners of his eyes crinkled at her defiant challenge. "Never?" he murmured.

He took a step toward her. Feeling menaced, Lara swung the curry rake at his face. His fingers closed over her wrist, twisting it until she was forced to drop her weapon. With a jerk she was pulled against his chest, his arms sliding around her waist. She wedged a breathing space with her elbows.

"You can say no. I'll back off," Rans laughed.

"Let me go!" Lara glared at him coldly.

She had learned in the orchard that where he was concerned, she would get what she gave. Lara had to admit but only to herself, that she'd gotten physical first.

He seemed content to hold her captive. It was almost as if he enjoyed provoking her smoldering temper.

His voice was soft when he spoke again. "You know, Lara, a friend asked me once to break in a half-wild filly for him. The secret was that she needed a lot of handling to remind her who was boss. Mostly she had to learn that a man's touch really wasn't so bad."

"What do you want me to do? Neigh my agreement?" she retorted, intrigued and frightened by the dark glint in his eyes. "Let me go."

Rans merely smiled, lean dimples appearing around his mouth. Lara breathed in sharply as his hands moved suggestively along the sides of her waist inches from the swell of her breasts. Her own hands moved to intercept his, frantically pushing them away from his objective.

"You don't like that?" he murmured. A hand left her waist to move to the back of her head. "I don't suppose you like it when a man runs his fingers though your hair, either."

This time he didn't allow her to deter him. The tortoiseshell clasp was unsnapped and tossed to the floor. He raked his fingers through the silken fire of her hair, sending it cascading around her shoulders and neck.

Its release did the same for her temper. No matter how useless it might be, Lara struggled, twisting and turning, trying to elude his exploring hands. The struggle was simultaneously infuriating and exciting, but she desperately wanted to win it. Finally she started to bring her knee up between his legs, but he blocked her attack and she fell heavily against him, momentarily knocking him off balance.

In that split second she twisted free.

Chapter Six

Breathing hard, Lara backed away warily. Rans was between her and the door. With the swiftness of his reflexes, there wasn't a chance that she could run by him and escape. He made no move toward her, standing there with his hands resting on his hips, dimples carved by the arrogant smile, brown eyes caressing her.

Rumpled red-gold hair fell loosely around her shoulders in alluring disarray. The top two buttons of her blouse had come undone during the struggle, revealing the curving swell of her breasts, rising and falling with her agitated breaths.

Her face was flushed—she hoped it was a becoming shade of pink. Her widened eyes were a turbulent green, alert to the slightest movement by Rans. Nervously Lara moistened her lips.

"Get out of here." Her voice quivered and Rans only shrugged, as if he thought the situation was funny.

Her foot came in contact with an object behind her. Lara knew she must be close to the stable wall. She let her gaze leave Rans for the split second it took to glance over her shoulder. A pitchfork was leaning against the wall. Before the thought was formed in her mind, she was grabbing it, pointing the pronged ends at Rans.

"I mean it. Get out of here," she ordered, more certain now with a weapon in her hands that she was able to defend herself.

The amusement faded from his smile and his eyes narrowed with measuring thoughtfulness.

With a flash of intuition, Lara realized she had made a mistake. Ráns had never intended to try to recapture her as she'd feared. If he had, he would have done it already. No, he had only been playing with her the way a cat played with a mouse for the fun of it, then walked away and let the mouse go free for another day's game.

Lara wavered. Brandishing the pitchfork had changed the game, but it was too late to put it down now. The threat was made and she had to follow through with it, or seem like she had given in. That she would never do.

Apparently, neither would he. With slow purposeful strides, Rans walked toward her, narrowing the gap between himself and the pointed tines of the pitchfork. She tried to swallow away the tightness in her throat.

"Stay away from me," Lara warned, raising the pitchfork a fraction of an inch.

Rans didn't, stopping only when the pitchfork was pricking the front of his shirt. Nervously her fingers clenched and unclenched the handle. She almost admired the blasé way he was ignoring her threat.

"Go ahead. Do your worst." His gaze bored into her

troubled green eyes. "A woman is entitled to defend her honor."

"Leave me alone," Lara murmured desperately.

The pitchfork wavered, as if it had become too heavy. Before she could steady her shaking arms, his hand sliced upward, gripped the handle just in front of the prongs and shoved it away from his chest. Lara forgot to let go of her end and his twisting, pulling motion drew her within his reach as he yanked the weapon from her hands.

The bay whinnied nervously in his stall, the uneasy shifting of metal hooves echoing loudly in the stable. The hammering of Lara's frightened heart drowned out even that as she kicked and clawed at Rans.

An iron band circled her waist, lifting her feet off the floor. Her fists flailed at his head and he turned her in his arms so she had no target. The heel of her shoe found his shinbone. His grip loosened and her feet touched the ground. Lara nearly spun out of his hold for the second time.

Instead she went crashing onto the floor, her fall cushioned by the mound of hay. Rans was there immediately, the weight of his body holding her down while he clasped her wrists and stretched her arms above her head.

"Let me go!" she cried in angry frustration, glaring at the hewn face above her own.

"Not a chance, hellcat," Rans chuckled. "Not until you've learned your lesson."

The smoldering light in his eyes warned her of his intentions. Frantically she turned her face into her arm to elude the mouth moving toward her. She didn't want to kiss him—then she did—and she finally realized she didn't know what she wanted from this enigmatic, powerfully sensual man.

Holding her slender wrists with one hand, he brought her chin gently around with the other . . . and kissed her.

She liked it. And she couldn't escape. Her body writhed beneath his, suddenly alive with pleasure. The strength to resist and struggle ebbed to nothing.

His masterful kiss grew even more tender. Lara noted the change with relief as Rans seemed to breathe life into her instead of stealing it away. His fingers left her chin to tangle themselves in the silken mass of her flame-colored hair.

Lara gulped in shaky breaths, inhaling his musky scent at the same time. Absently she was aware of his mouth moving along her jaw, pausing to nibble the lobe of her ear, then trailing down the sensitive nerves of her neck.

The hay scratched at her arms. Lara made a protesting movement against it and her wrists were released. Slowly she drew her arms down, and she became even more conscious of the seductive quality in his touch. Her skin was tingling where Rans was lightly nibbling on her neck.

"Ohh," Lara breathed. Her hands moved to strain against his muscular chest.

His mouth left her neck only to close sensuously over her lips. She realized then that he didn't intend to let her go until she told him to. Her heartbeat quickened. Instantly his hand began caressing her shoulder and neck in the most soothing manner, easing the rigid tension the thought had evoked.

"Relax," Rans murmured huskily against the corner of her lips.

Seemingly without a will of her own, Lara obeyed. His mouth opened over hers, reminding her how to kiss with passion, an art she thought she had forgotten until his expertise recalled it. The intimate exploration of the kiss aroused desires she had believed long dead.

The wild desire shooting through her melted what little cold resistance that remained. A leaping pulse hastened the thaw. The wonder of his touch filled Lara with awe. A million new sensations had been aroused in her and she welcomed them.

Her hand inched closer to the curling thickness of the hair on his neck. His own fingers loosened themselves from the silken tangle of her hair, trailing erotically down her neck to the hollow of her throat.

A sighing moan of surrender came from her throat when his fingers undid the buttons of her blouse. Her breast swelled to the cup of his hand. Lara slid her hand inside his shirt, reveling in the burning nakedness of his skin. What was happening to her was crazy—crazy and glorious.

A whirlpool of emotion had her spinning. The warm moistness of his lips moved down her neck to kiss the rounded curve of her breast while his hand moved along her hip, molding her pliant flesh against his hard length. Senses vibrated with secret longings. Of its own volition her body moved suggestively against his.

His head raised to claim her mouth again, tasting the hunger of her parted lips, the kiss deepening with elemental desire. A radiant glow of ecstasy filled Lara's heart with a joy beyond expression. The abandonment of her response was her way of sharing the profound emotion awakening within her.

There was a withdrawal of his lips from hers. Lara waited to feel the fiery trail touch her again. Rans's weight shifted slightly away from her. The red-gold tips of her lashes fluttered upward, an expectant glow in her green eyes, the ardent fire no longer veiled by her lashes.

Rans was watching her, a mysteriously hard light in his eyes. A sensual chill ran down her spine.

"You are full of surprises, aren't you?" he murmured, drawing a deep, calming breath. "Maybe I should let your husband in on your little secret."

"Wh-what secret?" Lara whispered shakily.

What did he mean? Was he going to tell Trevor what he'd done? The way he'd kissed her and she had kissed back? Why? For what possible purpose?

"That all it takes is a little assertiveness to turn you on sexually," Rans said softly.

She didn't want to agree with that blunt statement. Scarlet stained her cheeks as waves of unbearable heat swept through her. Swiftly Lara rolled from beneath him, sitting up with her legs curled beneath her in the hay, her back turned to him, her head bent in shame.

What had gotten into her? Rolling around in the hay like that like Lady Chatterley—she was no better than her philandering husband. "That's not true," she protested in a choked voice. Her fingers fumbled with the buttons of her blouse, fastening only two when the hay rustled beside her.

"It's true and you know it." Rans turned her partially around, his hand sliding under her blouse onto her ribs. "Let me prove it."

Her head remained downcast, the fiery curtain of her hair concealing her expression from his probing gaze. Tears of shame burned her eyes as Lara silently acknowledged the power Rans seemed to have over her flesh. Even if she struggled, she knew she would be ultimately overpowered by the potent force of his masculinity.

In her heart she knew it would only be a token struggle. The rapture she had felt at his caress was still too fresh in her mind. There was no need for him to prove her susceptibility to his lovemaking.

"Don't." Her whisper was weak and shaky as the rest of her from the desire he had awakened. "Please," she added, asking for his mercy.

Her heart hammered wildly as he withdrew his hand from her bare skin, then crooked a forefinger under her chin to raise it. Her front teeth were holding her quivering lower lip still. At his continued lack of movement and silence, Lara lifted her lashes to gaze imploringly at him. One crystal teardrop hovered on the tip of a lash.

The unreadable depths of his brown eyes held her attention while a finger touched the lash holding the tear. It slipped onto his fingers.

"You wanted to make love with me, didn't you?" Rans stated, his chiseled expression revealing nothing, not even the effects of the lust-filled moments they had shared.

"Yes. Yes. *Yes!*" Her reply rose in a crescendo of hurt and humiliation, ending with, "I hate you!"

He seemed to find her vehemence amusing. He studied the movement of his thumb as it rubbed the wetness of her tear on his finger. With animal litheness, he rolled to his feet, towering above her while Lara glared at him, her head thrown back proudly.

"Poor Lara," he said. "You are human, after all."

Her eyes filled with tears, as if somewhere a dam had burst. Lara didn't see Rans leave, only heard the closing of the stable door. Salty tears ran down her cheeks, their briny taste coating her lips.

It was nearly half an hour before she had sufficient control of herself to sneak back into the house. In the privacy of her room it started all over again. She had once sworn that she would never let a man hurt her again, but she had never expected to meet anyone like Rans MacQuade.

The next morning Lara had to force herself to go downstairs to join her father and Trevor at the breakfast table. She was certain they would notice the change in her. The shell that had protected her was gone. She was a vulnerable woman again. Neither of them—and not even Sally, who knew her so well—appeared to see any difference in her. She felt temporarily safe for a little while longer.

But the moment she dreaded most of all had not yet occurred. She still had to meet Rans face to face. The more days that went by without it happening, the more she dreaded the confrontation. Would pride keep her composed or would she dissolve at the sight of him, remembering what had happened to her in his arms?

When the moment came, Lara still wasn't prepared for it. She and Sally had finished in the kitchen and Lara was on her way to her room, intending to hide there behind the pages of a book. As she crossed the entry hall to the staircase, the study door opened and her father stepped out.

"Lara, are you busy?" Martin Alexander halted just outside the opened door.

She hesitated, then turned away from the stairs to walk toward her father. "Not particularly. Why?"

"Would you bring a pot of coffee into the study?" he asked. "Rans and I are discussing the chapter outlines of my book."

Her gaze flew past him through the open door, riveting on the man in the chair facing the desk. The study light gleamed on the dark golden brown of his hair. Her pulse leaped and for an instant Lara was afraid she would faint. She forced herself to get a grip.

"Sure, Daddy," she agreed, planning to deputize Sally to carry in the pot.

"And bring three cups," he instructed.

"Three?" she frowned.

"Yes, I want you to join us."

Lara swallowed, smiling nervously. "Another time, maybe. There were, uh, some things I wanted to get done tonight."

He waved the protest aside. "Let them wait."

"But you will be talking about the book, technical things—"

"Exactly," Martin nodded. "Rans seems to think I should have separate chapters on disease and insects, because—well, never mind. We'll go into the reasons later, but I want your opinion too." The matter was settled as far as he was concerned and he turned to reenter the study, pausing to add, "You might bring some of Sally's pecan tarts with the coffee."

Then he was inside, closing the door. Lara was left standing there, her mind still racing to find a suitable excuse to refuse. She stared at the door for a long second before deciding that she was foolish to prolong this meeting. It was best to get it over with.

Wings from a million butterflies fluttered madly in her stomach she walked to the kitchen. Her throat was dry and tight, with hardly enough moisture in her mouth to swallow. She poured the coffee into the insulated server and set it on the tray with cups and saucers, adding a plate of Sally's tarts.

At the study door, Lara took a deep breath to steady her jumping nerves, balanced the tray on one hand and opened the door. As she walked in, her gaze was magnetically drawn to Rans, sliding away when he politely rose at her entrance.

"Here's coffee and dessert." She walked to the second leather chair in front of the desk, setting the tray atop the cleared space on the desk. Her glance ricocheted off Rans's carved features. "Hello."

"Mrs. Cochran." He acknowledged her greeting smoothly.

He continued to stand, setting off the butterflies again in her stomach. Did he have to be so damn well-built? It wasn't fair, not at all. "Please sit down," Lara insisted with a forced smile.

Another glance in his direction was caught by his brown eyes. He appeared aloof and remarkably indifferent to her, as if their sexy battle in the stable had happened to two other people. Nothing in his expression revealed even a hint of emotion.

A little sigh of relief quivered through her as she turned to her father. "Would you like me to pour?"

"Please." He looked up from the notes in his hand. "Do you take anything in your coffee, Rans? Sugar? Cream? Honey?"

"Nothing, thank you."

There was only a slight trembling of her hand as Lara poured the coffee into the three cups, adding honey to her father's and setting it to the right of him. The cup for Rans jiggled in its saucer when she picked it up to hand it to him.

His strong fingers were reaching out for it, but his attention was diverted by her father bringing up some point about his book. Lara didn't hear it. She was too busy concentrating on maintaining her composure.

As his hand closed over the saucer, it accidentally came in contact with Lara's. An electric current seemed to spring from his touch, jolting her so that she jerked her fingers back. Her action was not swift enough to elude the cup of coffee as it tipped, spilling its nearly boiling contents on the back of her hand.

The clatter of the cup in its china saucer and Lara's stifled cry of pain instantly had both men's attention. She was gripping her wrist, the fingers of her injured hand spread. Her skin was already turning a fiery red from the scalding liquid.

"What happened?" her father said concernedly.

Rans was already on his feet, the emptied cup shoved on the desk. "She's burned her hand with the coffee." An inner instinct had backed Lara away from him, but she was too distracted by the pain to increase the distance when Rans moved toward her. "We'd better get some cold water on it right away."

His hand was under her elbow, guiding her from the room, taking charge of the situation before Lara could protest. "It's n-not serious." Her teeth were slightly clenched. "I can take care of it myself. Really."

But he was already opening the door to the bathroom on the ground floor and escorting her inside. The cold-water faucet in the sink was turned on and her injured hand unceremoniously thrust into the water.

"Is there any salve around to put on it?" Rans inquired briskly.

He was standing so close beside her that Lara could feel the heat of his body. Disturbed by his nearness, she moved to the side of the sink, keeping her head down and her gaze on her hand beneath the running water.

"There should be some in the medicine cabinet behind the sink mirror. On the second shelf, I think." She swallowed, her heart beating overly fast as she tried once more to reject his aid. "There's really no need for you to stay. I can take care of it."

Her statement was ignored as he opened the mirrored door above the sink. He found the tube of salve immediately, removing it from the shelf and closing the door. Lara could feel his gaze studying her and hoped her profile didn't reveal the tension that strained her poise.

"Does it feel better?" he asked after another minute had passed with cooling water running over her hand.

"Yes, it . . . it doesn't burn anymore." The brief shake of her head was designed to flip the hair away from her face, a self-conscious movement since her red-gold hair was securely pinned in an impeccable coil.

Rans turned off the faucet and reached for the towel hanging in the ringed rack. He ignored her outstretched hand to take it from him and gently wrapped the soft towel around her other hand. Carefully he pressed the towel against injured skin to absorb the moisture.

With his attention diverted to her hand, Lara allowed herself to glance at his face. The strong lines were so masculine, sun-browned and rugged. And yet he could be this tender. His thick and spiky lashes, not long and curling like Trevor's, veiled the brown of his piercing eyes, a deceptively friendly color that concealed the steel in his gaze. There was a hardness to his mouth that she actually liked. She remembered its mastery when it had taken intimate possession of hers.

The memory stirred the physical longings within her, and Lara hastily glanced away from his mouth. Instead she concentrated on the drying motion of his hands. They were large and powerful like their owner, and amazingly capable. Her breasts tingled with the memory of the erotic caress of those hands. Lara breathed in sharply at how vividly she recalled the sensation.

Instantly his gaze narrowed on her face. "Does it still bother you?"

For a startled second, she thought he had read her mind, blushing self-consciously when she realized he was referring to the burn on her hand.

"No, it hardly hurts at all." Which was not exactly true since her hand was still uncomfortably sore. "I was thinking about something else."

His mouth quirked with amusement as Rans darted her a meaningful look. "Hmm. What else is there that makes you gasp?" he said, unwrapping the towel from her hand.

Lara hesitated, unwilling to answer what amounted

to a leading question. "I didn't gasp." She reached for the tube of salve. "I'll put it on."

"I'll do it. It'll be faster," Rans rejected her offer, then resumed the former subject. "If it wasn't a gasp, what was it?"

His fingers began to rub the cream onto the faint pink area of her hand, his gentle touch nearly as soothing as the burn ointment. Her throat ached and Lara couldn't answer his question. The rhythmic massage of his fingers was making her weak.

"That's good enough. It's much better now, thank you," she said stiffly. She took her hand away from his.

"You look a little pale. Are you sure you're all right?" he questioned.

Lara wavered. The small size of the bathroom meant she couldn't get to the door without brushing past him. At this moment she needed to avoid any contact. As much as she was reluctant to admit it, she was disturbingly attracted to him physically.

Rans misunderstood the reason for her silence. When her lashes fluttered in silent frustration, he reached out to steady her. Flinching from his hand, Lara took a step backward.

"Leave me alone, please." It was a breathless order.

Their eyes locked. He looked deeply into her eyes, reading the emotions that she tried to conceal.

"Lara, I wasn't trying to make a move here."

His words chilled her. Lara tried to tell herself that she wanted to hear what he was saying. She really didn't want him to touch her again or hold her in his arms. In fact, she wanted to forget the struggle in the stable had ever happened.

"Good," she said shortly. "I'm glad."

"Not that I didn't enjoy our little romp in the hay the other night." His husky voice laughed at the prim tilt of her chin.

"I don't wish to discuss that." Lara broke away from his steady gaze.

"Has your husband discovered that you're really not made of marble?" His gaze roamed over her with suggestive laziness. "Or don't you let him get that close?"

"My private life is none of your business!" she retorted sharply.

Rans chuckled. "Maybe I should give him a few lessons on how to make you purr."

"You are disgusting! I hoped you'd have enough manners not to bring up the subject!" Her eyes flashed with offended fury. "Oh—I hate the sight of you!"

"Too bad. I'm just not that much of a gentleman. And you're not that much of a lady"—his gaze flicked down to her hands—"or you wouldn't be about to claw my eyes out. Believe me," Rans continued with an incredibly annoying grin, "the dislike is mutual. I don't think much of a woman who tries to have sex with someone else to bring her husband to heel. Okay, it was—interesting, I'll say that much for you. But it's probably best for both of us that nothing really happened."

Nothing? She had felt a lot of things in that passionate clinch, but not one could be described as nothing. Instinctively her hand swung in an arc, the palm stinging against his cheek. He didn't even blink. Lara faced him, trembling with the rage at his insult.

"Do you feel better?" Rans said softly.

"Yes!" Lara hissed.

"Then let's call it even."

She was wary. "What do you mean?"

"You live here and I work here. That makes it inevitable that we'll run into each other again. I can learn to tolerate you if we don't keep crossing swords every time we meet," he concluded.

"Tolerate me?" Lara gasped. He was the one who had come and disrupted everything. She hadn't been happy exactly, but she hadn't been discontented with her life, either. Now she wasn't certain that was true at all. "You are incredibly arrogant."

"Point taken and thank you for being honest. By the way, you are an insensitive bitch." He was still grinning. "Are we going to continue to trade insults or shall we make a pact of peaceful coexistence?"

Fuming inwardly, she held her silence for several seconds before she grudgingly agreed. "A pact."

He nodded. "Good. Shall we return to the study before your father decides that you seriously burned your hand?"

"You go ahead," Lara said tightly. "Make my excuses. I'm sure you can come up with something that's convincing."

After letting Rans have a head start, Lara hurried up the stairs to her room. The pact would never work. Whenever Rans MacQuade was around, her reaction to him was inevitably warlike . . . or loverlike, a small voice added.

Chapter Seven

The leather reins were looped around her wrist as Lara walked between the rows of trees. The branches arched above her head, covered with new leaves of a bright spring green. The bay hunter blew softly against her shoulder. Lara paused to stroke its velvet nose.

A tear slid down her cheek, tickling the corner of her mouth. Impatiently she brushed it away, wondering where it had come from. It was spring. The pecan trees were bursting with life. She should feel happy, instead of trapped in this melancholy mood.

Not even Angie's letter in the morning mail had cheered her up as it usually did. It was so nice to get a handwritten letter instead of an e-mail, but Angie's friendly prattle about her husband, Bob, and the redecoration of their house had struck a sad chord. The topics were routine, no different from what Angie usually went on about, but Lara was different.

Once she had found a strange kind of contentment in the emptiness of her marriage. If nothing else it was predictable. She had honestly believed her life to be fulfilling. She had even boasted to Angie that it was everything she wanted. Now she wondered.

A pickup track drove past the orchard, stirring up dust. Lara recognized it as Rans before she heard the brakes being applied. Quickly she scrubbed her cheeks, to be certain there was no trace of tears.

A slam of the truck door confirmed that he had stopped. Within seconds Lara saw him vaulting the white fence and walking toward her. Surprisingly, their tentative pact had worked thus far. It had only been tested in meetings that had included her father.

She couldn't begin to guess why he was stopping to see her now. He was definitely not someone she wanted to see at this particular moment when her spirits were so downcast.

"Hello!" he called. "Problems?"

Lara shook her head. "No." Her hand continued to stroke the blazed face of the bay, avoiding the directness of Rans's gaze when he reached them.

"I thought your horse might have gone lame again. That's why I stopped," Rans explained.

"He's fine. Fully recovered," she assured him. "I was just cooling him off before we got back to the stable." She could feel the piercing examination of his eyes and wished the pact didn't exist. She didn't feel like being polite to him. "I'm sorry you were delayed without cause."

"You've been crying. Is something wrong?" he observed quietly.

"You're mistaken." A hand moved defensively to her face.

"Your mascara is smudged."

Lara ran a quick finger beneath each eye, a telltale

dark brown staining her finger. "Sweat," she lied. "We galloped nearly all the way here."

"Really?" Rans didn't seem to buy that excuse. "That's also why your eyes are red and swollen, too, I suppose."

"Hey, I'm tired and in no mood to match words with you." Irritation flashed through her at his perceptiveness. She gathered up the horse's reins and looped them over its head. "It's time I was getting back to the house."

"The No Trespassing message came through loud and clear," he replied dryly, stepping to the horse's head and taking hold of the bridle.

"Good."

Her coordination was jerky as she gripped the reins along the hunter's neck and held the stirrup to mount. When she started to swing into the saddle her boot slipped off the metal stirrup, sending her down. She stumbled and would have fallen to the ground if Rans hadn't been there to check her fall.

Her flesh melted at the searing contact with his masculine form. The bay's hindquarters swung away from the pair while Rans's grip immediately tightened around her waist. He was so strong. Lara wanted to lean against him and just soak it up.

For a few seconds she allowed herself to do that. Her head rested against his chest, listening to the steady beat of his heart, and feeling the warmth of his breath near her skin. The brushing touch of his mouth against her hair triggered an awareness of what she was doing. Her defenses had crumbled to the point where she was inviting his caress.

Her hands stiffened against the rippling muscles in

his arms as Lara pushed herself from the warmth of his body. His grip loosened, making no attempt to check her withdrawal.

"I'm sorry." Lara didn't know why she was apologizing to him. Maybe the words were really spoken for herself. "I was more tired than I realized."

"Let me give you a leg up." His voice was tautly controlled.

"Thank you," she murmured, feeling choked by a sudden surge of emotion.

The bay was swung back into position. His large hand was offered palm upward for her boot. Effortlessly Lara was boosted into the saddle. She had lacked the courage to look at Rans until she was safely removed from his nearness.

The enigmatic light in his brown eyes held her captive, her heartbeat skipping erratically all over the place. His left hand held the reins while his right rested on her knee. An empty ache started devouring her insides.

"I have to go," Lara murmured desperately, as if he was asking her to stay.

"Tell your father I'll stop by with the quarterly reports tonight." Rans stepped away. He seemed suddenly aloof and indifferent.

"Yes. Yes, I will," she answered tightly, reining the horse away from him as scalding tears welled in her green eyes.

Lara barely remembered any of the ride to the house. She simply gave the bay hunter his lead and let him take her back. Trevor was on his way out when she rounded the corner of the house.

He paused to wait for her. "I'm glad I saw you

before I left," he said. "I left a note in the kitchen to let Sally know I wouldn't be here for dinner this evening. Knowing her, she's liable to throw it away, thinking it's a scrap of wastepaper, so would you pass the message on to her to be safe?"

"Yes," she agreed automatically. "Where will you be?"

"Do you care?" Trevor asked.

Lara sighed and ran a weary hand over her forehead. "No." She started to walk past him to the front door, but he caught her arm.

"You seem different," he said curiously. "I can't put my finger on why."

His touch made her skin crawl. "You're mistaken, Trevor," she said with freezing scorn.

"Am I?" His dark head tipped to the side in considering thoughtfulness. "I'm not sure."

"Don't you have some place you have to be?" Lara snapped, not wanting to be subjected to his probing for fear of what he might discover . . . or what she might discover about herself.

His dark eyes flicked impatiently to his watch. "Yes, I'm late now. We'll talk another time, Lara."

Not if she could help it, she thought as he released her arm and walked swiftly to his car parked in the driveway. Lara didn't wait to see him leave, but hurried into the house, rubbing her arm where he had touched her.

The courtyard was darkened by evening shadows. Lara turned away from the glass-paned door, twirling the liquor in her glass and listening to the clink of ice against the sides. She ran a nervous hand along the waistband of her long skirt, a vivid floral pattern against a background of black.

After the quiet meal shared with her father, Lara had not wanted her own company. To be alone meant to think. That was one thing she didn't want to do. So she had accompanied her father to his study, sharing an after-dinner drink with him, breaking her usual custom of abstinence.

But his company hadn't proved to be the distraction she had hoped. Soon after they had entered the study, Martin Alexander had become immersed in the notes she had typed for him today, leaving Lara to restlessly wander about the room.

"What time is it?" he asked with a frowning glance.

Looking at the delicate gold oval of her wristwatch, she answered, "Nearly half past eight." How could time go by so slowly?

His mouth straightened with grim impatience. "That mechanic said he'd have my car out here by no later than eight o'clock. I shouldn't have left it with him. I could have waited to have the oil changed and the tires rotated another time when I wouldn't be needing it the next day."

"I'm sure he'll be here if he said he would bring it tonight," Lara assured him absently.

"I hope so or—" His sentence was interrupted by a knock at the front door. "Maybe he's finally here," he grumbled, rising from his desk to answer the door.

Taking one of the books from the shelf, Lara flipped through it disinterestedly and slid it back in its place. With a dispirited sigh, she wandered to the red brick fireplace. Through the open study door, she heard the voices in the entry hall and stiffened.

"Rans. Come in," Martin instructed in a surprised and pleased tone. "I didn't expect to see you tonight."

"I mentioned to your daughter this morning that I would be bringing the quarterly reports to you."

"It probably slipped her mind," was the dismissing reply. "Come into the study."

In a flash of honesty, Lara realized that everything had been a lie. It had not been a mere whim that had prompted her to wear the decidedly flattering outfit of a black chiffon blouse and complementing flowered skirt. Nor had it been a desire for a change that had led her to style her hair to flow freely down her back, gold combs holding it away from her face.

She'd joined her father in his study not to avoid the solitude of her own company or because she had wanted to be with him. Subconsciously she had plotted her actions, arranging circumstances so that she could see Rans MacQuade and hopefully have him notice her.

The discovery panicked Lara. Even the drink in her hand had been calculated in a weak attempt to gain courage. She wanted to run but it was already too late. Footsteps were approaching the door. Quickly she swallowed the remainder of her drink, then turned toward the door.

"Hello, Rans." A polite smile curved her mouth as he stepped into the room, tall and vital and compellingly attractive. "I'm afraid I didn't pass on your message to Daddy. I forgot all about running into you this morning while I was riding." A half truth since she had forgot the message but not their meeting.

"No harm done." Rans shrugged, running an impersonal eye over her.

"How about a drink, Rans?" Martin Alexander inquired. "A whiskey, maybe?"

"Sounds fine."

As her father started toward the built-in bar near the door, there was another knock on the front door. He glanced at his daughter. "Maybe that's the mechanic." He shook his head, not holding out much hope. "Do you want to help yourself, Rans, while I answer the door? Lara can show you where things are if you can't find what you want."

But Rans didn't require her assistance as he stepped behind the bar. She covertly watched him dump several cubes of ice in a squat glass and pour a shot of whiskey from the bottle beneath the counter over the ice.

He glanced at the empty glass in her hand. "Would you like another?"

"Please." She carried her glass to the bar for him to refill. "A Bacardi cocktail. Sweet."

A few minutes later he handed the glass back. "How's that?"

Lara sipped it experimentally. "Perfect," she smiled nervously, clutching the glass in her trembling hands. "I'll have to remember your bartending talent."

His mouth quirked in dry amusement. At that moment her father reentered the room, smiling in a slightly harried fashion.

"The mechanic is here with my car," he announced. "I have to drive him back to town. Can you stay for a few minutes, Rans? I'd like to go over these reports with you since you're here. I shouldn't be gone long."

"I can stay for a while," Rans agreed.

"Good." Martin Alexander nodded. "Lara can keep you entertained while I'm gone."

With that, he left the room. Lara had seen the look of pleased surprise in Rans's eyes at her father's last remark. His attitude didn't lessen the tension that scraped at her raw nerves.

The silence was beginning to build in the room. Rans walked leisurely to the fireplace, resting a foot on the raised hearth and leaning an arm against the mantel. He appeared relaxed while Lara was as taut as a violin string.

"There was something else I forgot to mention this morning." She tried to sound nonchalant as she wandered to a chair near the fireplace, standing behind it as if it offered protection.

"What's that?" He slid her a lazy glance.

Lara had difficulty meeting it, feeling guilty because her reasons for being in the room were less than honorable. "My father's birthday is a week from Saturday. We're having a small dinner party for him in town to celebrate. I know he'd like you to be there if you're free that evening."

"I have nothing planned."

"Good. I'll count on you to be there, then," Lara replied, feeling very awkward. "You're welcome to bring a friend, by the way." It was an attempt to deny that Rans had the power to attract her. "You do have a girlfriend?"

"I have someone I can invite if you are sure you don't mind." His tone was bland.

"Why should I mind?" She forced a careless shrug. "It's perfectly all right with me if you bring someone." She took a bolstering sip of her drink and looked away. "I just didn't know one way or another, so that's why I made the suggestion."

"Thank you for assuming I have a life apart from the Alexander ranch, Mrs. Cochran."

Lara flinched at his cutting tone but refused to let the conversation turn into an exchange of insults. "Is she from Hattiesburg?"

"Yes."

"Have you known her long . . . or is that too personal?" A faint bitterness crept into her voice.

"It is personal, but I don't mind answering it," he replied evenly. "I met her shortly after I came to work here."

"Really. Obviously you like her or you wouldn't still be seeing her." Lara stared at the pink liquid of her drink, fighting the constriction that gripped her throat. She tossed her head back in a gesture of uncaring pride.

"That's right."

"What does she do . . . for a living, I mean?" she faltered.

"She has a respectable profession, if that's what you're asking." Those damn dimples appeared in his tanned cheeks. "She's a nurse."

"I didn't mean to imply anything of the kind." Lara laughed uncomfortably, trying to make a joke out of his sarcastic remark.

The liquor didn't seem to be able to settle her nerves. Lara looked around for a coaster to set the glass down on, but Rans seemed to read her mind. He took the glass and set it on a circle of cork on the round table beside the chair.

"Ann is twenty-six, divorced and has a four-year-old boy," Rans continued. "She's taller than you with blond hair and blue eyes, pretty in a quiet, gentle way. Would you like her vital statistics?"

"No." Hurt flashed in her eyes, and Lara quickly veiled it with her lashes.

He was standing much too close. Out of the corner of her eye she could see the dark hairs on his chest curling above the unbuttoned collar of his shirt.

"Where is Trevor tonight?" He reversed the roles and became the inquisitor.

"I don't know." Red-gold curls danced between her shoulder blades as she shook her head.

"Did you ask where he was going?"

"Yes, I did but he didn't tell me." She lifted her chin proudly. "If he had, it would probably have been a lie anyway."

"Why do you say that?" The brown eyes subjected her to a measured look.

"Because Trevor doesn't know how to tell the truth." A resigned sigh accompanied the remark. "'Men are deceivers, ever,'" Lara quoted a line she had once heard, the author forgotten.

"That's a cynical remark from one so young and beautiful," Rans observed dryly.

"It's the truth." Her eyes challenged him to deny it. "I know you will find this hard to believe, but I was once a very happy bride. Of course the happiness barely lasted past the honeymoon. Prince Charming turned out to be Prince Chaser."

Momentarily preoccupied by that thought, Rans clinked the ice in his glass. Then his narrowed gaze studied her expression, a disconcerting appraisal in his eyes.

"So you've sworn off all men," he said quietly.

A soul-deep weariness rushed through her. She was tired of being alone, of constantly holding herself aloof. She wanted to be touched, to be caressed, to be the object of someone's affections. She wanted to be needed and cared for and to lean on someone else instead of always being apart. She wanted to share her joy and her sorrow with someone. Before she could give in to her own emotional weakness, Lara walked slowly to the fireplace.

"At least I won't be disillusioned anymore."

"You haven't stopped being disillusioned, Lara."

"My, this conversation is getting personal." She smiled wryly, glancing at him.

His compelling gaze refused to let her look away. "Sorry." Rans drained his glass, a grimness in the line of his mouth.

"Why?" Lara breathed, her heart pounding almost louder than her voice.

"Sometimes I have to remind myself that you're married." Rans slid her another raking glance. "And that you're my boss's daughter. Two strikes. I'm almost out."

She wanted to read more into his words and knew she didn't dare. The air was suddenly crackling with high-voltage tension. Rans snapped the connection by walking to the bar and setting his glass on the counter.

"When Martin returns, explain that I wasn't able to stay any longer," he said curtly. "Good night."

His abrupt exit left Lara with the sensation that he had taken some part of her with him. It frightened her. Everything that had happened that night had its implications. She had arranged to see him. She had dressed so that he would notice her. She had directed the conversation to a personal level. Now Lara wanted to erase the knowledge of what that meant.

As the hour of her father's birthday dinner drew closer, Lara wished she could cancel it. Of course it was impossible. All the arrangements had been made, and the guests were on their way.

Lara pressed a hand to her throbbing temple, knowing an excuse of a headache would be true. There were two reasons why she couldn't use it. A glance at the dark-haired man behind the wheel of the car reminded her of one of the reasons. If Trevor attended the dinner alone, the gossip about their loveless marriage would increase to the point where it would become unbearable.

The second reason was that she had to conquer her physical attraction where Rans was concerned. She couldn't avoid the inevitable. No matter how much pain it caused, it was best that she attend the dinner tonight and see him with another woman. That's all it had taken to kill her feelings for Trevor.

"Do you suppose there is anything going on between Martin and Charlotte Thompson?" Trevor broke the silence as they entered the city limits of Hattiesburg.

Charlotte Thompson was the widow of Clayton Thompson, who had been one of her father's oldest and dearest friends. He had decided to escort her to the dinner tonight rather than have her come alone.

"I doubt if it was more than a friendly gesture," Lara replied indifferently.

Trevor chuckled softly. "Honey, your father isn't so old that he wouldn't enjoy some feminine companionship."

"Is that all you ever think about?" Lara felt a flash of irritation.

"Don't you *ever* think about it?" Trevor said with biting quietness.

Yes, she could have said. Much too often lately. And the desires were aroused by the wrong man. Instead Lara let his question slide past unanswered. The other couples had just begun to arrive when Lara and Trevor reached the private dining hall that they had reserved for the evening. Lara didn't see Rans and his date arrive. She turned and he was standing near the portable bar with a drink already in his hand, and one in the blonde's.

Her breath caught in her throat at the way Rans was smiling at the woman, his eyes crinkling at the corners. Lara had to admit the girl was attractive in a freshly scrubbed, gee-whiz way. Her ash blond hair was short, cut in a boyish style that was appealing. Her lips seemed permanently curved in a friendly smile.

A few seconds later, Rans looked up and met Lara's gaze. His expression seemed to harden without a perceptible change showing in his smile. Then his hand was gripping the woman's elbow, and he was guiding her across the room to where Lara stood with Trevor and a few other guests.

Dismayed, Lara survived the introduction, saying all the right things at the right times. Using Trevor as a shield, Lara directed as much attention as she could to him. She knew her husband well enough to recognize the symptoms of a budding interest in Rans's companion, Ann Koffman.

Gratefully, another couple approached to divert them from Rans and his blond nurse. Afterward Lara took care to avoid the area of the large room where he was, and Trevor, portraying the model husband, stayed at her side. It was impossible to ignore Rans's presence. He was the only one in the room who was alive to her. The rest of the guests could have been robots instead of people.

At the announcement of dinner, Trevor directed the seating arrangements, splitting up the couples—to keep the conversation lively at the table, he said. As hostess, Lara took the chair at the opposite end of the table from her father, relieved to see Rans seated beside him, although still very much within her line of vision.

Trevor was making a show of seating Mrs. Thompson on his right, closer to the middle of the table. The reasoning behind his seating arrangements became apparent when Lara noticed Ann Koffman sitting in the chair to Trevor's left. The fact was noted by Rans, whose keen glance strayed to Lara. She avoided it quickly.

The food seemed tasteless to Lara. She ate mechanically, adding a token comment now and then to the conversation around her. Silently she observed Trevor's discreet maneuverings, knowing she wasn't the only one interested in what was happening.

Trevor was good at working his charm, asking a few polite questions of the blonde without appearing to devote all of his attention to her. By the time the meal was over, Ann Koffman was talking to him quite animatedly, a victim of his magnetic spell even if she wasn't consciously aware of it. But Lara was and Rans had to be.

The tables were cleared swiftly of the dishes by efficient waiters. Just as quickly the tables were removed from the room, almost without the guests being aware of it. A small dance combo slipped into the room, played a few testing notes, then offered a rousing rendition of Happy Birthday.

Trevor was at her side to claim the waltz that followed, leading her onto the small dance floor after her father and Mrs. Thompson had made the initial circle. At least in his arms, Lara didn't have to keep up the pretense of conversation.

Which was a good thing, because when she saw Rans dancing with Ann pain gripped her heart. The knowledge that she had no right to be jealous only increased her misery. Afraid her expression might reveal her inner feelings, Lara glanced hesitantly at Trevor. His gaze was on the same couple.

"Did MacQuade tell you much about Miss Koffman?" he asked casually.

"No." Her lips mouthed the word as she shook her head briefly. Lara was too preoccupied by her own misery to truly be aware that her husband was questioning her about another woman.

"He didn't mention whether they were serious?"

"He only said he had been seeing her for some time." She forced her answer out. "You'll have to do your own investigating to find out more than that."

The sharpness of her tone drew his darkened gaze. "I was just curious," Trevor smiled.

"Why do you bother to lie?" Lara's sigh had a cynical edge. "You know very well that you've singled her out for your next conquest, no matter what's going on between her and Rans McQuade."

"Are you giving me your blessing?" There was definite amusement in his voice.

"Trevor, you could go jump into a bottomless pit, for all I care," she returned caustically.

"My sweet little wifey," he mocked.

"And you're my devoted husband."

"Why do you stay married to me?"

He looked down at her—literally and figuratively, Lara thought. "Don't ask that question," she answered with taut control, "or I might find that I don't have any reason anymore." Her green eyes flashed at him. "And you don't want a divorce, do you? It's so much more convenient to be married and have your affairs on the side. You never have to make a commitment because you're married but you always have a good reason to fool around. I guess I make a convenient scapegoat." She laughed bitterly. "What do you tell them? You're a poor misunderstood husband with a frigid wife at home. Oh, God, you make me sick, Trevor."

He was angry. Angry and a little bit uncertain that perhaps he had pushed her too far. His tight-lipped silence brought a measure of satisfaction to Lara. He seemed to understand that her reference to a divorce had not been an idle threat.

"Have you ever considered that I might be more of a husband if you were more of a wife?" he said finally.

"But I'm not interested in being more of a wife to you," she pointed out to him. "If I were, I wouldn't look the other way when you carry on your flirtations right in front of me."

The song ended. As Lara turned out of Trevor's arms, she was facing Rans, his expression impassive as he met her startled look. Her gaze darted to the hand resting lightly and possessively along the blond-haired woman's wrist. A stab of envy pierced her, remembering the firm touch of those masculine hands.

She would have turned and walked away, unable to bear the sight of the two of them together, if Trevor had not stepped forward.

"Good band, isn't it?" Trevor commented as the combo swung into a lively tune.

"Yes, it is," the blonde agreed enthusiastically, an added sparkle entering her blue eyes under the influence of Trevor's flashing smile.

"Lara doesn't care to dance to the faster songs. Would you like to dance, Ann? May I call you Ann?" Trevor tacked on with old-fashioned courtesy.

"Yes, please, call me Ann." Before she accepted his invitation, she glanced to Rans and received a curt nod of permission, accompanied by a smile as an afterthought. "And I would like to dance, thank you. Rans claims not to be very good at it."

"You don't mind, do you, dear?" Trevor inclined his head toward Lara, a faint challenge in his dark eyes.

"No," she murmured.

The truth was she minded very much. She didn't want to be left alone with Rans. Her strained nerves were already too sensitive to his presence. But a protest at this point was impossible, as Trevor very well knew.

Lara watched the two of them step onto the dance

floor, one tall and darkly handsome and the other willowy, slender and fair. Rans was aware of Trevor's reputation. A covert glance out of the corner of her eye noted the iron set of his jaw as he, too, watched the pair. She dodged his gaze when he suddenly glanced her way.

"You look like you need a drink. May I get you one?" Rans offered in a slightly forbidding tone.

"Please," she replied, grateful for any distraction, however brief.

Chapter Eight

Within a few minutes Rans was back. "A Bacardi cocktail, sweet and on the rocks," he said dryly as he handed it to her.

"Thank you." Lara almost wished he had forgotten.

His gaze strayed to the dance floor, picking out Trevor and Ann among the couples. Their steps matched well together, as naturally as a couple who had danced together many times before. There was a grimness about Rans's mouth as he glanced at the whiskey he held in his hand. Lara could guess how angry he was at the way Trevor was making a play for his girl.

"I'm sorry, but Trevor has a penchant for blondes."

"Jealous?" came his soft, husky voice.

"Yes." The answer was instinctive, but it wasn't entirely the truth. Lara was jealous of the blonde because she was Rans's date. Not because Trevor was hitting on her.

As the music faded, the pair stopped dancing, yet

didn't seem to be in any hurry to leave the floor as they talked and laughed. Another song began, a slower melody this time, and Rans turned to Lara.

"Shall we dance?" A challenging light glinted in his eyes.

Lara fought the impulse to accept wholeheartedly, glancing at her drink, intending to use it as an excuse not to have to endure the torture of being held in his arms. But his strong fingers closed around the glass and removed it from her hand, deliberately interpreting her silence as an acceptance.

"I—" Lara attempted a protest.

With the glasses set aside, his hand closed around hers and led her to the dance floor. Then Rans was bringing her into his arms, a hand sliding around her waist.

"I guess I accept," she laughed, the sound brittle with tension.

"Did you want to wait there for them to come back?" Rans asked flatly.

Glancing to the edge of the dance floor, Lara saw Trevor eyeing her curiously. He knew she generally avoided dancing with anyone but old friends of her father's when they attended social functions. Her actions surprised him, but Trevor never let anything bother him too long. His dark head bent closer to the blond woman at his side. In the next moment they were returning to the floor.

"No, I didn't want to wait," Lara answered his question finally.

Her first few steps were awkward and uncoordinated as they began to dance to the slow music. She was trying desperately to control the desire to relax against Rans and let him lead her wherever he wanted to go. His physical attraction made desire too dangerous.

Her stiffness didn't ease when he held her. His touch was hard and firm as though something inside him had to be kept under control. Lara stared at the knot of his tie, her heart hammering wildly. Peeking through her lashes, she studied the strong line of his jaw and moved her gaze upward. His brown eyes were looking beyond her, anger in their depths.

Hesitantly Lara glanced over her shoulder, finding the target of his look. Ann Koffman was molded against Trevor's length, her head resting against his shoulder as they moved sinuously to the slow tempo. Trevor's dark head was bent toward hers, smiling as he murmured near her ear.

Sharply averting her head, Lara met the rapier thrust of Rans's eyes. She paled under his piercing regard and looked swiftly away.

"Is this what he usually does when you go out?" The question was laced with sarcasm.

"We rarely go out together," Lara said and paused nervously before continuing. "If there's an attractive woman, Trevor usually pays attention to her. His ego can't tolerate it if a woman doesn't like him."

"Don't you do anything about it?"

"There isn't anything I can do." Or that I want to do, she could have added, but didn't.

"Isn't there?" He smiled crookedly, a wicked gleam in his eyes.

His forearm moved over hers, drawing her hand

against the solid wall of his chest, her fingers clasped in the firm grip of his. The arm around her waist tightened to bring her closer until she was wrapped in a near embrace. Only a struggle would have freed her from his iron hold.

"Rans!" Just token resistance. She didn't mind what he was doing at all.

"Quiet," he ordered. "We are being observed, so just listen to the music."

Out of the corner of her eye, Lara saw the frowning look Trevor was directing at them. Then the melody of the song captured her attention as she remembered a line from its lyrics. *My darling . . . what a long, lonely time I've waited . . . for your touch.* With eyes closed, she surrendered to its truth and relaxed in Rans's strong arms.

It took all of her willpower to leave his arms when the song ended. Her ivory complexion was paler than normal, but her expression was composed. She didn't cringe under Trevor's scrutiny when they rejoined them.

Her father and Charlotte Thompson joined the four of them on the sidelines. Martin Alexander was in one of his garrulous moods, directing the conversation to his favorite topic—pecans. His presence in the group brought a continuous stream of guests stopping to chat for a minute or two before moving on to the dance floor or to the bar.

Rans had retrieved Lara's drink shortly after they had left the dance floor and had obtained one for Ann, who was now at his side. As much as she tried, Lara couldn't keep her attention focused on the conversation around her. She was too conscious of Rans.

He was listening to her father, nodding now and then at some statement, yet he seemed aloof, as if most of his thoughts were elsewhere. His glass was refilled for the third time and Lara knew something was eating away at him. She could only guess that it had to do with Ann, whose gaze kept straying to Trevor.

A hand gripped her elbow and Lara glanced at its owner. Trevor smiled at her—the smug smile of a cat licking the cream from its whiskers.

"Let's dance," he said.

If she had expected him to ask anyone, it would have been the willowy blonde with Rans. The invitation had been issued loud enough for the others to hear. Under the circumstances Lara didn't see how she could refuse, so she let him escort her onto the dance floor.

Slipping an arm around her waist, Trevor murmured complacently, "You seem very interested in MacQuade tonight. Is there anything I should know?"

Her poise cracked only for an instant. "I haven't the slightest idea what you're talking about," An icy chill ran down her spine. If her preoccupation with Rans had been so obvious, perhaps others had noticed.

"Don't you?" he mocked. "I noticed you didn't object when he held you so closely while the two of you were dancing."

"Was there something wrong with that?" Lara remarked haughtily. "The way we were dancing wasn't much different from you and that Ann."

A dark brow arched in quizzical amusement. "Hmm. I detect a note of jealousy in your tone. Maybe you aren't as indifferent to me as you like to pretend."

"You have a very vivid imagination, Trevor." She tipped her head back to glare at him with cold contempt.

"If it's not my attention you are trying to gain, then it must be MacQuade's," he pointed out with a speculative gleam in his dark eyes.

"Don't be absurd." But she had to look away.

"Why don't you be honest with yourself for once, Lara?" Trevor smirked. "I know MacQuade isn't your type, so why don't you simply admit that you're trying to make me jealous?"

Lara sincerely doubted that anyone could possess an ego as big as Trevor's. He was so absolutely positive that no woman would want another man if she could have him that Lara nearly laughed in his face. The only thing that stopped her was the sight of Rans guiding his date onto the floor.

She shrugged eloquently. "I couldn't lie about a thing like that."

"I didn't realize you were so adept at playing games, Lara," he commented after considering a moment. "I'm willing to prolong the chase if that's what you want. It tends to heighten the thrill of capture."

His hand slid suggestively downward from her

hip. Her own hand quickly left his shoulder to check his caress. "Stop it," Lara warned beneath her breath.

And Trevor chuckled. "It's still too soon, is it? Does it seem wrong?"

"It always has," she stated acidly.

"Whatever you say." He smiled confidently. "I'm willing to play by your rules, with a few variations of my own."

In the next few steps, his cryptic statement was explained when he paused alongside another couple. Lara's glance of vague curiosity encountered the sparkling blue of Ann's eyes. Suddenly wary, she looked back at Trevor. His dark gaze was directed at Rans.

"Shall we change partners?" Trevor suggested.

Lara sent up a silent prayer that Rans would refuse. He looked at her, the smoldering dark brown of his gaze almost curling her toes. Then it flicked arrogantly to Trevor.

"Permanently?" Rans questioned in a deceptively lazy tone.

Her heart leaped in spite of the common sense that told her it was only a joke. Trevor was momentarily disconcerted, too, but he recovered with a laugh.

"It's a thought, isn't it?" he replied with bogus sophistication as he released Lara to Rans's waiting arms.

A thrill of pleasure quivered through her at Ransom MacQuade's firm touch. She had difficulty breathing when she felt the hardness of his thighs against her legs. Lara swayed closer until she felt his smoothly shaven jaw against her hair. His head jerked back as if she had burned him.

"I'm sorry," Lara mumbled self-consciously, trying to move away.

"No. Stay with me." His voice was hard and his head bent slightly to rest alongside her face.

She swallowed. "Please." His breath was warm against her cheek, smelling of alcohol. A strong thumb was absently rubbing the inside of her wrist. "I think you've had too much to drink," Lara breathed, feeling the heady intoxication of his body pressed against hers.

"Maybe just enough to have a good time," Rans said in a low voice, drawing back to gaze into her troubled eyes, "I want to make you purr the way you once did."

"Don't," she protested.

"Don't you want to make your husband jealous?"

Lara shook her head, needing to escape. "Let me go," she insisted shakily.

"The song isn't over yet," he reminded her complacently.

Blindly she stared at a button on his shirt. "Let me go," Lara repeated desperately.

There was an expressive shrug of his wide shoulders as his hold slackened. Unmindful of the curious looks, Lara walked unhurriedly from the dance floor, aware that Rans was following with leisurely strides. She knew he didn't intend to let her escape completely. She supposed that Rans was flirting with her to get revenge on Trevor for flirting with Ann. And

Lara didn't like being used that way, not when she was trying to control her own wayward emotions.

There was one place Rans couldn't follow and she slipped into the ladies' powder room. She took her time applying fresh lipstick and patting the smooth coiffure of her hair. When she peered out the door into the hall, there was no sign of Rans.

Cautiously she stepped out, avoiding the door leading into the private banquet room in favor of a rear exit door opening to the outside. The night was still, its quiet broken only by a few crickets chirping in the landscaped bushes. Lara stepped farther into the cool darkness, wrapping her arms around her middle in an attempt to ease the aching emptiness she felt. She was in the kind of mood that made her wish she hadn't given up smoking. Reflexively, she touched her small evening purse, then remembered it had been over a year since it had held a pack.

"Would you like a cigarette?"

At the familiar sound of the sensually husky voice, Lara jumped, pivoting sharply in alarm. A tall figure separated itself from the concealing shadows.

Light from a three-quarter moon touched Rans MacQuade's face. His rugged features were twisted in an odd smile. "I've been waiting for you."

A cigarette burned in his hand as he placed a second between his lips and snapped a lighter flame to the end, handing it to Lara after an initial puff.

"I . . . I needed some fresh air," Lara faltered. "But I need this more at the moment." She took a long drag and exhaled the smoke. It wasn't as satisfying as she'd thought it would be.

"That's what I thought," he responded dryly.

"Why are you here?"

"Because you are."

Lara turned away, unable to endure the lazy thoroughness of his gaze. "Why don't you leave me alone?" she murmured in despair. "Your date will be wondering where you are."

"And so will Trevor. Isn't that the whole point of this?" inquired Rans, moving forward into her line of sight and glancing casually skyward at the stars overhead.

"Trevor won't care," Lara replied tightly.

In fact, he would probably find the whole thing amusing. It would reinforce his opinion that Lara was attempting to make him jealous—which was preposterous and impossible since he felt no deep emotion for her—and it would give him a clear field with Ann Koffman.

"You've forgotten Trevor's ego." He studied the burning tip of his cigarette and the smoke curling in a gauzy gray ribbon from its tip.

"What do you mean?" she frowned, eyeing him uncomfortably.

"He isn't going to like it if he thinks his wife finds another man more attractive. If nothing else, curiosity will make him come after you."

"I don't particularly care." She stared stonily into the night, knowing that what Rans was really hoping was that Trevor would leave Ann alone.

"Don't you?" His cigarette was ground out beneath the heel of his shoe.

"No, I don't."

"You went along very willingly with the idea of making him jealous of you tonight," Rans pointed out. "You even admitted you were jealous when he was dancing with Ann. Is it pride that's making you say that you don't care?"

"I wasn't jealous!" Lara protested with irritation, and realized that she didn't want to explain that statement. "Will you please go away and leave me alone?" she demanded.

"I swear half the time you don't know what you are saying or doing!" he muttered, his hand snaking out to grasp her wrist. "You keep contradicting yourself." Lara strained against his grip to no avail. "You swear you can't stand to be touched when the actual truth is just the opposite."

"Let me go, please." She was breathing quickly, and unevenly, seeing the light in his eyes and knowing she had neither the strength nor the desire to fight him off.

"No." He shook his sun-streaked head, a hand moving her waist to draw her toward him. "We're going to see this thing through to the end."

His mouth closed over hers in hard possession, parting her unresisting lips in sensual exploration. An explosion of fire raged through her veins. She didn't need the molding caress of his hands as she willingly arched her body against his solid outline, her fingers clutching the material of his jacket.

Lara's hungry response released a torrent of kisses that rained over her eyes and cheek and neck. Each one jolted her to her toes. She tried to return his passion and thrilled when she felt the trembling of his muscles. A large hand roughly cupped the swelling curve of her breast as his mouth blazed a fiery trail to the shadowy cleft at the vee neckline of her dress.

The outside door swished shut, bringing Lara somewhat to her senses, enough to realize that someone had seen them. Her hands pushed against his chest.

"Rans, please," she begged for him to stop, while every fiber of her body wanted only for him to continue, to not stop until they were both satisfied.

It was the latter that he responded to, laughing huskily as he nuzzled the side of her throat, nibbling sensuously at her earlobe until she moaned with the erotic mastery of his touch.

With the last ounce of her will, Lara protested sharply. "Stop." Rans started to ignore her again and she added, "You're drunk."

"Drunk?" Harsh laughter erupted from his throat as he drew his head back, his chest rising and falling in deep, disturbed breaths that didn't help Lara's emotions. "Yeah. I am drunk. With liquor or with you, I don't know. They both make me lose my head."

But he was in control of himself, Lara could see that in the piercing hardness of his eyes. His arms fell to his sides, leaving her skin cold where his touch had burned her minutes before. Inside she was crying, desiring him more than ever.

Everything had gone wrong. She hadn't wanted to come tonight. Now she regretted bitterly that she had. Instead of remembering Rans with another woman, the memory of what had happened this moment would be forever with her.

"Someone saw us," she breathed shakily.

"So?" Rans taunted. "Are you worried about your reputation?"

She turned abruptly away. His jeering words hurt more than they should have. "No." Her chin dipped downward in defeat.

"Don't worry," he said. "I doubt if it was anyone other than your husband. I know you'll excuse me now. Good night, Lara."

Her chin was lifted and a hard kiss was branded on her mouth. Before her hands could touch him—to protest or deepen the kiss—he was gone, striding away toward the building. Lost and alone, Lara remained outside for several more minutes, wishing she didn't have to go in and face Rans again or argue with Trevor.

There wasn't any choice. Soon someone would come looking for her, more than likely Trevor if he had seen her locked in that embrace with Rans. She didn't want to see her husband alone yet, not until she had better control of herself.

She dropped the forgotten cigarette in her hand on the pavement and crushed it out.

Lara delayed rejoining the party by slipping into the powder room. Her eyes were red and swollen from unshed tears. While she was rinsing them with cold water, one of the dinner guests, Nora Evans, walked in.

"Oh, hello, Lara," she said with only mild surprise. "That secondhand smoke really burns your eyes, doesn't it? It's almost a relief to get in here."

"Yes, it is," Lara agreed, drying her eyes and reaching for her evening purse on the counter top. Quickly she reapplied her makeup, finishing as the woman was about to leave, and walked with her into the party room.

Trevor was at her side immediately, his dark eyes glittering with a knowing look. Lara had little doubt that he had seen her with Rans.

"There you are." His possessive arm circled her shoulders. The gesture was fake, all the way. "I was beginning to worry about you."

The woman, old enough to be Trevor's mother, smiled with a trace of envy at the romantically handsome man and moved off in search of her balding husband. Lara remained rigidly erect against his touch.

His dark head bent to whisper in her ear. "MacQuade returned some time ago. What took you so long?"

"That's none of your business," she murmured.

He clicked his tongue in mock reproof. "You forget, my love, that I'm your husband."

Lara flashed him a cold look. "I try."

His eyes widened at her rejection, his nostrils flaring in anger. Then, slowly, a nasty look replaced the stagy surprise.

"It was all part of your game, wasn't it?" Trevor smiled. "You had me going there, Lara. I always thought you had too much moral pride. It seems I don't know you as well as I thought."

"You don't know me at all, Trevor. You never will. You're too self-centered to bother about anyone but yourself," she retorted. "Let's rejoin the others."

Trevor laughed softly and guided her toward the

group dominated by her father. He was too arrogantly sure of his own attraction to believe there was any truth in her words, and he was making his own interpretations of her actions.

Covertly Lara searched the faces in the room. None belonged to Rans or Ann Koffman. Had they left? She longed to ask yet knew she didn't dare if she wanted to avoid more of Trevor's infuriating comments.

The pounding in her head that had been with her all evening in various degrees began to increase. The steady chatter of voices, the loud music of the band and the crowdedness room didn't help her headache. Overriding all of those was the tension.

A half an hour later, when Trevor suggested they leave, Lara could have cried with relief. She didn't even care why he wanted to leave the party so early. But Martin Alexander objected to their departure.

"Lara, you are the hostess. You can't leave," her father protested.

"I have a terrible headache, Daddy. Besides," she said coaxingly, "you're the guest of honor and your friends will be less inhibited if the under-forty riff-raff leaves."

"You do have a point there." His eyes twinkled merrily and Lara knew she had won.

She kissed him lightly on the cheek. "Happy birthday, Daddy," she murmured. "And give our goodbyes to the others."

Minutes later she was relaxing against the plush upholstery of Trevor's Seville. Closing her eyes, she listened to the silence, the powerful motor no more than a contented purr inside the car. Pine trees crowded the sides of the road, serrated silhouettes against a moonlit sky.

The car made a turn and slowed to a stop. Lara opened her eyes, expecting to see the lighted entrance of her home. There wasn't a building in sight, only the forests and the tan ribbon of the dirt road. Her gaze swung warily to Trevor. He was sitting sideways in his seat, quietly watching her.

"Why have we stopped here?" Lara was instantly on guard.

His hand moved toward the dashboard of the car. There was a click, then soft music floated out and filled the night. Trevor took his time in answering.

"Do you remember when we were dating?" he mused. From the shadowy darkness of his side of the car, Lara could feel his gaze roaming over her. "We used to park along some isolated stretch of the road, listen to music and talk . . . and kiss."

"I remember." She was wondering how she could have been so naive to believe all the lies and romantic compliments he had made then. "It was all very long ago, Trevor." There was a hint of acid distaste for the subject in her tone as she leaned her head against the raised seat back. "Please take me home now."

Not a sound betrayed his movement. The spicy scent of his cologne warned Lara of his nearness an instant before his lips pressed against hers. Repulsed, she twisted her mouth away, her hands raising to push against his chest.

"Stop it!" she snapped angrily, hunching her

shoulder against his attempt to bury his mouth along her neck. "I'm not in the mood for a wrestling match with you. I have a headache and I want to go home!"

Trevor simply laughed, pressing her back against the seat with his weight. "That's not much of an excuse, even for a wife."

Sickened, Lara realized that he wasn't going to be put off with mere words. He had seen the way she had responded to Rans and intended to penetrate her glacial coldness. She fought his mouth and roving hands that left her feeling dirty and unclean. The more she struggled, the more excited he seemed to become.

The nightmare grew to terrifying proportions as Lara felt the fragile material of her dress ripping at the shoulder. He bit at her bared skin in a way that would leave a mark, sending shudders of revulsion down her spine. She freed an arm from the pinning weight of his chest and raked her fingernails across his face.

With a yelping curse, Trevor moved away, a hand instinctively cupping his wounded cheek. He held it away, staring at the traces of smeared blood in the palm with disbelief. A black rage distorted his handsome features.

Lara didn't wait for the explosion. With wrenching sobs of panic, she pushed open the door, her legs quivering with fear. Trevor reached for her, his fingers closing over the skirt of her dress. She tore it away, not caring about the second rip that ruined the expensive gown.

"Come back here!" Trevor snarled, moving across the seat to follow her.

She tried to slam the door in his face, but his arm reached out to stop it. Wildly she glanced around for help, but the road was completely deserted.

Trevor was stepping out of the car, the moonlight illuminating the scratches disfiguring his cheek. "I'll get even with you for this," he threatened. "Now get back in the car."

There was a brief, negative shake of her head, then Lara bolted, running down the road. She could hear the crunch of gravel behind her and realized Trevor was chasing her. Her high heels were slowing her down. It was only a matter of seconds before he caught up with her.

Turning abruptly, she stumbled down the ditch alongside the road and raced into the pine woods. The towering trunks closed around her protectively, hiding her from his sight within seconds. She was making too much noise of her own to tell if he was still following her, but Lara could hear him angrily yelling her name. It made her run faster.

Chapter Nine

Ahead, a light shone through the trees. Winded and sobbing between gulps for air, Lara staggered toward it, her heels sinking in the soft mulch of pine needles. She had no idea where she was or which direction to go to reach her home, but the light promised safety.

As she drew nearer, a small house took shape, standing alone in a clearing in the pines. A dirt road stretched in front of it. The light she had seen gleaming through a window beckoned her toward the porch.

Out of the darkness, a hand grabbed her, then a second. A gasping scream ripped from her throat. Lara struggled wildly like a frightened animal trapped in a snare, but the iron hands easily overcame her attempt, giving her a hard shake that rattled her teeth.

"Lara, stop it!" a voice commanded harshly.

Her gaze focused on the bronzed features of Rans MacQuade and she collapsed weakly against him, winding her arms around his neck and sobbing her relief into his shirt.

"What are you doing here? Oh, Rans, help me." The breathless plea released a torrent of tears.

"I was taking a shortcut."

"Who—whose house is that?"

"I don't know. Maybe it belongs to the three bears. It doesn't matter." The hands at her waist denied her the support of his body, holding her away from him. His piercing gaze swept over her in rapid inspection noting the torn material at the shoulder of her dress. "What the hell happened?"

"Oh, please," Lara swayed toward him and he gathered her against his chest. "You've got to help me," she sobbed as his hand gently smoothed the hair away from her face. "He—he—" Convulsive shudders wracked her body, making her words incoherent.

"Who?" His voice was rough but he was making every attempt to soothe her. "Who did this to you?" he demanded savagely.

At first Lara could only shake her head mutely, not wanting to talk. She only wanted to be held in his arms and feel his warmth while she tried to forget the horrible memory of Trevor's repulsive touch.

"Answer me!" Rans insisted. "Who did this?"

"Tr-Trevor," she answered through her choking sobs. "He . . . he tried to m-make love to m-me I . . . I—" Lara shuddered uncontrollably again.

Rans made a visible effort to control a reaction that was very male and almost entirely instinctive. "Just so we're on the same page," he said at last, "I did think that you wanted to make him jealous. I can't judge you for that, considering how he was acting."

"No." She shook her head disbelievingly.

"Hey, I was there," he laughed harshly.

"I never wanted him to touch me," Lara breathed, tears drenching her face.

"He's your husband. He feels entitled."

"He isn't." Closing her eyes, she fought the revulsion that quaked through her. "He makes me feel . . . dirty." Tears blurred her vision when she look at Rans. "No one . . . no one understands. No one."

Tiredness engulfed her, the tiredness of defeat. It was no good explaining. Rans wasn't listening to her. Nothing she said made the slightest impression. She turned away, silent sobs of wretched misery shaking her shoulders.

Behind her, Rans swore softly, then his hands were turning her into his arms. Lara resisted briefly then buried her head in the inviting expanse of his chest and wept. His hand stroked her hair in a soothing caress.

Finally there were only hiccupping sobs left. She had cried out all her pain until she felt hollow and completely empty inside. She was numb to any emotion.

Wearily Lara lifted her head. A crisp white handkerchief touched her cheek, wiping the dampness from her skin. She glanced up gratefully to see his faint smile.

"Your mascara is running all over the place," Rans murmured.

He stood silently, inches from her as she took the handkerchief and scrubbed her face. A few minutes later she handed it back, her breathing still shaky and uneven.

"Come on." His hand closed firmly on her elbow. "I'll drive you home."

The pickup truck was parked on the opposite side of the house. In the cab, Lara leaned weakly against the seat, too tired to care where she was going or what might be waiting for her when she reached her destination. Rans was sitting beside her and temporarily at least, she felt safe.

When the truck stopped in the cul de sac drive, Lara stared woodenly at the light streaming from the long windows flanking the front door. Her door was opened and Rans reached forward to help her out. She fumbled through her purse for the door key and placed it in his hand. It was several seconds before his fingers closed around it in acceptance.

Once the door was unlocked, he followed her into the entry hall, glancing around the silent house. There was no sign or sound of anyone else in the house. Returning the key, Rans studied the dispirited lines etched in her pale features.

"You're tired," he said quietly. "Sleep will help you forget what happened."

Instantly an image of Trevor flashed in her mind's eye. The rage that had been in his expression sent a shiver down her spine. Her widened green eyes swung to the staircase. Was he upstairs waiting for her? The thought chilled her to the bone. Mutely Lara appealed to Rans. She didn't know where her father was and she didn't want to be here alone.

Rans gave an impatient sigh. "Come on."

A guiding hand rested lightly on the small of her back as he turned her toward the stairs. Their footsteps echoed hollowly through the empty house. Without a word, Rans checked her room and the locked adjoining door to Trevor's room. There was no one upstairs, either. Lara hovered near the foot of her bed, feeling awkward and foolish. Her gaze skittered away when he glanced at her.

"I don't think you have anything to worry about. I'm going to call your father's cell, though—I'm not going to say anything about what happened, just find out when he'll be home and tell him that you're, uh, a little under the weather. I'll stick around in the driveway until he gets home, just to be on the safe side," he said.

"All right," she agreed with a self-conscious nod. The last thing she wanted to do was explain to her father, who still seemed to think that his son-in-law walked on water.

Rans went to the door. "Thank you," Lara offered hesitantly. Rans nodded curtly, stepping into the second-floor hallway and closing her bedroom door.

For several seconds she listened to his departing footsteps. Sighing, she realized that Rans had a lot to think about too. But he hadn't abandoned her and he wasn't far away. Trevor wouldn't dare pick a fight with him.

Most likely Trevor wouldn't even come home tonight. No doubt his injured pride would make him seek solace in some other woman's arms tonight.

Slowly Lara undressed and slipped on the mint-green nightgown, the lightweight material falling loosely around her ankles. Sitting in front of the vanity mirror, she began to brush her hair, prolonging the moment when she had to crawl into the empty bed. She was exhausted and overwrought, but she was afraid that once in bed she would start thinking.

There were only two things to think about, and she didn't want to face the truth of either of them. She didn't even want to admit there was anything to face. However, she couldn't spend the rest of the night brushing her hair.

Resolutely, Lara set the brush down and walked to the table lamp at her bedside, turning it on. As she turned to walk to the overhead light switch on the wall, her bedroom door was opened. Lara halted in surprise when Rans stood in the opening.

Behind her, the light from the bedside lamp made the thin fabric of her nightgown appear transparent, revealing the nakedness it was meant to conceal. Tension gripped both of them, electric and sensual.

"I thought you—you were waiting in the driveway," Lara whispered at last. Her pulse skipped rapidly with joy that he had come back to her.

"I—" Rans breathed in deeply, seeming to gather his control. He looked down at the cup in his hand, its expression impassive when it returned to her. "I fixed you some cocoa. Figured you needed something to relax you."

He set the cup and saucer on the dresser near the door and turned as if to leave. Lara stepped quickly forward, desperately wanting him to stay.

"Don't go!" she called to him, and hesitated when

he turned toward her. "Can't you stay and . . . and talk to me? I don't want to be alone."

"Talk?" His gaze raked her. "With you dressed like that, do you think if I stayed we would talk? My God, what do you think I am?"

Her hands crossed defensively over the bodice of her gown. Lara reached quickly for the robe lying across the bed, holding it in front of her, but not putting it on.

"I don't want you to leave," she protested weakly.

"I don't want to be caught in your bedroom. Good night, Mrs. Cochran." His sardonic voice underlined the marital term of address.

"Don't call me that!" she flared.

Lara crossed the room on wings of hurt anger only to have it fade to nothing when she reached him. Her green eyes searched his impassive face for some sign that would give her hope. There wasn't one.

"Don't you want to stay?" Lara's whispered plea throbbed with the aching need she felt.

He reached out and rested his hands on her shoulders, while a muscle twitched uncontrollably along his jaw. His hands moved down, almost against his will. Languidly, Lara melted against his body, masculine and strong.

"Do you think I don't want to?" The smoldering light of desire shone in his brown eyes. Her heart rocketed as his gaze swept possessively over her face and the lacy neckline of her nightgown. "Damn, you're beautiful, Lara," Rans muttered thickly. "I—"

Her fingertips touched his lips, checking their flow of words. She felt utterly feminine and enticing, no longer struggling against the waywardness of her emotions.

"I love the way you just said my name," she murmured. "There's something different about your voice now . . . something softer. Oh, Rans . . ." Lovingly she let his name roll from her tongue.

He turned his head away, breaking free from her touch. "You are making me crazy," Rans breathed heavily.

"Why?" Lara smiled, knowing she was disturbing him as he had disturbed her so often.

"I have only one rule as far as women are concerned," he said flatly. "I stay away from the ones who are married. And like it or not"—his voice was as firm as the strong hands that pushed her away from him—"you are married."

"Y-yes." She stopped herself for a moment and instead she asked breathlessly, "And if I wasn't?"

He shot her a guarded look. "Is there any likelihood of that?"

Lara hesitated, unable to answer him immediately.

"That's what I thought. No point in getting carried away."

"Rans, no!" she called out to him as he turned to stride into the hall.

He seemed determined to get as far away from her as possible in the shortest amount of time, but Lara followed him. She reached the top of the stairs as he opened the front door on the ground floor.

"Rans, wait." The door was slammed shut. "I love you." The admission was out in the open, her voice trailing forlornly into a whisper when Lara realized she was the only one who had heard it.

The pickup truck roared out of the driveway. Slowly Lara retraced her steps to the bedroom, ignoring the cup of cocoa on her dresser to curl into a tight ball of misery beneath the covers of her bed.

At least she was no longer afraid of the worst. It could be argued that it had just happened.

The next morning Lara slept late, mentally and physically exhausted from the turmoil. She had just dressed and was walking toward the stairs when she heard voices in the hall below. One was her father's and the second belonged to Rans. Lara hurried to catch him, wanting to speak to him even if it was too soon, but the front door was closing as she reached the landing.

"Was that Rans?" she questioned her father, taking the last few steps a little too fast. She almost stumbled. "Is he leaving?"

A puzzled frown creased his forehead when he turned to her. "How did you know?"

"I heard his voice. I have to talk to him." Lara raced toward the door in time to see the rear of the pickup driving down the lane. "Did he say where he was going?"

"No." Martin Alexander shook his head, running his fingers through the sides of his hair. "Where's Trevor? I've got to talk to him about this." Lara noticed the paper her father had clutched in his hand. "I imagine if Rans told you, he told Trevor, too. I just don't understand," he sighed.

"What?" He was confusing her. "What was Rans supposed to have told me?" Was her father referring to last night? She didn't understand.

"About him leaving, of course," he answered impatiently. "Did he explain his reasons to you?"

"Oh no," Lara breathed, her face growing pale.

"Oh yes. He's leaving!" Her father waved the paper in the air. "He even put his resignation in writing. A two-week notice and the name of a man qualified to replace him."

"Why?" In her heart she guessed the reason.

"That's what I'm asking you!" he retorted. "You were the one who said you knew he was leaving."

"No, I . . . I only meant was he leaving the house. I had no idea at all that he'd quit," Lara explained. "What . . . what reason did he give?"

"Oh, some excuse about the job not turning out to be the kind of thing he wanted." Her father shrugged absently, his brow furrowed in concentration.

"Surely you tried to talk him out of it?"

"Of course," he sighed, and rubbed his forehead. "I offered him more money, a part ownership in the farm, a new house, a new car. I tried everything, but he kept insisting that he was still dissatisfied and nothing would change that. I nearly got down on my hands and knees and begged him to stay. I couldn't have found a better man for the job than Rans if I had ordered him directly from heaven. And now what?" He lifted his hands in a helpless gesture.

"He can't leave," Lara whispered. Her father was

too concerned with his own problem to hear the unusual degree of emotion in her soft voice.

"Maybe Trevor can talk him out of it, or at least we can put our heads together and come up with some kind of a plan. Where is he?" Martin glanced toward the stairs. "Is he still in bed?"

"He didn't come home last night," she answered, swallowing the lump in her throat.

"What? You two left the party together last night? How could he bring you home and not come home himself?" he demanded incredulously. "Where is he?"

"I don't know and I don't care!" The details of last night would require too much telling for Lara to want to spend the time explaining. "It doesn't matter what you think anymore, Daddy. I'm divorcing Trevor as quickly as I can see an attorney and get the legal papers filed. Our marriage has been dead for a long while. It's time it was buried. So Trevor isn't going to be much help to you whenever he does come back. And you can tell him what I said, if I'm not here."

"What are you talking about? What's going on?" His confusion increased as Lara opened the front door. "Where are you going?"

"To talk to Rans."

"Well, see if you can talk him into staying!" he called after her. "Rans might be at the cattle barns."

Racing around the side of the house, Lara realized that now that she had faced the truth, it really hadn't been such a difficult thing. What would hurt was if she had left it too late. Her fear now was that Rans would really leave.

Behind the wheel of her blue Mustang, she stepped on the accelerator, the tires churning up a cloud of dust as they tried to answer the demand for speed. The pace didn't slacken until she reached the breeding pens two miles from the main house. The rust-colored head of a Santa Gertrudis bull lifted curiously when she turned into the lane to the barns.

Rans's pickup truck was parked beneath a large oak. Lara stopped her car beside it, stepping out before the engine died. At first glance there was no sign of activity in any of the barns. Despairing, Lara thought she would have to search each one, then she saw someone move near one of the large double doors.

She held her breath, letting it out slowly when Rans appeared. Sunlight glinted on the amber highlights in his brown hair. The white of his shirt contrasted sharply with the dark tan of his sun-browned features, chiseled into an expressionless mask. Snug-fitting, faded Levi's molded the muscular length of his legs, striding purposefully forward.

There was a slight narrowing of his gaze as he saw Lara poised beside her car. His stride faltered for an instant, then continued in a direct line toward his truck. Lara realized he had no intention of speaking to her and she walked swiftly to intercept him.

"Rans, please, I want to talk to you," she explained hurriedly as he drew near her.

His glance, dispassionate and aloof, swept over her briefly. "We don't have anything to discuss."

"Yes, we do," Lara protested. "You can't leave, Rans, not now."

"Guess your father told you I was quitting," he interrupted briskly, not slackening his long stride to match her smaller steps.

"Yes. Rans, I have to know why, please."

"I gave him my reason. I'll let it stand." He opened the door of his pickup and would have gotten in if Lara hadn't caught at his arm to stop him. He looked down at her coldly.

"You have to listen to me. I wanted to explain to you last night, but you left before I had a chance," Lara declared earnestly.

"I've heard it all before," Rans replied disinterestedly. "As far as I'm concerned, last night never happened. I've handed in my resignation, and there is nothing you can say that will change my mind. Do I need to make it any plainer than that?"

Recoiling as if he had struck her, she stared at him, unable to believe the rejection his words implied. When her hand fell away from his arm, he stepped into the cab of the truck, started the motor and drove away without another glance at Lara as she stood in stunned silence.

The truck had disappeared on the graveled road before she moved, walking numbly to her own car. Her hands clasped the steering wheel and Lara bowed her head against them, intense emotion sweeping through her. She didn't want to believe what she had heard.

He hadn't even listened to her, or given her a chance to explain. The only sentence that gave her any hope at all was his comment that he had heard it all before.

It was a hope as slim as a wishbone, but it was the only one she had. She needed it. The next few days would not be easy. Lifting her head, Lara smiled tightly. First things first, she told herself, turning the key in the ignition.

But if Rans MacQuade thought he had heard the last from her, he was very much mistaken. Alexanders did not give up very easily, as he would soon discover. She shifted the car into gear, driving at a much slower rate back to the main house, using the time to think of how she was going to deal with her father and Trevor. Again the thought returned that the next few days would not be easy, but nothing really worthwhile ever was.

Chapter Ten

Lara nibbled at her fingernail. Her anxious gaze swung from the sun-bathed courtyard to her father, who was seated behind the mahogany desk. A black telephone receiver was in one hand while the other tapped the eraser end of a pencil on the table.

"See that he gets the message immediately, Tom," Martin Alexander said into the phone, then replaced it in its cradle.

"Well?" Lara prompted. "Is he coming?"

"I don't see how he can possibly avoid it," he answered with a smiling shake of his head.

Suppressing a shiver, Lara turned back to the courtyard scene. "What are we going to do if this doesn't work, Daddy?" she murmured.

"We'll think of something." The chair squeaked. A few seconds later she felt his hands curving around the soft flesh of her upper arms. "I'm sorry, pet. I don't know if I've got around to saying that yet or not. I wasn't a very understanding father."

"You meant well." Lara turned her head, glancing

up to the concerned eyes. "I just didn't tell you everything, that's all." She smiled reassuringly. "Let's face it, Daddy, we are both Alexanders, and sometimes we have to be hit in the face with the truth before we'll accept it."

"We have too much damned pride." He winked and lightly kissed her cheek. "If we don't want our plan to fall apart, I'd better leave. It's not going to take Rans long to get here from the sheds once Tom delivers the message."

If he comes, Lara thought silently. In the last ten days, Rans had avoided her and the house like the plague. Every attempt she had made to speak to him had been met with defeat. But Martin Alexander was still his employer for a few more days, and he could hardly ignore a direct order—she hoped.

"I'll be back in, oh, about two hours." Her father moved away toward the hall door. "Good luck, pet."

"Daddy?" Lara turned, her voice checking his departure at the door. "Thanks . . . for all you're doing."

A rueful smile curved his mouth. "After the callous advice I gave you the last time you came to me, this is the least I can do."

With a wave of his hand, he was out the door. Several minutes later, Lara heard the sound of his car pulling out of the drive. The antique clock ticked loudly in the silent house, the hands on the dial moving much too slowly.

Restlessly she walked from the study to the living room, counting the ticking seconds as she twisted her hands nervously, her left hand bare of any rings. She hovered beside a window looking out onto the front lawn.

Her heart stopped when a pickup truck turned into the driveway. The plan had worked thus far. Stifling the impulse to race to the front door, Lara waited at the window, well back so she couldn't be observed from the outside.

Rans swung his long frame out of the truck, hesitated as he glanced at the house, then slammed the cab door. There was an impatient spring to his stride and his mouth had thinned to a forbidding line. Inhaling deeply, Lara didn't move until she heard the knock at the door.

Her palms were moist with nervous perspiration. She dried them self-consciously in a smoothing gesture down the sides of her slacks. Her pulse was throbbing erratically and her legs only just carried her to the front door.

Rans looked at her as she opened it, his expression granite-hard. "Your father left a message that it was imperative he see me at once," he said tersely, without even offering a polite greeting.

Lara swallowed, unable to smile even stiffly. With a nod of her head, she stepped away from the door, holding it open until he had walked into the hall. Rans didn't stop, but continued toward the study, ignoring her existence completely.

Her heart was in her throat as she followed him. A step inside the empty room, he pivoted. His gaze flicked to her. The blood mounted in her face at his accusing look.

"He's not here," she explained unnecessarily. "He had to leave unexpectedly."

"I'll come back when he's here."

"No, wait," Lara hurried, trying to remain calm but

unnerved by his uncompromising hardness. "He asked me to give you something."

"Very well." Rans moved to one side as Lara entered the room, his mouth thinning into a grim line.

His alert gaze watched her walk to the desk and pick up the folded paper lying on it. She held it for an instant as she sent up a silent prayer, then turned, holding it out for Rans to take. His hand reached forward, but stopped short when he recognized it.

"You have the wrong paper." His hand fell back to his side. "That's my letter of resignation."

"Yes, I know." Lara's voice quivered in spite of her efforts. "My father wants you to reconsider it.

"No." Rans turned abruptly, terminating the conversation with his action.

"Not to stay on permanently," Lara rushed, "but just for a few more weeks. That's all he's asking. Things are in somewhat of a mess around here. I don't know if you've heard."

Rans paused near the door, but kept his back to her. "Martin has my notice. If my leaving has caused difficulties, then that's his problem. I made my recommendation for a replacement and would have been able to work with him this past week if your father had hired him, or anyone else. Since he didn't see fit to do it, I don't see any reason to stay any longer than my two weeks."

"He's been busy trying to find someone to take over Trevor's work." Lara held her breath as Rans hesitated again, letting it out slowly in relief when he turned. "You haven't heard?" she breathed.

His gaze sliced over her. "I've been too busy to listen to gossip. What happened?" he said coldly.

"Was he sued for breach of promise by one of his mistresses? What a scandal that would be. And quite a blow to your self-righteous pride, too. He was supposed to keep his affairs discreet."

His words were meant to hurt, and Lara winced at the pain they inflicted. "I've filed for divorce. Trevor has left."

She had been afraid that Rans had known and that it hadn't made any difference to his decision. But the flicker of surprise in his expression dismissed that possibility.

"Since when?" He clipped out the question.

"Since a week ago Sunday." Lara waited. When he didn't respond, but kept studying her with a narrowed look, she continued anxiously. "With both you and Trevor leaving within days of each other, it puts a heavy burden on my father. Would you consider staying for a while longer?"

A frown creased his forehead as Rans thought it over and walked to the courtyard doors. "Is Trevor's absence supposed to make a difference to me?"

Nervously, she clasped the paper in both hands. "I hoped it would." She stared at it, the words blurring in front of her eyes.

"Why?"

Her widened eyes, shimmering and green, met his without flinching. "Because I want you to stay."

"Because of your father?" Rans persisted, not lessening the intensity of his piercing gaze.

There was a tenseness about him. He seemed to be holding himself rigidly still as if his tall, muscular frame was carved from stone. Lara kept wondering if she was up against a rock wall that nothing she said would penetrate.

"Partly," she acknowledged, dipping her chin. "He does need you."

"What's the other part?"

Achingly Lara studied his face, the roughly hewn jaw and chin, the faint lines around his eyes that crinkled when he smiled and the clefts that framed the firm line of his mouth, the wide tanned forehead and his thick, tobacco-brown hair. He was so aggressively virile that her whole body throbbed when he was near.

"Don't you know?" she whispered.

"No."

A heavy silence weighted the room while Rans waited for her answer. Lara gathered what little of her pride that remained and threw it away.

"Because I'm in love with you, Rans." Her voice quivered. "In my heart I divorced Trevor a long time ago."

Slowly he crossed the room, not releasing her from his pinning gaze. His hands settled on her shoulders, their touch making her sway toward him, but he firmly kept her away.

"Are you sure?" His fingers dug into her flesh as if he meant to shake the truth out of her.

"Very sure." She smiled tremulously.

Some of the hardness began to leave his expression as if the rock wall had started to crumble. "Am I a fool to believe you?" he mused absently, his gaze traveling over the cascading red-gold curls falling loosely around her shoulders and returning to the jewel brightness of her eyes.

"Probably," Lara murmured. "I'm headstrong and independent and spoiled. I lose my temper at the drop of a hat. And I'll turn into a jealous shrew when I'm old and wrinkled and not pretty enough anymore to make you—"

His mouth closed over hers in a passionate kiss to stop the enumeration of her faults. She melted against him, deepening the kiss with the hungry response of her own lips. Roughly his hands pulled her nearer. The torrid embrace stretched into minutes until Rans regained some self-control. Lara's arms remained locked around him as she nestled her head against his chest, the pounding of his heart sounding joyfully in her ears.

"You will stay. Promise me you will never leave." She tipped her head back to gaze at him.

"It'll be hell getting rid of me, wildcat," Rans growled affectionately, his fingers twisting into the flame gold of her long hair.

The light radiating from the velvet brown of his eyes took her breath away, at once possessive and passionate and gentle. A sensation of buoyancy seemed to fill her as if she was floating on a cloud.

"Tell me why, Rans," whispered Lara, watching the hard lips and waiting for them to form the three precious words she was aching to hear.

He didn't disappoint her. "I love you. That's why." He pressed his mouth against her temple, murmuring against her skin, "I love you, Lara. I love you." Repeating it as if the words had been bottled up too long inside of him.

Her fingers spread, moving over his back and shoulders in an exploring caress. "I love you too,

Rans." She rubbed her head against his chin and mouth, dissolving with emotion.

A tenseness seemed to grip him. "The way you loved Trevor?"

"Oh, no," Lara denied with a smiling sigh. "I loved his image. I was in love with love. His touch never shattered. His kiss never destroyed. I never felt alive with him the way I do with you. There was always something missing that made me feel incomplete. But not anymore, not when you hold me. It's as if I've come home at last."

"To stay, Lara," he declared firmly, "because I'll never let you go."

"I'll hold you to that." She shuddered, remembering the desolation that nearly entered her life when she'd thought she might never see him again. "You quit because of me, didn't you?"

"Why else?" His mouth crooked into a dry smile as he drew his head back to let his gaze rove possessively over her upturned face. "The job, the work, was everything I ever wanted. I knew that within a few weeks after I arrived. What I hadn't counted on was a beautiful redhead complicating the situation. I managed to ignore you quite successfully for a while. But you kept getting under my skin." Rans chuckled softly, his hands lightly caressing her feminine curves. "Even if you were like a block of ice. It was a challenge to keep chipping away to see if it was solid."

Lara leaned back against his arms, her hands sliding to his broad chest. An impish light gleamed in her green eyes as she met the glittering fire of his gaze.

"My first impression of you was that you were

arrogant." Her lips trying to conceal the smile hovering at the corners. "And I haven't revised my opinion at all."

The dimples came into play, carving sexy clefts in his tanned cheeks while his eyes crinkled at the corners. "You should have," Rans told her, "because with you I was never certain about anything except how much I wanted you. The night I walked home from the stable was possibly the longest walk I ever took. I had to come to grips with the way I was really feeling toward you."

"That night was a revelation to me, too," Lara admitted. "I had thought I was immune to any physical need. Before, I was revolted by a man's touch. But not that night. You wiped out the illusion that I was somehow different from everyone else. It was a little scary. No, a lot scary."

"How do you think I felt, realizing I was falling in love with another man's wife?" A muscle twitched in his jaw. Lara caressed it tenderly to ease his remembered pain. "I had to keep reminding myself you were married and didn't belong to me. And you didn't make things any easier," Rans accused with mock gruffness.

"I couldn't help it. I wanted you, too," she defended herself.

"I know. That's why I was leaving." He smiled fleetingly. "I knew that if I stayed, it was only a matter of time and I'd have you. I also knew I could never be satisfied with merely possessing you. I wanted you for my wife, to live with me, bear my name and my children. The prospect of an affair filled me with a bitterness that could have destroyed both of us." His mouth closed briefly over hers in a hard kiss. "And that is my proposal of marriage, honey. Do you accept?"

"Yes." Lara breathed the answer that had been written in her face since Rans had taken her in his arms.

His hold tightened around her. An almost inaudible groan came from his throat as he crushed her against him. "How in the world are we going to make it until your divorce is final?" he muttered into the fiery silk of her hair.

"I can survive anything as long as you love me," was her whispered reply.

"Maybe you can fly to Reno or Mexico," Rans suggested while her fingers lovingly explored the rugged contours of his face. "I don't want to wait another day."

"Neither do I. We'll find a way, and we'll find it together," Lara promised.

"We'll start a new tradition." There was a wicked glint in his eyes as a roguish smile spread across his face. "The MacQuade brides always live happily ever after."

THE MATING SEASON

Chapter One

The couple walked unhurriedly along the curved corridor of the airport terminal. Tall and willowy, the woman was unaware of the attention she was receiving from the men she passed. Her ash blond hair, a little longer than shoulder length, was cut in a windblown style that framed her face and its picture-perfect features.

Her jeans were of polished cotton in a sophisticated color. A black suede jacket was belted at the waist, permitting only a glimpse of her print blouse, which was open at the throat. Her black boots were high-heeled, clicking on the polished floor.

The man at her side matched her graceful, long-legged strides. He was only an inch or so taller than she was. His gray topcoat carried an expensive label inside, as did the charcoal suit beneath it. With dark, almost black hair, he was as good-looking as she was in his own way.

As they approached a newsstand in the terminal, he caught her hand and drew her inside to the magazine rack. Standing out among all the others was the cover of a fashion magazine. It was a portrait, caught forever by the camera, of the woman now gazing at it. Glistening lips held the hint of a smile while blue eyes radiated the brilliance of inner pleasure.

He took a copy from the shelf to examine the cover more closely. "Another one for your already full scrapbook." He cast her a sideways glance that was both assessing and admiring. "Jonni Starr, the hottest model in the country. How does it feel to have the most sought-after face?"

Jonni smiled somewhat wryly. "It doesn't feel any different until someone asks me a question like that," she admitted. She stared at the photograph on the magazine cover, knowing the face belonged to her yet seeing a stranger. "Sometimes it feels as if the woman is someone else, not me."

"There's only one Jonni Starr." He crooked a finger under her chin to lift her head and bring her eyes level with his. There was a teasing glint in his look. "And I don't care what your birth certificate says, I still believe your agent made up that name."

Soft laughter rolled from her throat. It was the same accusation Ted Matlin had made when they first met almost two years ago. They had met at a theater party for a new Broadway show Ted had produced, one of Jonni's rare evenings out.

"My mother will verify it for you, if you like." She repeated the same two-year-old answer. "Jonni was the closest she could come to naming me after my father, John Starr."

"I promise I'm going to ask your mother about it when I meet her," Ted warned, but with a smile. "I'll buy this magazine for her. Since it's only just come out on the stands, she probably hasn't seen it yet."

"She'd like that." Jonni smiled her agreement with his thoughtful gesture. Ted would have little difficulty charming his way into her mother's affection, but Jonni knew her father was a different matter. She waited while Ted walked to the cash register and paid for the magazine. He was a persistent and determined man. It had taken him two years, but he had finally won her over.

When she had first met him, Ted had seemed too charming, too sophisticated, too worldly to be trustworthy. She hadn't been impressed by his wealth. The Starr family of Kansas, with its oil and cattle, could have matched him asset for asset. The expensive presents he'd showered her with didn't turn her head.

When they'd met she'd lived in the spacious and beautiful apartment she'd had since arriving in New York six years ago. The rent had been paid by her father until her modeling income allowed her to take care of it herself. She shared the apartment with a fellow fashion model, strictly for reasons of companionship, not for financial help. There had been nothing material Ted could offer Jonni that she didn't have or couldn't get.

His status in the social and theatrical circles of Manhattan had not made an impression on her either. At their first meeting Jonni was already a highly paid and frequently booked model. She didn't need the reflection of his power and success to give herself importance, so the usual ploys hadn't worked with her. She had kept Ted at arm's length until he had eventually proved that his attentions were serious. It gave Jonni a secure feeling to know it had been a conscious decision and she hadn't been swept off her feet.

Tucking the magazine under his arm, Ted returned to her side and curved an arm behind her waist. "Shall we go and claim our luggage and find that air charter company? Or would you rather relax and have a cup of coffee at the restaurant first?"

"No coffee for me, thank you." Jonni glanced at the large wall clock in the Kansas City terminal. "We still have to fly all the way across the state. I don't want to run any risks of arriving after dark—the runaway at the ranch isn't equipped with lights for night landings."

"There's plenty of time," Ted assured her, but he didn't argue any further as he directed her down the corridor toward the baggage claim area. At a row of telephone booths he stopped and suggested, not for the first time, "Are you positive you don't need to call your parents so they'll be expecting us?"

"No." Jonni dismissed that suggestion with a firm shake of her head. "I want to surprise them," she insisted.

A raised eyebrow showed that he disagreed with her. "Surely there are some preparations that will be necessary before our arrival. I don't think it's right for us to come without giving them some warning."

Jonni just laughed at that. "What you don't understand, Ted, is that in this part of the country the latchstring is always out. My mother doesn't need to get ready for company. She's always ready, just in case. Besides, I don't want the red carpet rolled out. I want to go home without any fanfare."

"It's one thing for you to do it. You're the daughter. But what about me?" he pointed out. "What kind of an impression am I going to make as their future son-in-law?"

"I don't want them to know I'm bringing my fiancé home." She didn't attempt to check her frank admission. "When Mother and Dad meet you for the first time, I want it to be without any preconceived ideas about what you'll be like."

"What you mean is that they'll be blindsided by the arrival of the man who's stealing their daughter from them." Ted flashed her a smooth smile as they continued along the corridor.

"More or less," Jonni agreed. "Once they meet you, I know they'll love you. Besides, they're both eager to have grandchildren."

"Not too eager, I hope," he murmured dryly. At her quizzical look, he explained, "I'd like you all to myself for a while."

"If I haven't forgotten some of the things I learned in my rural upbringing, such things take time." The gleam in her blue eyes laughed at the serious tone of her answer.

"So I've heard." Ted's glance was both worldly and indulgent.

Her gaze dropped to the engagement ring on her finger. An enormous diamond solitaire reflected a rainbow of lights. "I only wish you hadn't been so extravagant over this ring. It's way too big."

Ted didn't seem too concerned by her vague criticism. "I wanted it to be large enough for anyone to see it. There can't be any question that you belong to someone, namely me."

"No one could miss seeing it." Jonni adjusted the ring on her finger, not accustomed to the heavy weight.

"I've never claimed modesty as one of my virtues," Ted admitted without remorse. His innate arrogance was part of his special brand of charm. Jonni accepted that, even though it irritated her at times. "I'm grateful you aren't cursed with any sense of false modesty. You're beautiful and successful, and you know it." An idle curiosity flickered across his handsome features. "You know, I've never asked what your parents think about your career."

"They're proud, naturally." Jonni shrugged. "In their eyes, I could never do any wrong."

"Then why are you so concerned about them finding out about me before the fact, so to speak?" questioned Ted.

"Because they'd ask where we'd live after we're married, and I'd have to tell them New York," she explained. "They still think it's a terrible place to live. They won't believe the statistics that say crime is decreasing—well, maybe they would if they saw it in *USA Today*. I haven't been able to convince them any differently."

"Didn't you mention that they'd visited you in New York?" He looked amused by her comment.

"Yes, I usually see them twice, sometimes three times a year. But this is the first time I've been back to Kansas since I left for New York six years ago." It didn't seem that long ago to Jonni. Yet, at the same time, it seemed much longer. Conflicting statements that were still true.

"Any particular reason?" he asked.

"The first year I was in New York, I didn't want to go back until I'd achieved some success. When my career took off, I didn't have time to go back. If Mom and Dad hadn't visited me so often, I would probably have arranged to have enough free time to come home," Jonni admitted. "With Gabe in charge, it was easier for Mom and Dad to visit me."

"Gabe? Who's Gabe? I don't remember his name being mentioned before," Ted commented with a thoughtful look.

"Gabe Stockman is dad's general manager." They arrived at the baggage claim area and Jonni's thoughts veered from Gabe Stockman. "There's the carousel with the luggage from our flight," she said, pointing.

When their luggage was retrieved from the rotating belt, Ted signaled for a porter. The man guided them to the gate where the chartered, twin-engine aircraft was waiting to fly them across Kansas to the Starr ranch. They climbed aboard while the pilot stowed their luggage in the baggage compartment.

"All buckled in?" the pilot inquired, glancing over his shoulder at his passengers in the rear seat as he settled into the left seat.

"Yes," Jonni answered, but Ted responded with only an uninterested nod.

"It'll just take me a couple of minutes to run through this checklist and we'll be on our way," the pilot promised. He was past middle age, all crisp and professional with a decidedly military air.

The next few minutes were filled with revving motors and lifting ailerons and flaps. Then the pilot requested permission from ground control to taxi.

A staccato response over the radio gave him the go-ahead and relevant information.

When it was their turn to roll down the runway, Jonni felt that familiar exhilaration. As the plane's wheels left the ground and tucked with a thump into the belly of the aircraft, she experienced a leap of excitement that came with flying. She glanced at Ted, who was passively looking out the window as the plane gained altitude, then settled back in her seat, realizing Ted didn't feel the same tug at his heart because she was the one winging her way home, not him.

Soon the plane turned west, crossing the Missouri River and flying over the flat wheatfields of eastern Kansas. After six years of living in the concrete city of New York, where the closest Jonni got to grass and trees was Central Park and occasional forays into the surrounding suburbs, she suddenly realized how much she missed the wide open feel of the country.

Below, the ground was laid out like a patchwork quilt in fields of varying shades of brown and green. The green of spring was tinting the pastures. The horizon stretched almost without limit. The vastness of the sky was a clear blue, broken only by a puffy cloud and the glare of the sun.

The drone of the engines meant conversation was difficult, but Ted made an attempt. "Rather monotonous, isn't it?" he remarked, referring to the almost unchanging landscape below them.

"Concrete buildings are monotonous. Mother Earth is always changing her clothes." Jonni corrected him without trying to argue. His expression revealed disagreement and she laughed. "Not everything west of the Allegheny Mountains is wasteland, Ted."

"No, there's Los Angeles," he conceded.

"Look below," she instructed. "We're flying over the Flint Hills. Aren't they fascinating?"

"If you say so." But his agreement was strictly an indulgence, not an endorsement. "I'm still waiting to see a sunflower. Kansas is the Sunflower State, isn't it?"

"Yes, but they don't grow all year round," Jonni chided him, then smiled. "I should be grateful you didn't get it mixed up with Iowa, the Corn State."

If Ted had exhibited more interest Jonni would have pointed out the route of the old Santa Fe Trail, which had wound across Kansas in the pioneer days. Instead she kept silent, watching the changing terrain the plane's shadow covered. When the plane banked southwest, the lowlands of the Arkansas River were beneath them. Farther along the river, out of sight, was the historic town of Dodge City where the trail bosses from Texas had driven their beef to the railhead.

They were nearing Starr country, where the Cimarron River snaked through the red hills. It was too soon to look for the ranch boundaries yet. Jonni leaned back in her seat. So much of the flight had been in silence that she glanced at Ted to see if he was still awake. He was, his gaze steadily watching her.

"I'm glad I insisted on taking two weeks off," she said. "It's going to be good to be home for a while. Are you certain you can't stay longer than the weekend?"

"I definitely have to be back by Tuesday," Ted stated. "Business, my dear. Besides, I would rather arrange to spend my free time on a long honeymoon than share it with you chaperoned by your parents. From all you've told me, they sound old-fashioned."

"Yes, but they're very nice. You'll like them," Jonni responded with total confidence. Being old-fashioned was a trait Ted made fun of, but it was also one he admired. Jonni was fully aware that part of her appeal had been the fact that she hadn't been easy to win. Once he had won her, he had no intention of letting her go, which suited Jonni just fine.

"Couldn't you stay a couple of extra days?" she asked. Saturday and Sunday would speed by so quickly. He would barely have time to become acquainted with her parents before he left. "I'd like to show you around the place."

"I'm afraid not," he replied without hesitation. "It would probably be all very interesting, but the great outdoors is not my style. A view from the air is all I need."

Jonni knew that and had become resigned to it. "Daddy will want to show you the operation. He's quite proud of what the Starr family has built."

"I promise you I'll be dutifully attentive and interested when he does," Ted assured her in a dryly mocking tone.

"You absolutely can't stay longer?" She repeated the statement as a question.

"I absolutely can't." Ted took hold of her hand and carried it to his lips. "We haven't even arrived and you're already missing me before I leave. No wonder I'm in love with you!"

"I love you, too, Ted," Jonni murmured.

Her hand patted his strong jaw. His skin was tanned brown by the rays of a tanning bed he kept in his enormous apartment. Kind of vain of him, but she had made use of it herself on one or two occasions. Leaning over, she placed a lingering kiss on his mouth.

The changing pitch of the engine's drone informed her that they were losing altitude and beginning their descent. She straightened back to her own seat, exchanging a warm look with Ted as the pilot glanced over his shoulder.

"We'll be seeing the airstrip soon," he told them.

After rechecking her seat belt to be sure it was securely fastened, Jonni glanced out the window. She was positive they were flying over Starr acreage even though it had been six years since last she saw it.

"Do you know what kind of condition this private runway is in?"

"It's a grass runway, but you can be sure it's in the best condition. My father has always insisted on that," Jonni replied with quiet authority. "It's on that plateau just beyond the buildings coming up on the right."

"I hope your parents are home," Ted remarked. "I'd hate to think we've come all this way only to find out they're on vacation."

"Don't worry, I talk to them every week. Last Sunday they were very definite they wouldn't be going anywhere until the heat of the summer," she reassured him.

The white, two-story building of the main house stood like a quiet sentinel on the plateau. The branches of the towering trees that surrounded it looked bare from the plane's height, but a new carpet of green grass was on the ground. Hay was stacked in great mounds near the barns and equipment sheds.

Red Hereford cattle dotted the rugged land around the ranch yard.

The pilot cautiously made a pass at the landing strip to inspect its condition. A warm feeling of pride spread through Jonni as the statement she had made echoed true. The grass strip was in flawless condition, freshly mowed as if they were expected. The wind sock on the small metal hangar was barely moving. Painted on the roof of the hangar was a large star, to signify Starr Ranch. The next time around, the pilot set up for the actual landing.

"It's quite a walk from the airstrip to the main house," Ted observed. "I hope you aren't planning a late-afternoon stroll."

"Someone will hear the plane land and come to investigate. We'll have a ride," Jonni stated prophetically.

With flaps down for a soft field landing, the pilot slowed the aircraft to near stall speed and gently set it down on the grass runaway. Short of the end of the strip, he turned the plane and taxied it to the hangar, cutting the engines. As the pilot climbed out to help his two passengers disembark, a pickup truck braked to a stop at the building and a tall man dressed in Levi's, Stetson and a denim jacket stepped out.

"You've landed on a private airstrip," he announced in a low-pitched voice that could border on a growl with the right intonation. At the moment it was only a politely worded demand to state their business or be gone. "There are several municipal fields in the area I can direct you to—unless you're having mechanical problems."

"I have chartered passengers for the Starr Ranch," the pilot replied evenly.

"Passengers?" The word was snapped out in wary disbelief.

At that moment Jonni stepped out of the plane onto the wing's steps. A throaty laugh came from her, rich with happiness to be home, yet controlled in its jubilation.

"Stop trying to order me off before I've even had a chance to set foot on home ground, Gabe," she declared in mock reproof.

She was met with silence as she negotiated her way off the wing. Standing on Starr grass, she lifted her gaze to the man standing near the wing tip. It was Gabe Stockman, who managed the ranch for her father.

Accustomed to being around men of her stature or only slightly taller, Jonni discovered she had to look up to meet his gaze, a fact she had forgotten after six years. Broad-shouldered, with a tautly muscled stomach and hips, Gabe Stockman was on the wrong side of thirty. The sun had weathered his hard-bitten features to the color of finely grained leather, tanned and smooth, with wavy lines at the corners of his dark eyes from squinting into the Kansas sun. A neatly trimmed mustache, as black as the hair beneath his dusty hat, was his only touch of masculine vanity.

The steady gaze of his eyes boring into hers, inspecting and appraising how she'd changed, was disconcerting to Jonni. There was something so frankly sensual about the way he was studying her that it made her nervous.

"Aren't you going to say something, Gabe?" she prompted to end the silence, which was beginning to make her uneasy.

His mouth quirked in that familiar, hard way, a corner disappearing into the edge of his black mustache. "It's about time you came back."

That warm feeling of coming home enveloped Jonni again. Gabe wasn't a stranger. He was a comfortable friend from the past, someone who had taunted her unmercifully about the boys she dated, who had questioned her ambition to become a famous model, but who had always listened to all her troubles, no matter how large or small.

"Is that any way to say welcome home after six years?" She laughed and crossed the space that separated them.

Her arms went naturally around his neck as she rose on tiptoe to kiss him. Automatically his large hands reached to grasp her waist, their size spanning her rib cage. Her lips had hardly touched the smooth mouth beneath the black mustache when his grip tightened. She exhaled with a whoosh, feeling her breath mingle with the warmth of his. Her heels rocked onto the ground as Gabe relaxed his grip, his face losing all its expression.

It was on the tip of her tongue to ask him what was wrong. Too late, she realized her mistake. Had startled him, that was all. She was no longer in New York where people who were practically strangers hugged and kissed in greeting. Gabe's inbred aloofness would not permit so demonstrative a greeting. She smiled and tried to ignore the incident.

That was easy, because Ted was walking toward her. Taking a step away from Gabe, Jonni turned to include him, stretching out a hand to be enclosed in Ted's grip.

"Gabe, I want you to meet Ted Maltin, my fiancé." She noticed Gabe's dark eyes narrow in piercing inspection. "Ted, this is Gable Stockman, the manager of Starr Ranch."

"I'm pleased to meet you, Mr. Stockman. Jonni has mentioned you often," Ted lied smoothly. He hadn't learned of Gabe's existence until that day.

He offered to shake hands but Gabe was already turning to look at Jonni. She couldn't tell if Gabe was deliberately ignoring the outstretched hand of her fiancé or didn't see it. But she had never been able to read his expression. He could summon up a perfect poker face, masked and unblinking in its regard.

"I suppose he's the reason you finally came home," Gabe observed with a grimness that implied censure.

Anger flashed in Jonni at Gabe's rudeness. He was talking about Ted as if he wasn't standing right there. "Ted is the main reason I've come home now," she admitted. "He only proposed to me last week." She moved closer to Ted's side. "Naturally I wanted Mom and Dad to meet him right away."

"I tried to persuade Jonni that we should call ahead to let them know we were coming," Ted explained, "but she insisted on surprising them. I hope Mr. and Mrs. Starr are here. They haven't gone away for the weekend, have they?"

"No, they're at the house." It was a clipped, precise answer, without elaboration or comment.

"Aren't you going to offer us your congratulations?" Jonni challenged, irritated and off balance because of his attitude.

"Congratulations," Gabe responded in a flat voice, devoid of emotion. His gaze flicked to the huge diamond in her engagement ring. "Don't wear that around the animals, it's liable to spook them." He issued the warning with a straight face, without a trace of humor.

Gabe brushed past Jonni and Ted to take charge of the luggage. "We'll load them in the back of the pickup." He picked up one of the heavier suitcases and started to reach for the second, of an equal size, when he glanced back to see Ted still standing beside Jonni, making no move to help. Gabe altered his choice to one of the lighter bags. With a nod of his head toward the remaining heavy bag, he said, "You can bring that one, Mr. Matlin."

Jonni felt Ted stiffen in resentment. A second later, he changed his mind and walked over to take the second suitcase. Her lips thinned into a straight line as her gaze met Gabe's shuttered look.

She was caught in the middle, aware of both sides of the situation. Ted had been accustomed all his life to having someone else do the heavy work. It was a natural oversight on his part to let Gabe and the pilot carry the bags.

On the other hand, Gabe was not a hired hand. He was the ranch manager, in total authority. He carried no man's luggage and would not assume the role of servant for anyone, not even a guest. He was Ted's equal, willing to help but not to do it all.

What bothered Jonni was the terse way Gabe had put across his point. It could have been accomplished with a bit more finesse, less bluntness. If Gabe had used friendlier wording Ted would not have bristled. Jonni suspected Ted might have even apologized for his oversight. Now there was an open breach between the two men. Jonni blamed Gabe, knowing he could have been more understanding.

With the luggage arranged in the back of the pickup the pilot climbed back into the plane. Its twin engines were revving up as Jonni slid into the cab of the truck. She sat in the middle between the two men, her shoulders rubbing against theirs. Ted held her hand in his, affectionately winding their fingers together. When Gabe reached forward to start the engine, his gaze flicked to their entwined hands. Jonni noticed the way his square jaw hardened in disapproval.

"Where are you from, Mr. Maltin? New York?" Gabe shot out the question, making the foregone conclusion become a condemnation. There was a harsh, abrasive thrust to his voice that reminded Jonni of the serrated edge of a knife blade.

"Manhattan, yes," Ted replied, and added deliberately, "Manhattan is in New York City."

Gabe shifted the truck into gear, coldly smiling. "I've heard that. What do you do for a living?"

"I have several interests—investments in real estate, office and apartment buildings and the like, as well as stocks and whatnot. And a few Broadway productions."

"It sounds as if you won't have too much trouble taking on the added responsibilities of a wife." The remark sounded offhand and indifferent as Gabe slowed the truck to make the bend in the dirt road ahead.

"I doubt that I'll have any trouble," Ted said cockily. "It will be a case where two can live as cheaply as one, since we won't have two apartment payments along with food and utilities."

"Do you mean you aren't living together already?" Gabe issued the question with the lazy surprise of someone expecting to hear differently.

"No, we're not." Jonni's cheeks flamed as his gaze slid slowly over the two of them. Jonni blamed the heat on outraged anger and Gabe's total lack of tact, rather than embarrassment, which was usually alien to her.

She shifted in her seat, trying to inch closer to Ted before the bend in the road slid her toward Gabe. Jonni ached a little where Gabe's hands had gripped her for an instant.

"I don't think you know Jonni very well, Mr. Stockman," Ted stated, coming to her defense.

"I don't think *you* know Jon very well." Gabe abbreviated her name, the glint in his dark eyes indicating an inner secret not to be shared with Ted. "'Johnny be good' used to be the catchword for Jonni around here. It was more often a plea."

What Gabe said was true, but not the way he implied it. She had always been too curious, eager to explore new territory, riding farther afield on the ranch than she was usually allowed. She was bold, not wild.

The bend in the road was negotiated without Jonni sliding into Gabe. Ahead of them was the house, her childhood home. The skeletal branches of the trees were dotted with green buds. Spring was only a few warm days from bursting out in an explosion of green. Gabe stopped the truck at the end of a stone path leading to the house.

"How long are you planning to stay?" He addressed

the question to Ted as he swung his long frame out of the cab.

"I'll have to leave on Monday. Jonni is staying for two weeks." This time Ted didn't need to be prompted, and walked to the rear of the truck to remove two of the suitcases.

Without the pilot to assist them, Jonni offered to help. "I'll carry some."

Gabe handed her the two lightest ones. "Two weeks isn't a very long time, compared with six years." There was condemnation in his brooding look. "What does that break down to? Two and a half days for every year you've been gone?"

"I was lucky to arrange that," she said defensively.

"Jonni is very much in demand." Ted smiled at her with pride.

Lifting the last of the bags over the tailgate of the truck, Gabe appeared unimpressed by the statement. "I don't think the world would come to an end if she took a couple of months off."

"It could seriously affect her career, though," Ted murmured with faint arrogance.

"So what?" Gabe said with an offhand shrug. "She'll be marrying you. Or are you going to continue working after you're married?" The question was directed at Jonni.

"Well, yes, naturally." She glanced at Ted, who smiled encouragingly. "Why shouldn't I?"

"I wouldn't dream of suggesting that Jonni give up her very successful career simply because she's marrying me," Ted said.

Gabe's gaze raked Ted from the top of his head to the polished tips of his shoe, as if doubting his manhood. There was something dismissive about the way Gabe turned away from him, a disgusted sound coming from his throat.

An understandable anger flared in Ted's expression. He took a step toward Gabe as if to challenge him.

"Don't." Jonni whispered the warning. She knew who would be the victor in a fight, and it wouldn't be Ted. He had neither the muscle nor the experience. And for all his determination, Jonni doubted that he could be as ruthless as Gabe was.

With remarkable restraint, Ted schooled his expression to blandness. He cast Jonni a stiff smile and indicated with a nod of his head that she should precede the two of them to the house. As she walked along the stone path she visualized the two men walking behind her. She was struck by the startling contrast between the two.

Both were tall and dark, but Gabe was rough with all blunt edges; Ted was smooth and polished, like a fine gemstone. Ted was dressed in an expensive, hand-tailored suit and topcoat and fine leather shoes; Gabe wore durable denims and boots worn down at the heel. Ted was sophisticated and well mannered, fully aware of which fork to use at the most elaborate table setting.

Gabe said what he thought, leaving no one in doubt of his opinion. Shrewd and uncannily intelligent, he had obtained most of his education from life while Ted had attended the best schools available, including two years at a European university. Both were unmistakably men, one refined and the other, raw and totally real. Jonni felt slightly shaken by the comparison and didn't know why.

Before Jonni reached the steps to the porch the front door opened and her father walked out, tall and slim, his blond hair silvering to gray. A look of incredulous delight beamed from his handsome face.

"I saw you coming up the walk and couldn't believe my eyes!" he declared.

"Surprise!" she laughed.

He paused to shout into the house. "Caroline! It's Jonni! She's come home!"

Chapter Two

The next few minutes were lost in a confusion of laughter and hugs. Everyone was trying to talk at once with no one understanding what anyone else was saying. If her father hadn't noticed Ted standing quietly beside Gabe, the chaos might have continued longer.

"Who's the young man you brought with you?" he asked, drawing her mother's gaze to Ted as well.

Before Jonni had a chance to make the introduction, Gabe identified Ted. "This is her fiancé."

Jonni hurried to fill the sudden silence that followed his announcement. "Mom, Dad, this is Ted Maltin, my fiancé," she confirmed Gabe's statement. "Ted, this is my mother, Caroline, and my dad, John Starr."

Ted shook hands with each of them, exhibiting his charm as he lingered over her mother's hand. "Now I understand where Jonni inherited her looks. It was obviously from you, Mrs. Starr. May I call you Caroline? Mrs. Starr seems too formal. You don't look old enough to be her mother—or my mother-in-law, for that matter."

"Flattery will get you anywhere with me, Ted." Her mother laughed at the lavish compliment. "And please feel free to call me Caroline."

"Thank you, Caroline." Ted made a mocking half bow over her hand.

Jonni accidentally glanced at Gabe during the exchange between her mother and Ted. She saw the look of disgust that flashed across his expression, quickly concealed by a very masculine scowl. *Damn him,* she thought angrily.

"I can't get over it, John. Our little girl is engaged." Caroline shook her head in disbelief, smiling and catching her lower lip between her teeth as if expecting it to quiver.

"Now don't start crying, Caroline," John Starr ordered, putting an arm around his wife's shoulders and giving them an affectionate squeeze.

"I'm not. I'm happy," was the reply. A questing pair of blue eyes turned their attention to Jonni, their shade the same vivid blue as her own. "You do love him, don't you? Oh, now what kind of a question is that?" Caroline Starr remonstrated with herself for asking it. "Of course you do, otherwise you wouldn't be marrying him."

"I do love him, Mom." Jonni said the words anyway, knowing they would reassure her mother. She raised her left hand to offer her engagement ring for her parents' inspection. "See?"

"It's beautiful!" her mother breathed.

"It's as big as a spotlight," her father remarked, and glanced at Ted. "She'll have you in the poorhouse if you let her keep picking out jewelry like this."

"Jonni is worth it." Ted smiled at her, but didn't

bother to explain that the ring had been his choice, not hers.

"Good heavens, what are we doing still standing on the porch!" Caroline exclaimed. "Come inside. John, bring your daughter's suitcases in."

As they entered the house Ted said, "I hope our arriving so unexpectedly won't cause you too much inconvenience."

"John and Caroline won't tell you if it does," Gabe inserted in a cool, dry voice.

"Don't listen to him." Caroline spoke up, dismissing Gabe's remark with a wave of her hand. "We never know when we're going to have company, so we're always ready. My daughter—and my future son-in-law—would never be an inconvenience to us anyway. Let me hang up your coat for you, Ted."

As Ted shrugged out of his topcoat, Jonni saw her father eyeing the suit and tie Ted wore. In this part of Kansas, men dressed much more casually. Ties, especially, were reserved for more august occasions. John Starr had never been one for formality.

"Which suitcases are yours, Jonni?" Gabe interrupted her thoughts. "I'll carry them up to your room."

"All but the two tan ones with the brown straps." That left four containing her clothes.

Gabe's raised eyebrow was the only indication that he questioned why a man who only intended to stay for three days would need two suitcases, but the question wasn't voiced. Jonni found it impossible to explain to Gabe how meticulous Ted was about his wardrobe. Everything had to coordinate perfectly. Then she became irritated that Gabe was making her feel an explanation was necessary to justify the amount of luggage Ted had brought. She pivoted away toward her mother, trying to conceal the annoyance in her expression.

"Will I be sleeping in my old room, Mother?" she asked.

"Yes, dear," was the smiling answer. "I thought Ted could take the guest room at the end of the hallway. Will that be all right?"

"Fine," Jonni agreed.

"Let's go into the living room," Caroline Starr began to move in that direction. "I'll fix some coffee. Or would you rather have something to drink?"

"I think what they would like," her father intervened, "is some time to rest and freshen up after that long plane trip here."

"Of course. How foolish of me!" Caroline stopped and glanced apologetically at Ted. "You must think we're terrible hosts. I don't have any excuse, except that it's so wonderful to have Jonni home again that I don't want to let her out of my sight."

"I can fully understand that, Caroline." Ted smiled, inclining his head in agreement. "I feel that way about her myself."

The adoration in his response was calculated to draw a pleased smile from her mother, and it succeeded. "I'll take you upstairs and show you your room," Caroline offered.

"There's no need, Mother, I know the way. Why don't you put some coffee on instead?" Jonni suggested. "Ted may want a drink later, but I'd love a cup of coffee."

"I'll fix some," her mother agreed.

As Jonni turned toward the stairs, she saw Gabe

had separated her luggage from Ted's. Her weekend bag was tucked under an arm. He was already holding one of the heavier cases and he was reaching for the other. Her cosmetic case still sat on the floor.

"I'll take this one, Gabe." Jonni bent to pick it up.

"I planned on that." His expressionless reply reinforced his statement that he took it for granted she would carry part of her own luggage.

The absence of any protest, even a polite one, piqued Jonni no end. Gabe seemed to be implying that if she thought she was going to be waited on like a celebrity, she was wrong. Jonni expected nothing of the kind and resented him for thinking she did.

The sparkle of veiled temper was in the glance she shot at Ted. "This way," she said to him. She added over her shoulder to her parents, "We'll be down shortly."

Gabe was four steps up the stairs before they started. Jonni sent daggers into the broad expanse of his tapering back. Under the weight of the suitcases his muscles bulged to fill the shirt. Yet he carried the suitcases with seemingly little effort. At the top of the stairs Gabe paused to wait for them, his sun-leathered face impassive in its expression.

"Your room is at the end of this hall, Mr. Maltin." The rolled brim of Gabe's Stetson dipped toward the right.

"Thank you." There was a faintly condescending ring to Ted's voice. "By the way, you can call me Ted."

"Ted it is."

Jonni waited for the ranch foreman to say you can call me Gabe. He didn't say it.

"There's an adjoining bath, shared with the other

guest room, which is unoccupied at present," Gabe stated. "Caroline always keeps fresh towels in it."

"I'm sure it will all be satisfactory." But the glittering light in Ted's eyes indicated he thought Gabe knew too much about the house and its routine. He gave Jonni a rather severe smile. "I'll meet you downstairs in twenty minutes or so."

"All right," she agreed.

As Ted started down the hall to his room, Jonni turned in the opposite direction toward hers, but Gabe and the width of the suitcases he carried blocked her way. She saw the dark, calculating look that watched Ted walking away, and immediately a wary feeling stole through her.

"By the way"—Gabe's low, drawling voice halted Ted's steps—"Jonni has probably forgotten after six years, but the floorboards there in front of John's and Caroline's door squeak rather loudly. You might want to keep that in mind if you're planning any late-night wandering." The implication, of course, was "to Jonni's room."

A nerve twitched below Ted's left eye, betraying his incensed reaction to the information. There was an instant of electric silence before he responded.

"Thank you, I'll remember that," he said. With the next step he took the floorboards creaked loudly under his weight. Ted hesitated for a split second before continuing on his way.

Gabe turned toward Jonni's room but she saw the deadly smile of satisfaction on his face before he completed the pivot. She did a slow burn as she followed him to her bedroom and closed the door. Anger simmered to the forefront when Gabe set her luggage down and turned to face her. The blue sparks shooting in her look didn't seem to impress him at all.

"If I were a man, I'd punch you in the mouth, Gabe!" Jonni declared, issuing the statement through tightly clenched teeth.

Amusement flickered briefly in his eyes. "Your fiancé doesn't appear to share your opinion. Maybe that says something about him."

"Ted is a gentleman. He doesn't feel it's necessary to resort to violence over a mere insult," she retorted.

"I suppose he thinks it's beneath him." Gabe's mouth curled into the black mustache above his lip. Almost instantly, his gaze made a leisurely appraisal of her figure, lingering on the agitated rise and fall of her pretty breasts. "Of course, if you were a man, Jonni, this situation would never have occurred." His gaze lowered to take in the rounded curve of her hips. "Even without the Gucci label on your jeans, I can tell you aren't a man."

A tremor shivered through her nerve ends at his blatantly sexual regard. "They aren't Gucci jeans. These are knockoffs." She denied the designer label for want of a more cutting response.

"Does that mean fake?" Contemptuous amusement was in his quick exhalation of breath.

"Yes."

"Okay. Got it. Well, they sure as hell aren't Levi's." His long strides carried him past her to open the door leading into the hallway.

"Damn you!" Jonni choked on a mixture of hurt and anger. "I almost wish I hadn't come home!"

Gabe paused in the doorway, throwing her with a hard, cynical look. "We can agree on that. I'm beginning to wish you hadn't come back, too." He walked out of her bedroom, punctuating his sentence with the closing of the door.

Jonni wanted to throw something at the door to vent the aching rage inside her. But it was a childish impulse and she wouldn't submit to it. She turned her back on the door, digging her long fingernails into the palm of her hand until the subsequent pain made her relax the fist.

In a burst of agitated energy, she set the cosmetic case on the dresser and began unpacking the contents. Below, she heard the banging of the screen door. The window beside the dresser faced the front of the house. Dotted swiss curtains of pale yellow were drawn from the window panes by ties in matching material.

Compelled by an invisible force, she stepped to the window as Gabe emerged from the shadow of the porch overhang. His unhurried, rolling gait gave an impression of lightness that was unusual for a man his size. It reminded Jonni of the easy, natural stealth of some big animal.

A tightness gripped her throat. Her homecoming hadn't lived up to her expectations and it was Gabe's fault. His discordant welcome had set the tone, throwing everything else off-key. Why? What had gone wrong?

What had happened to that invisible link that had always made her feel close to him? Had it ever existed in anything other than her imagination? Maybe in the past six years she had created in her mind the idea that there was some special bond between them.

Her relationship to Gabe had been hard to define.

Not friends—the gap in their ages precluded that. Not brother and sister, either, since Gabe had never permitted her to be that familiar with him. Jonni found that she couldn't categorize it to save her life.

Once, in her teens, she remembered that she had attempted to idolize him. But as soon as Gabe realized it, he had figuratively removed himself from her pedestal and ignored her puppylike adoration until it went away. He had destroyed the dream she had tried to build around him with a callous indifference that had bordered on mean. After that painful experience, Jonni had never again made the mistake of fantasizing about him as a lover.

What did that leave? Jonni couldn't find a label that fit. In her confusion she watched the tall, well-muscled figure walking toward the pickup truck. Black hair, black eyes, black mustache, all that was familiar to her, even the features that had hardened to shut out the world. Yet Jonni had the feeling Gabe was a stranger, that she didn't really know him at all, and never had.

At the sound of her bedroom door being opened Jonni stepped guiltily away from the window as if she had been caught doing something she shouldn't. Her behavior irritated nerves that were already raw. She had nothing to hide, especially not from Ted. As he entered her room his gaze narrowed curiously, having caught her furtive movement away from the window.

"Hello, Ted. Is your room all right?" She attempted to assume a bright facade to mask her previous reaction to his entrance.

"It's comfortable, yes." He walked to the window where she had been standing and looked out.

Glancing sideways, Jonni saw Gabe walking around the pickup to the driver's side. He opened the cab door and paused to look up at the window. The wide brim of his Stetson no longer shadowed his sun-bronzed face. His features were drawn in a grimly set expression before his chin came down and the hat brim shielded his face once again.

"He's pretty full of himself," Ted remarked. "Do all Western men swagger like that?"

Looking away from the window, Jonni didn't pretend that she didn't know whom Ted was referring to. "Some of them do, yeah." The metal slam of the truck door closing echoed into the room. She began arranging the bottles of lotion, perfumes and powder in the proper order on the dresser top. "But I wouldn't say that to Gabe's face if I were you," Jonni murmured.

Ted laughed without humor. "I have no intention of doing so," he assured her. "Not that I wouldn't like to back it up with a pair of brass knuckles, just for the hell of it!"

"Maybe I should have warned you that Gabe never heard of tact," she offered ruefully.

"I would have been better prepared." He moved to stand behind her, lifting aside her ash blond hair to nibble at the curve of her neck. "I expected an inquisition like that about my background and our future plans from your father—not a hired hand."

"Gabe is a hired hand only in the loosest meaning of the term, like an executive in one of your firms," Jonni corrected him. She shrugged a shoulder in vague protest against the exploring caress of his mouth.

Ted straightened to take her by the shoulders and turn her to face him. "I didn't realize it was a touchy subject with you, too." He studied her closely. Jonni squirmed inwardly at his examination of her, although she didn't know why, since she had nothing to hide.

"It isn't that." She ran her fingers along the lapel of his jacket, unnecessarily smoothing the material. "I just don't want you to let something slip that might cause more hard feelings."

"You know me better than that," he admonished.

"I'm just being cautious. I want you to make a good impression on everyone." To make up for the way she had avoided his previous caress, Jonni let her lips seek his to initiate a kiss that his practiced skill would finish.

With studied passion he took possession of her mouth and held her tightly within the circle of his arms. Her lips parted under his. His hand slipped inside her sweater jacket to cup the rounded peak of her breast. Jonni yielded to the consummate experience of his embrace.

When his arm tightened around her to mold her more firmly to his male shape, it touched the tender spot where Gabe had squeezed too hard. "Oof" She broke away from the kiss, wincing at the brief but sharp pain.

"What's the matter, Jonni? Did I hurt you?" Ted was instantly concerned and curious.

"I got a little banged around from the ride on the dirt road," she lied, reluctant to mention the incident with Gabe since doing so would accomplish nothing.

An understanding smile shaped his mouth. "I don't know which was worse," he acknowledged, "the springs on that truck or the chuckholes in that so-called road."

"Probably a combination," Jonni suggested, and stepped out of his encircling arms. "The truck could never be mistaken for your Mercedes, although the condition of the road reminded me a lot of New York."

"The driver wasn't your local drugstore cowboy, either." Ted brought the subject back to Gabe. "Where does he live? Here in the house?"

"No." With the cosmetic case unpacked, Jonni set it on the floor and lifted the suitcase containing her lingerie onto the bed. "Dad took one of the bunkhouses and turned it into private living quarters for Gabe. Why?"

"He seemed to know the house really well." Ted shrugged, then elaborated, "The location of your bedroom and the squeaking floorboards in relationship to the guest room, to be specific."

"Gabe is practically a member of the family," Jonni replied a shade defensively. "He's free to come and go as he pleases. Besides, nothing escapes his attention, no matter how trivial," she explained. "He has an uncanny memory. He can be in a room once and remember every detail—the location of furniture, a sticking window, which drawer an item is kept in—everything."

"Uh-huh. So what was his reason for being in your room?"

Jonni didn't like the way. Ted was looking at her—or what he might be implying. "One of my windows was stuck and Dad needed his help to get it loose," she snapped. "What did you think he might have been doing in here?"

"Hey, temper!" he chided with amusement.

"I resent your insinuations," Jonni said, unpacking her lingerie and shoving the expensive lace garments in the empty drawers of her dresser.

"Why are you so upset? For a second I thought there might have been something going on between you two six years ago, that was all." Ted studied her with alert curiosity. "Is he married?"

"No, he isn't married." Telling herself she was overreacting, Jonni tried to calm down.

"That doesn't surprise me." Ted kept his tone deliberately offhand. "He has a kind of he-man toughness that might appeal to some women, especially teenagers. He looks as if he just stepped out of a Marlboro ad. Is it inconceivable that you might have developed a crush on all that brawn?"

"Brawn *and* brains. Don't make the mistake of underestimating his intelligence," Jonni warned. "It isn't inconceivable that I could have been infatuated with Gabe, but it so happens that I wasn't." She finally answered his question.

"I was just finding out where the competition is," Ted said. "The last thing I want to do is compete with an old love from the past. I dislike being jealous of ghosts."

His explanation relaxed her. She abandoned her defensive attitude and smiled. "Gabe doesn't rank among my list of old flames, so you have nothing to worry about."

"Good. I'll feel more at ease about leaving you here alone for two weeks." He lifted a sheer nightie from her suitcase. It was chocolate brown, trimmed with mocha-colored lace. "Very pretty. I bet you look totally tasty in this. Remind me to have you model it for me sometime."

His glance was deliberately suggestive, but it wasn't his unsubtle message that was sending a pleasant glow of warmth through Jonni. It was the prospect that Ted could be jealous.

"You really thought it was possible that I might have loved Gabe, didn't you?" she marveled. "And it worried you."

"It concerned me." Ted avoided the stronger word. "Is it so unlikely that you would have?"

"Gabe is so much older than I am, for one thing," Jonni pointed out.

"So much older?" He appeared skeptical of that reason. "He can't be more than thirty-seven, thirty-eight. And you're twenty-five. Twelve years, even thirteen years, is not that vast an age span. We're nine years apart. So, if you're trying to imply that Stockman is old enough to be your father—well, he isn't."

"I . . . I guess you're right," she conceded after a second's hesitation. "Gabe probably seemed older because I was younger."

"Probably," Ted agreed, and handed her the chocolate brown nightgown of thin silk he had admired. "Are you going to finish unpacking or shall we rejoin your parents downstairs?"

"I can finish unpacking later. Mom and Dad are probably anxious for us to come down." Despite her reply, Jonni began to fold the nightgown neatly to lay it in the drawer.

When she did so, Ted walked over to let his hands slide over her hips, careful to avoid her sore middle.

His mouth made a slow trail across her cheek to her mouth.

"My sweet country girl," he murmured, "all dolled up in silks and satins and designer jeans." He teased her lips with a nibbling kiss. "I should have thanked Stockman for warning me about those squeaking floorboards. It could have been awkward if your father had caught me stealing into your room in the middle of the night for a preview look at you in that nightgown."

"Ted!" Jonni drew her head back from his kiss, worry creasing her forehead.

"Don't worry, love," he mocked her. "I won't embarrass you, although I admit to being tempted."

"Don't tease about things like that." She moved out of his arms, not seeing any humor in his remark. "I want my parents to like you. It's bad enough that you're from New York City."

"I suppose they would like me more if I were some Kansas hick." Hidden in his voice was the sting of truth.

"I'm a Kansas hick," Jonni reminded him, using the term with a surge of pride.

Ted didn't want to argue. Catching her chin between his thumb and forefinger, he planted a hard, silencing kiss on her mouth.

"You're the world's most beautiful, elegant hick," he declared. "And soon to be Mrs. Ted Maltin—with your parents' approval and consent, of course. Shall we see what we can do about obtaining that?"

Next he'd be referring to her as a redneck. Well, a lot of Kansans were—and they took pride in their hardscrabble heritage, not giving a damn what anyone called them. She ought to follow their example. Jonni linked her arm with his and started toward the opened door to the hallway. Her return to her childhood home had started out wrong, but she was determined the day wouldn't end the same way.

Chapter Three

"What will you have to drink, Ted?" John Starr acted the host, handing Jonni her requested cup of coffee. "Besides coffee, we have cold beer in the refrigerator and some whiskey in the cupboard."

"Whiskey, please, with a splash of water." Ted hitched up his pants legs as he sat down beside Jonni on the living-room sofa.

"A man after my own heart," her father declared in approval of Ted's choice. "I'll have the same. My only allotted, and prescribed, alcoholic drink of the day," he added.

"Prescribed?" Jonni questioned his use of the word.

But her father ignored it. "If we'd known we had an engagement to celebrate tonight, we'd have bought a few bottles of champagne and had it chilled and waiting to drink to the two of you." He walked across the braided rug that covered nearly the entire oak floor of the living room. "It'll take me a minute to get some ice and water from the kitchen."

"What did he mean, prescribed?" She addressed the question to her mother.

"It's that heart condition of his. Dr. Murphy prescribed a shot of whiskey a day. It's supposed to help his blood or calm him down or something. Can you believe it?" Caroline Starr laughed in a show of unconcern. "Those two men! One lies and the other swears to it."

"Is it serious?" Ted questioned.

"When you get to be our age, nothing is ever dismissed lightly. But no, as long as John doesn't overdo it, he'll live to be a hundred," she assured them. "Luckily, Gabe doesn't give John a chance to do anything too strenuous."

"When was this discovered? Neither of you said anything to me." Jonni frowned.

"Not in detail, no," her mother admitted. "We glossed over it a few years ago when we told you John was retiring to take things easier. He doesn't like to talk about it. It isn't easy for him, Jonni, to admit he isn't the man he once was. You have to understand that. Besides, it honestly isn't anything to worry about or I would have told you."

Approaching footsteps forewarned them of John's imminent return, and Caroline Starr swiftly changed the subject. "Did you notice the new drapes, Jonni? I finally found some material that would match that unusual shade of blue in the sofa. The room is so much cooler in the summer with them to cut the sunlight."

"Yes, I saw them." Jonni followed her lead, glancing at the light blue drapes hanging at the windows. "And you've added to your collection of wood carvings."

She glanced at the mantel of the fireplace. "That eagle and his nest are breathtaking."

"Wait until you see the old cigar-store Indian John found in a junk shop. It's a treasure, isn't it, John?" She glanced at her husband with pride.

"To us, it is." He grinned back as he added whiskey to two glasses.

"It was in pretty bad shape," her mother explained, "but John managed to restore a lot of it. He has it in his den. We'll have to show it to you later."

"You've done a lot of changing since I was home." Jonni glanced around the room. The arrangement of the furniture looked the same, but there were two new chairs and a polished oak table that she didn't remember. The walls were a lighter shade of blue gray to contrast with the woodwork. "It all looks familiar, but with little differences."

The ensuing conversation became a discussion of the house and its contents, what had existed, been added or removed since Jonni had lived there. Each item seemed to make its own conversation, whether it was the leather recliner her father hadn't wanted to part with or the rickety antique table her mother had paid a dollar for and spent a fortune to restore.

When her father finished recounting his story about a massive Lincoln desk of walnut he'd bought only to discover there wasn't a door or window large enough to get it inside the house, they were all laughing.

Caroline Starr wiped the tears of laughter from her blue eyes. "As you can tell, Ted, John and I share a passion for old things, not all of them necessarily antique. But we seem to get sentimentally attached to them all the same. I hope we aren't boring you with our nonsense," she said.

"Not at all," he assured her, and Jonni reached over to slide her hand over his, silently thanking him for not being bored by her parents' less than sophisticated outlook.

"We may not be boring him," her father said, "but I'll bet we're starving him. When will dinner be ready?"

Her mother glanced at her watch in surprise. "I didn't realize it was so late." She hastened to her feet.

"I'll help you, Mother." Jonni started to rise.

"No, you stay here with Ted," she insisted. "Everything is either in the oven or steaming. The table is already set. I can manage this time."

"I'm sure you can, but four hands—" Jonni began.

"Sit," her father ordered, his eyes twinkling. "Obey your mother."

"Yes, Daddy." She smiled and sank back into the cushions beside Ted, knowing it was a lost cause to argue with the two of them.

"You already have Ted's ring on your finger. It's a little late now to be trying to impress him with your cooking. You still can cook, can't you?" John asked. "I remember some of your first meals. Fortunately you improved very quickly before we all acquired terminal ptomaine."

"Yes, I can still cook. And let's not bring up past disasters," Jonni insisted with a laugh.

"Has she fixed dinner for you yet, Ted?" her father quizzed.

"Yes, a couple of times," he admitted. "But we eat out a lot."

"I much prefer Caroline's cooking to anything served in a restaurant," her father stated. "Wait until you taste what she can do with a piece of beef. It absolutely melts in you mouth. Caroline is an excellent cook. Jonni takes after her."

"I enjoy cooking, although I haven't had the time or opportunity to do much of it." Jonni hoped it wasn't a skill she'd lost from lack of use.

"You will," her father winked.

Ted noticed the vague apprehension in her expression and misinterpreted its cause. He squeezed her hand in reassurance. "Don't worry, honey, I won't chain you in the kitchen after we're married. With the hours I keep we'll probably still eat out a lot. It will be much easier than you trying to keep a meal warm until I get there."

"You don't exactly have banker's hours," Jonni admitted, and turned her sigh into an exhaled breath.

"John." Her mother appeared in the living room archway. "You're going to have to come out to the kitchen and talk to Gabe. He feels he's intruding by joining us for dinner this evening. He insists he'll fix something at his place, but you know he can't even crack an egg."

"I'll speak to him." John's mouth thinned into a no-nonsense line as he left the room.

Caroline hovered in the doorway. "Gabe is so impossible sometimes," she said with a slight grimace of disgust. "He's been like a son to John—you know that, Jonni. Why on earth would he get the idea that you wouldn't want him to have dinner with us?" She continued to gaze in the direction her husband had gone.

It was the last thing Jonni wanted, but it was also the last thing she wanted to admit to her mother. She kept silent, knowing her mother didn't really expect her question to be answered. She darted a sideways glance at Ted. His look held the same reaction she felt. He lifted her hand to kiss the back of it, a gesture of understanding.

At that moment her mother turned, seeing the exchange but not its meaning. "Jonni, maybe if you spoke to him, Gabe would get this ridiculous idea out of his head," she suggested.

"Oh, Mother, really, I—" The words of refusal came instantly, but Ted interrupted them.

"Perhaps it would be a good idea, honey," he said. "We wouldn't want Gabe to feel left out."

Her startled look questioned his sanity but obviously he no longer regarded Gabe as a threat. Which, of course, he wasn't.

Or was he? The fact that she had asked herself that question sent a shiver of alarm down Jonni's spine. She did her best to ignore it.

"I'll see if I can persuade him to stay," she agreed, rising.

With a falsely cheerful smile at her mother, Jonni walked past her toward the kitchen. Before she reached it, she heard the placating tone of her father's voice although she couldn't make out the words. As she opened the kitchen door a fist slammed down on the counter top, rattling the dishes in the cupboard above with its force.

"Damn it, John! You don't know how the hell I feel!" Gabe didn't attempt to control his vehemence. His intensity almost took Jonni's breath away.

"If you break Mother's china, I can tell you how she'll feel," she declared with a shaky laugh.

Gabe's head snapped in her direction. An invisible shutter closed his expression, concealing the emotion she had glimpsed for only an instant. Her father wore a worried look when Jonni glanced his way.

"Have you talked Gabe into having dinner with us tonight?" she asked.

"Is that what you're doing in here?" Gabe responded in a low voice. "To lend your persuasions to John's?"

His dark, expressionless eyes were leveled at her. Jonni wanted to look away, but she couldn't break free of an odd compulsion to return his gaze.

"Yes," she admitted. She assumed a straight-on pose as if staring into the dark lens of a camera instead of his eyes. "You know they want you to eat with us," she reasoned.

"What about you and your . . . fiancé?" He hesitated over the term, as if there was an epithet he would have preferred to use.

Bristling, Jonni curved her lips into a honey-sweet smile. "We want you to join us, too," she lied.

He smiled with one side of his mouth. The resulting expression conveyed his very mixed emotions. "Well, who am I to deny what Jonni Starr wants?" Gabe said at last.

"Then you'll stay?" The lilt of her voice made it a question.

A resigned sigh came from him as he turned away. "I need a few minutes to get cleaned up." Both his hands were on the kitchen counter. They seemed to be supporting almost his full weight. He looked and sounded very tired.

In a flash of sympathy at his apparent weariness, Jonni offered, "Can I get you a cold beer from the refrigerator, Gabe?" She saw the wicked, laughing look he gave her father.

"Maybe that's the answer, John. Maybe I should get rip-roaring drunk," Gabe suggested with cynical humor. To Jonni, he said, "No, I don't want a beer." Shoving himself away from the counter, he walked toward the rear of the kitchen. "I'll use the back washroom to clean up. Tell Caroline I'll be at the table whenever she's ready to serve dinner."

His behavior puzzled Jonni. Everything about Gabe puzzled her. She stared after the man she had thought she'd known until the closing of the washroom door shut him out of her sight. Her confused gaze wandered to her father.

"What's the matter with Gabe, Dad?" she asked. "What's wrong?"

He didn't immediately answer as he took a deep, considering breath and walked toward her. Draping an arm around her shoulders, he hugged her to his side for an instant, a sad smile on his mouth.

"Gabe had a bad day, one of the frustrating kind where things happen that a mere human is powerless to prevent. It's been a long, cold winter, and a dry spring so far. It gets a man down, even the strongest."

"I suppose that explains why he was so rude and irritable today." Jonni's mouth tightened, remembering how infuriating he had been. "But that's no excuse for bad manners."

"Under the circumstances, I hope you'll be a little

understanding and overlook Gabe's faults for now." That same smile was still on his mouth. "After all, you're happy. You've got what you want—a tall, dark, handsome man and a great big diamond ring on your finger." Keeping his arm around her shoulder, he walked her toward the door. "And that man is waiting in the living room for you. You'd better get in there and rescue him from your mother before she starts telling him all those stories about you when you were a baby!"

As always, he succeeded in coaxing a smile from her. "I love you, Dad." She planted a kiss on his cheek before moving ahead so they could walk single file through the door. Jonni paused on the other side. "What do you think of Ted, by the way? Do you like him?" An anxious thread wound through her question.

"He seems to be a personable and prosperous man. But what's more important is your happiness. That's all your mother and I want—for you to be happy. Are you?" he asked, studying her.

"Yes, I'm happy. I'm very happy," she hurried to assure him.

"That's all that matters," her father insisted.

They entered the living room together. Jonni's blue eyes were sparkling with pleasure at her father's ready acceptance of her choice of the man she wanted to marry. Ted lived in such a different world from the one John Starr knew that Jonni had thought he might be reluctant to endorse Ted until he had an opportunity to know him better. Her attention was on the man smiling so warmly back at her and Jonni missed the concerned look of her mother.

"Did you speak to Gabe? Is he staying for dinner?" Caroline immediately began an interrogation.

"Yes, he's staying," her father answered. "Jonni and I talked him into it."

"What was his problem?"

As her mother asked that question aloud, Ted rose to stand beside Jonni and whisper in her ear, "Did you use that famous Starr smile to change his mind?"

"And a personal invitation from you and me," she whispered back.

"Gabe's had a hard day." John Starr responded to his wife's question. "He didn't want his bad mood putting a damper on Jonni's celebration." He shrugged away the reason as unimportant.

"Where is he now?" Her mother looked toward the kitchen.

"In the washroom cleaning up." Jonni supplied that information. "He said he'd be only a few minutes and for you to serve dinner whenever you're ready."

"I'd better get the food on the table, then." She hurried to the kitchen.

Ted glanced at his reflection in the mirror hanging on the wall opposite him. An ornately carved wooden frame surrounded the oval glass. It was an heirloom brought by the first of the Starr family to settle in Kansas, and was thus entitled to prominent display in the living room.

"Maybe I should have changed into a clean shirt," Ted commented as he smoothed the length of his tie inside his jacket and inspected the result.

"No, you shouldn't have," Jonni responded.

His comment had drawn an amused and slightly derisive look from her father. She had explained to

Ted that her parents didn't stand on ceremony, but the habit of changing for dinner was too deeply ingrained in him. He was simply too fastidious about his appearance.

"We seldom have reason to wear a suit and tie around here"—her father injected the comment into their exchange—"except to church on Sunday."

"New York's dress code isn't quite that relaxed." Ted turned from the mirror, looking a little dissatisfied.

It wasn't all that strict in New York. Jonni could have told him about a number of excellent restaurants and nightclubs that didn't require formal attire, and all the people she knew who dressed casually or even bizarrely. But what was the point when he didn't go to those places or associate with those people? She kept silent.

A few minutes later her mother asked them to come to the dining room table. With an odd number at the table, a balanced seating arrangement was impossible. Her parents were at opposite ends of the rectangular table with Jonni and Ted seated on one side facing Gabe. The arrangement was uncomfortable, but the alternatives weren't any better.

"How long have you two known each other?" Caroline Starr passed the sour cream and potato casserole while her husband carved the meat. "I know Jonni has mentioned you in her letters, Ted, she sent all those digital photos—"

"Took us forever to figure out how to download the dang things." Her father winked at Jonni.

"Yes, but it was worth it. And she spoke about you when we talked to her on the phone, but . . ." Caroline's voice trailed off so he could answer her first question.

"We met two years ago."

"That long?" Her mother looked surprised.

"It wasn't a whirlwind courtship." Jonni laughed and accidentally looked into a pair of hard black eyes across the table from her. There was a nervous fluttering in the pit of her stomach, ending her laughter, but she kept the smile on her face.

"She was elusive," Ted told her mother before smiling at Jonni.

"And he was persistent." There was a teasing inflection in her voice, but a little twinkle in her eyes.

"I regret that I never had the opportunity to meet you or John during your visits to New York to see Jonni. Unfortunately, I was always incredibly busy. Too many commitments, too many meetings—you know how it is," Ted said.

"If we'd suspected that it was serious between the two of you, we wouldn't have been so shocked when you arrived today," her father stated, setting down the carving knife and fork.

"How long will you be able to stay?" her mother asked, and instantly added, "I do hope you don't have to leave right away."

"I'll have to leave on Monday," Ted began the answer.

But Gabe finished it. "Jonni is staying for two weeks." It was his only contribution to the conversation thus far. There something faintly condemning in his tone, as if he implied that Jonni expected them to feel honored she was staying that long. But she was the only one who seemed to notice his biting dryness.

"Two weeks. How wonderful!" her mother exclaimed. "We'll have time to make plans about the wedding. Have you set the date yet?"

"Not yet," Jonni admitted.

"Soon," Ted said. "After the length of our courtship, I don't think we need a long engagement."

"You would make a beautiful June bride," her mother declared, passing the platter of beef to Gabe. "That's only two months away. We'll barely have time to have the invitations printed. We'll need to speak to Reverend Payton, too, about reserving the church." As Caroline Starr began listing the arrangements that had to be made, it occurred to her that she hadn't consulted her daughter about a few major decisions. "You are planning a church wedding, aren't you?"

"Yes." The answer was hesitant as Jonni darted a sideways glance at Ted and did her best to ignore the sharp, questioning look from the man seated opposite her.

Her mother looked from her daughter to her future son-in-law. "You were planning to be married here in Kansas, weren't you?"

"Actually we had discussed having the wedding in New York," Jonni said tentatively.

"But all our friends and family are here," her mother protested.

"Now, Caroline," her father interrupted to calm his wife, "it's *their* wedding. And you must remember that they have many friends in New York, plus Ted's family."

"I suppose so," she conceded. "I just always imagined Jonni walking down the aisle of the church where she'd been baptized and confirmed. There are so many endless details in planning a wedding—flowers, the wedding cake, gown fittings, the reception, wedding music. How will you ever be able to arrange all that, Jonni, and work, too?" Her mother made it sound totally impossible.

"We can have most of it done for us," Ted stated. "There are professional firms that arrange entire weddings down to the last details."

Her mother's forthright nature made her speak her heart. "But that's so impersonal!"

Jonni tended to agree with her, but under the circumstances it was the most logical route to take. Across the table, Gabe was subjecting her to a meaningful look she didn't know the meaning of.

"Part of the fun of having a big church wedding is picking out the little things like the bouquets on the pews or the champagne glasses, or racing to the printers because a name is misspelled. It builds up the excitement to a wedding. The ceremony itself is usually an anticlimax," said Caroline.

"After all these years, I finally know how she felt when we exchanged our vows," her father joked.

"Oh, John, you know that's not what I mean," Caroline returned impatiently.

"What she means is—if you two are getting married in New York, we will probably have to move there so she can take charge of the wedding." He continued to tease his wife even as he made the serious suggestion.

"That's a wonderful idea, Mother," Jonni agreed

with it. She laughed. "And it'll save on the expense of phone calls to Kansas."

"We could do that, couldn't we, John?" Her mother latched on to the suggestion with growing enthusiasm. "Gabe can look after things here," she added to enforce it.

Jonni shot Gabe a questioning look, but his gaze was focused on his plate. A muscle flexed along his jawline, contracting sharply.

"Not a problem, Caroline. I can see to the ranch," he agreed.

"It's all settled, then," the older woman announced with a lightened expression. "When you go back to New York, Jonni, will you look for a small apartment your father and I can rent for a couple of months?"

"There's no need to rent an apartment. Vickie, my roommate, is moving out at the end of the month—the firm she's working for is transferring its headquarters to California. You and Dad can have her bedroom." It was all working out so perfectly it seemed predestined, Jonni thought.

"That's ideal," her mother enthused. "While you're here these next two weeks, we'll have to start making up a list of family and friends we'll want to invite to the wedding."

"It's a bit early for that, isn't it?" her father asked.

"It's better than leaving it until the last minute," was Caroline's argument. "Have you looked for a place to live after you're married?" She addressed the question to both of them, but Jonni answered.

"We don't have to. Ted's apartment is huge and beautifully decorated. It's much nicer than mine, too. Wait until you see it."

"Have you been in it?" A faintly shocked expression registered in Caroline Starr's face at the thought that her daughter had been in a man's apartment.

Jonni knew her mother thought every handsome New York bachelor's bed had a giant, woman-attracting magnet under it.

"Yes, Mother," Jonni replied, and refused to elaborate.

"Excuse me." Gabe rose abruptly from the table, his water glass in his hand. "I need some more water."

"I'll get it for you," Caroline volunteered.

"I can manage," he insisted, halfway to the kitchen door.

His sudden departure left a confused silence, the rhythm of their conversation broken. It was several seconds before anyone attempted to resume it. Then it was Caroline.

"Wouldn't you rather have a house than an apartment, Jonni?" she asked. "A place with a lawn and some trees, your own space?"

"Naturally I would. But you'd have to have a penthouse with a terrace to do that, and even then the lawn would be about the size of a postage stamp. And it would cost, oh, about ten or twelve million in Manhattan," Jonni explained tongue-in-cheekily. "A plain old apartment is much more practical and convenient. You'll understand what I mean once you see Ted's."

"I know there are real houses in New York," her mother persisted.

"Yes, there are. But they're in the outer boroughs or the real suburbs, which means Ted and I would have to commute. It's definitely more logical to live in the center of everything," Jonni insisted.

"But in the center of New York?" Her mother grimaced.

"I've been living there for the past six years," Jonni reminded her. "You make it sound awful! New York is an amazing, exciting city."

"It's so crowded and congested—and all that concrete. I should think you would miss the country. You were such an outdoors person," her mother declared.

"I still am," Jonni assured her. "I have my own horse and I go riding several times a week. I'm outdoors whenever it's possible. There's lots of places to swim and you can ice skate any time of year at Chelsea Piers. And I like to jog through Central Park."

"That's dangerous." Her mother frowned at her in sharp reproof.

"Not if you're pounding the pavement with ten thousand other joggers, it isn't." She tried not to smile in the face of her mother's genuine concern. But the twinkling sparkle of amusement was in her blue eyes when she looked up to see Gabe return to the dining room. His black gaze looked and held her. A funny breathlessness got to her and her heart beat unevenly. It was really quite strange. The contact was broken as he pulled out his chair and sat down, placing the filled water glass by his plate. Ice cubes clinked against the crystal sides.

"Actually, Caroline," Ted was saying, "I'm more concerned about Jonni being injured while riding her horse than I am about her jogging though Central

Park with her friends. I've tried repeatedly to persuade her to sell the beast, but she refuses."

"Where do you ride?" her father asked.

"Surely not in all that traffic?" her mother protested. "And where on earth do you keep it?"

"At the Claremont Riding Academy on the Upper West Side. It's a really nice old building, oh, five or six stories high, that looks just like the other ones next to it. But the horses go up ramps inside it to get to the stables. And Central Park has a network of beautiful, well-maintained bridle paths," Jonni explained. "So you see, I'm really still a country girl at heart."

"You would never know it when she's in New York," Ted stated. "She's smooth and polished, a real sophisticate."

"I don't think there's enough water in New York to wash away the dirt between Jonni's toes." Gabe ran an assessing eye over her that seemed a little too penetrating. Jonni wasn't sure that she wanted him to see that deeply into her. "It's part of her," he concluded.

"You could be right." Ted's grudging admission indicated that he didn't like the idea of agreeing with Gabe about anything but for the sake of harmony, he would.

There was a lull in the conversation before her mother sighed. "I still can't get over the fact that our little girl is finally going to be married. I was beginning to think you would never find anyone and settle down, Jonni. Now, it's happened so suddenly that I don't seem to be able to believe it."

"Not all that suddenly," Jonni protested. "I've known Ted for two years."

"I know, I know, but you never even hinted it was serious between you." Her mother picked up the bowl of potatoes and offered it to Gabe. "More potatoes?"

"No, thank you." He took the bowl and passed it on to her father at the head of the table.

"I may work slowly, but I'm very thorough," Ted responded to her mother's comment. "When I proposed to Jonni, I wanted to be certain she'd have no doubts about accepting."

"Just think, John." Caroline Starr beamed a smile to the man at the opposite end of the table. "We're finally going to have our grandchildren after all this time!" Her loving glance encompassed Jonni and Ted. "I do hope you two aren't going to be one of those couples who wait years to have your children?"

Jonni hesitated, darting a look at Ted. Planning a family was one of the few things they hadn't discussed. She had no idea what his views were on the subject.

Ted laughed easily. "I think it would be better if Jonni and I were married before we become concerned about how soon we'll start a family." He had avoided a direct response and Jonni knew no more than anyone else about how he really felt about the subject.

"I think you'd better switch topics, Caroline," John Starr suggested, "before you end up asking something that might prove embarrassing to everyone."

"If you say so," she conceded, but couldn't resist adding, "I've never kept it a secret from Jonni how much I want grandchildren."

"Would you excuse me?" Gabe rose from his chair. "I have some paperwork to do."

"But what about dessert?" Caroline looked at him in surprise.

"Not tonight, thanks." His sweeping gaze included everyone at the table. "Good night." He didn't look any too happy. In fact, his eyes were brooding when they touched on Jonni. It ruffled her fur. She hadn't said or done anything to make him upset.

After the front door had closed, her mother said, "Gabe is pushing himself too hard, John."

"Nonsense. He's simply very conscientious." He leaned back in his chair and rubbed his full stomach. "Did you say something about dessert?"

Chapter Four

After dinner, Jonni and Ted went for an evening walk. Hand in hand they strolled along the rutted lane. The air was brisk and the velvet sky overhead was littered with stars. Jonni's gaze searched out the Big Dipper.

"You'd better watch where you're going," Ted suggested dryly, reproaching her star-gazing activities. "This ground is pretty rough and uneven."

"If I stumble you'll catch me, won't you?" she asked with a flirtatious tilt of her head.

"I intend to spend the rest of my life catching you," he told her with loving warmth.

Something black swooped down at them. Ted flung up an arm to protect his face and ducked, but the thing had already flown off into the night.

"What was that? A bat?"

Jonni laughed. "It was probably a bird."

He stopped and pulled her into his arms. "So you think I'm funny, do you?"

"I think you're a big, good-looking dude," she declared.

"A city dude who's very much in love with you."

His mouth covered hers in a long and satisfying kiss. She snuggled closer to the warmth of his body, sliding her arms inside his topcoat. It was very enjoyable in his embrace and it led her to think of other things.

"How do you feel about having children, Ted?" she asked.

He shifted her to his side, keeping an arm around her as he started walking again. She fell into step beside him. It was too dark for her to see his face clearly, so she couldn't read his expression.

"Any plans for a family will definitely have to wait a while," he said. "We have to consider the effect it would have on your career."

"Why should it affect it?" She frowned at his answer.

"Well, pregnant celebrities get on the covers of *Vogue* and *Vanity Fair,*" Ted said. "Pregnant models don't."

"They still get work," Jonni argued. "Up to a point."

"It wouldn't be wise to have to limit the kind of assignments you can accept. Besides, you're just reaching the peak of your success. Why throw it all away? Your popularity won't begin to wane for another four to six years. We can think about a family then," he reasoned. The arm around her waist tightened in a reassuring hug.

"But by then I'll be in my thirties and my biological clock will really be ticking."

"That's true," he acknowledged.

Jonni strained to see his face. A tiny shaft of fear splintered through her. He was staring straight ahead, not looking at her. A question loomed in her mind.

"Ted, do you want to have children?" Jonni forced her voice to be calm.

He hesitated. "Sure. Especially if we can improve the odds on the sex. I'd prefer a son. That's only natural. My height, your looks, smarter than the two of us put together." But his voice lacked enthusiasm for the idea. He had said it because it was expected of him.

"You can't pick and choose. There's no such thing as a designer baby. That's not natural at all."

"Well, maybe by the time we get around to it, we'll be able to," he said noncommittally.

Something died inside her and Jonni felt cold. "Brr!"

Ted shivered as if feeling the sudden drop in temperature, too. "It's getting cold out here. Let's go back to the house."

"Yes, I'm getting tired anyway," she agreed in a listless voice.

Dressed in a faded pair of denim jeans and a blue pullover sweater that showed equal signs of wear, Jonni tiptoed down the steps. Ted was a late sleeper and she didn't want to wake him. It was early, only a few minutes past six, but she was accustomed to rising with the sun. Outside the birds were singing and the morning sun was warming the air.

At the bottom of the stairs she began humming to herself, a happy, whimsical tune. She sauntered toward the kitchen. At this hour, that was where she would find her parents. The tips of her fingers were hooked inside the back pockets of her blue jeans. A silk scarf of blue and gold paisley print formed a wide band around her head. The ends escaped from the ash-blond length of her hair to trail over the front of her shoulder.

Her parents were seated at the small breakfast table when she entered the kitchen. They looked up, surprise changing to smiles at the sight of her.

"Good morning, Mom, Dad."

"Good morning, Jonni," The greeting was echoed in unison.

"You're up early this morning," her mother commented.

"I always am," Jonni replied, and walked to the refrigerator.

"We just finished breakfast. You remember how your father always likes to eat the very first thing after he wakes up. Can I fix you something?" her mother offered.

"No, thank you. I'll just have some juice." She took the pitcher of orange juice from the refrigerator and moved to the cupboard where the glasses were kept. As she filled one of the glasses with juice, she realized how comforting it was to find things still in the same places, routines unchanging. It rolled back the time to the years when she had lived here.

"Something more than juice, surely. How about some toast?" her mother suggested.

Jonni laughed. She had never been able to eat in the mornings, but her mother had always tried to persuade her to have something. Not even that had changed.

"This is all I want." She took a sip from her glass and winked at her father. "I have to watch my figure."

"I thought that was Ted's job," he teased dryly.

"Yes, and he makes the most of it."

"Is Ted awake? Will he be coming down?" Her mother rose to refill the two coffee cups on the table.

"He's still in bed, I think," Jonni answered, and joked, "he's a city boy, accustomed to sleeping until a saner hour in the morning."

"I was up around midnight," her father said. "I saw a light shining from under his door."

"He was probably reading." Jonni shrugged the observation aside as nothing to be concerned about. She wandered to the window above the kitchen sink and drank the last of her juice. "It's a beautiful morning, isn't it?"

"It looks as if it's going to be a warm spring day," her father agreed.

"I think I'll go walk around. Explore a bit," Jonni said and set her glass on the sink counter. As she walked to the back door, she glanced over her shoulder and waved. "See you later."

Outside, Jonni followed the path worn through the lawn. Its route was the most direct line to the barns. The air was crisp, the sky a pale morning blue. The temperature was low enough that she was glad she'd worn her old pullover sweater over her long-sleeved white blouse. It kept the chill from her skin.

Shoving her hands in the front pockets of her jeans to keep them warm, she strolled toward the barns. She could smell the hay mixed with the freshness of clean air. The large sliding door at the first barn was open.

From inside she could hear the noises of horses eating, blowing the grain dust from their noses and bumping the sides of their feed troughs to get every last grain. The warm, pungent scent of horses wafted through the door. It sounded crazy, but she liked that smell. It was like perfume to her, but she doubted that everyone would agree. Ted didn't. She had always been careful to shower and shampoo when she returned from riding before seeing him.

Metal pails clanged together inside the shadowed interior of the barn. The sound came from the feed bin. Jonni paused inside the wide opening to let her eyes adjust to the absence of direct sunlight. The door to the grain room closed and she turned.

A man walked toward her, dressed in the rough clothes of a cowboy, his short legs slightly bowed. He hesitated in midstride when he saw her, then continued forward.

Gloved fingers reached up to touch his hat brim. "Mornin', miss."

As he walked past her outside, he carefully averted his eyes. Jonni smiled. She had forgotten how shy some Western men could be. There had been recognition in his first brief glance. He knew who she was, but he hadn't forced an introduction of himself, a gesture of respect for her privacy. Jonni had missed that in the six years she had been living in the East. There, it seemed only aggressiveness was recognized.

A bale of hay was dropped from above to land on the barn floor in front of her. It bounced once, sending up a cloud of chaff and dust. Some of it filtered into Jonni's lungs. She coughed and waved to clear the air she was breathing.

Looking up, she saw Gabe standing at the edge of the opening to the hayloft. His stance was relaxed, one knee slightly bent. His arms were at his side, leather gloves protecting his hands. Instead of a jacket, he was wearing a suede vest lined with sheepskin. Wisps of hay and chaff were clinging to the rough denim fabric covering his muscled legs. He looked tough and fit, a man of the West with his hat pulled low and that dark mustache shadowing his mouth.

Irritation simmered through Jonni as she realized he had tossed that bale of hay down without checking to see if anyone was below. But she hadn't been anywhere close so it was pointless to say anything.

"Good morning." Her greeting was sharp with a ring of challenge.

"You're up early." He lifted his hat and settled it back onto his head in almost the same position as before.

"Why does everyone seem so surprised by it?" Jonni asked. "First Mom and Dad, now you. I've always been an early riser."

"Were you? You've been gone six years. We've probably forgotten." His comment on her prolonged absence struck a sore nerve, but he was already turning away before she could retaliate. "I've got a couple more bales coming down. You'd better step out of the way."

"You could have warned me the last time," Jonni retorted, and moved to stand close to the door.

"I saw you."

Jonni could hear his flat voice and the sound of his footsteps walking in the loft above her, but she couldn't see him. "You could have said something just the same."

"Like what?" Gabe appeared briefly in the loft opening to toss down the bale he carried, then disappeared.

"Like 'good morning.' It's considered good manners to greet people when you see them."

Gabe came back with the third bale and it tumbled to the floor with the others. "Good morning." He recited the phrase she had prompted. He jumped down from the loft, landing on his feet like a big cat.

Jonni shook her head in exasperation, frustrated and at a loss as to how to cope with his terseness.

"Do you want to give me a hand with these bales?" Without waiting for an answer, Gabe picked up the nearest one and started toward the row of partitioned mangers.

Hesitating for a mutinous instant, Jonni walked to a second and reached down to pick it up by the parallel bands of twine. The taut string bit into her fingers as she tried to lift. It was too heavy. She could barely get it off the ground.

"It weighs a ton!" Jonni dropped it within an inch of where it had been, groaning from the exertion.

Gabe stopped, carrying his with little obvious effort. "About eighty pounds is all. You're out of condition."

"Eighty pounds is all." She repeated his words sarcastically.

"Maybe less." He shrugged. Down the row of stalls, a horse stretched its neck over the manger and whickered at the delay. "Here." Gabe set the bale he was carrying on the floor and broke the twine to free the square bale of hay. "Put some hay in the mangers for the horses. I'll bring the other bales."

Jonni took a portion of the unbound hay and deposited it in the first manger. A chestnut horse plunged its nose into the strands. "Who was that man who left when I came in? Is he somebody new you've hired?" she asked as she walked back to the bale for another armload of hay.

Gabe carried the second bale farther down the line. "Bill Higgins. He's not exactly new—he's been working here four years now. He and his wife have rented the old Digby house. He was in town all day yesterday. His wife is in the hospital."

"Oh? Is it serious?" As Jonni emptied the hay into the manger and turned back for more, she fell in step beside Gabe.

He looked down at her, his expression cold and remote. "What do you care? You're only going to be here two weeks."

She stopped short, his response acting like a slap in the face. "Damn you, Gabe Stockman!" She trembled with indignant anger. "I asked because I was interested. I care about people."

"You have a hell of a way of showing it." He continued forward and picked up the last bale.

Jonni planted herself in his path. "Exactly what is that supposed to mean?"

Gabe stopped, resting much of the weight of the bale against his leg. "It means for the past six years you've been waltzing around New York in your fancy clothes and jewelry. You didn't have time for anyone but yourself. Then you get a notion to come back here. What are we supposed to do? Get down on our knees and be grateful a Kansas Starr has decided to come back to our heavens for two weeks?"

When he started to push his way by her, Jonni grabbed at his forearm to stop him. "I couldn't come back before now. I was working."

"Sure." His tone was derisive.

"I was working!" she repeated angrily.

"Very hard work it was, too," Gabe mocked. "Getting your picture taken."

"Does it sound easy?" Jonni snapped. "You should try it sometime. Get up at the crack of dawn and rush to some studio. Sit in a chair for two hours to have your makeup done and your hair styled. Then pose in front of hot, bright lights for hours and smile until the muscles in your cheeks quiver and ache. Some designer is usually standing in the background screaming that you're sweating all over his magnificent creation. Oh, I have an absolute ball every minute, Gabe!"

"It sounds like it," he commented, some of the coldness leaving his look.

"It doesn't end when the shoot is over," Jonni continued, still steaming from his previous remark. "No, you have to watch what you eat so you don't gain weight or so your face doesn't break out. And you have to go to bed early so the camera won't discover any shadows under your eyes the next day. It's a very glamorous profession, but not when you're in it. It's work, hot, tiring work. If you want to stay on top, you have to look better than the super-skinny teenagers on their way up. There's a lot of competition and I'm pretty sick of it." Her voice rang with six years of tiredness, frustration and disillusionment.

Sensing that the heat of her temper had been vented, Gabe stepped around her with the bale and walked down the row, speaking as he walked. "I told you six years ago you wouldn't like it. That kind of life isn't for you. But you wouldn't listen to me."

"Is that what all this has been leading up to?"

Jonni asked with incredulity. "You just wanted an opportunity to say 'I told you so,' didn't you? You're forgetting that when you tried to talk me out of going six years ago, you also told me I wouldn't make it. Well, I didn't fail, Gabe. I'm the best in the business." She was stating facts, not bragging.

"So?" He dropped the bale and reached down to snap the twine. "Is that why you stuck it out even after you discovered you didn't like it?"

"Partly," she admitted. "You were so positive I was going to fall flat on my face that I was determined to prove you were wrong. And the money was really good. I've invested a lot of it. I should be okay, financially speaking, when I quit."

Gabe straightened, drawing his head back to study he and gauge the truth of her statement. "Okay, so you've proved me wrong. Now what? Since it hasn't turned out to be a bed of roses and you don't like it, why go on with it after you're married?"

For an instant, Jonni faltered over the answer. "It isn't that many more years before I'll be too old. It's rare for someone over thirty to be on a magazine cover. A few of the top models keep working, but only a few. Ted and I have discussed it and decided that it's only logical for me to continue while I'm still in demand," she reasoned.

"Was that your decision? Or Ted's?" A dark brow lifted in silent challenge.

"Ours," she retorted. "Besides, what else would I do?"

"Be a wife and mother, if that's what you want."

"My God, is that old-fashioned!" She laughed

scornfully at his answer. "You're out of step with the times, Gabe."

"Am I?" he countered. "I think women should make their own decisions. There's no living with them otherwise." He winked at her and Jonni fumed. "Anyway, from what you say, it sounds like Ted's in charge." He picked up the loose hay and began distributing it in the mangers of the remaining stalls. "By the way, where's lover boy this morning?"

Jonni took a deep breath and made a rapid mental count to ten. "He's still in bed, sleeping." At Gabe's brief snort of laughter, she found herself rushing to defend Ted and was irritated. "Ted rarely goes to bed before midnight, so he's accustomed to sleeping late."

"That's some marriage you're going to have," Gabe scoffed. All the horses were now munching their hay. Finished, Gabe walked toward the open barn door, removing his gloves as he went.

"What do you mean?"

"You get up with the sun and he sleeps late. He stays up until all hours of the night and you go to bed early. About the only time you'll be able to spend with each other is over the dinner table," he concluded as they emerged into the morning sunshine.

Slightly stunned, Jonni realized that she had never really thought about it. Being very busy hardly left any time for the luxury of thinking things through.

"I'm sure we can arrange our schedules so we can spend time together." But she was wondering how.

"Marriage by appointment," Gabe mocked. "Dinner at seven, make love at eight. At nine, wife goes to sleep, husband leaves bedroom."

Phrased that way, it sounded very cold-blooded. It

annoyed Jonni that Gabe had instinctively seized on a very real difference between her and Ted—and she realized that he understood her in a way that Ted never could. The regimen he'd outlined was uncomfortably close to home.

"What is it about Ted that you don't like?" she demanded impatiently. As Gabe veered away from her Jonni added another sharp question. "Where are you going?"

"My truck is parked near the pond by the other barn," he said, without breaking stride.

Her long legs continued to follow him. "I don't even know why I asked you about Ted," she grumbled. "You've found fault with everyone I've dated."

"I don't see that it matters whether or not I like him," Gabe pointed out. "You're the one who's going to marry him."

"It doesn't matter," she insisted.

Ahead of them was the pickup truck. Gabe continued toward it, tapping the leather gloves in his hand against the side of his leg as he walked. The sound picked at Jonni's nerves, stretched as taut as banjo strings.

Chapter Five

"The pond is low," Jonni observed.

She stood on the knoll overlooking the man-made catch basin. The truck was parked on the other side of Gabe. An earthen dam had been built across a natural hollow in the land to trap the runoff of melting snows and spring rains, to insure water for the livestock through the long summer. A two-foot-wide ring of mud encircled the water. A duck waddled across the slowly drying band toward the encroaching grass.

"The wind blew away what little snowfall we had last winter. So far it's been a dry spring with barely enough rain to get the ground wet," Gabe explained, and Jonni recalled her father's similar comment last night. "Another week of this and everything around here is going to be as dry as a tinderbox. Even the Cimarron is low."

Jonni heard the morning breeze rustling through the grass, a dry sound. She was a rancher's daughter; she knew what a drought could mean. She watched Gabe remove his hat and comb his fingers through the thickness of his dark hair. It was a troubled gesture. He turned slightly to study the sky to the south as if hoping to see moisture-laden clouds coming up from the Gulf, graying the horizon.

There wasn't a cloud in sight, not even a puffy marshmallow one. The creases around his eyes deepened as he squinted into the sun. Sighing, Gabe looked away and settled the wide-brimmed hat firmly on his head.

"I've got to be going," he said. "With no rain to stimulate new growth, the grazing isn't good. We're moving the cattle again today—this time to the river pasture." His mouth quirked. "The boys are waiting for me and, as usual, you've held me up."

"Yes." Jonni smiled at the remark. "You were always telling me I was keeping you from your work," she remembered. "You used to say if I wanted to talk to you, I had to do it while you were working. And you usually made me help."

"You were in better condition then. An eighty-pound bale would have been heavy, but you'd have been able to lift it." A hint of a smile softened his mouth.

Suddenly everything seemed all right again. Their sharp bickering a few moments ago was forgotten as a warm smile spread across Jonni's face.

"Oh, quit trying to get my goat. Seems like old times when you do, though. It's good to be home again," she said. "It's wonderful to breathe fresh air again and walk under a wide-open sky. I won't have to worry about how I look." She laughed. "I don't even have to put on make up if I don't want to. It will be a glorious two weeks—riding wherever I want to and as far as I want to." There was a faintly wistful look in her blue eyes. "I wish I could go with you to move the cattle. That really would be like old times."

"Why don't you come?" His low-pitched drawl extended a persuasive invitation. Jonni glanced uncertainly in the direction of the house, hidden from view by the barn. The curve of Gabe's mouth became twisted. "I forgot—you'll want to be here when lover boy gets up."

Turning to face him, Jonni forgot to take offense at his remark. They weren't standing that far apart. Something Ted had said about him the day before make her look at Gabe as a man and not someone she had known for years.

She was tall, but Gabe was taller. Well-muscled, he radiated virility and hadn't lost his frankly sexual way of looking at a woman. There was a fluttering in the pit of her stomach. She guessed he affected a lot of women that way. She felt a surge of unexpected curiosity about his personal life.

"Why haven't you ever married, Gabe?" she asked, tipping her head to one side. "Haven't you ever thought about it?"

"Yeah, I thought about it seriously, once," he acknowledged, but Jonni had the impression of a door slamming in his expression, shutting her out of his inner thoughts.

"What happened?" she persisted.

"It didn't work out," was all he said.

Jonni wanted a more specific answer, but the squawking of a duck diverted her attention. A courting drake with his wings spread was approaching the duck that had just left the pond. The female was resisting his advances. The drake put up with her foolishness for only a few seconds before he began chasing her across the grass. The female immediately tried to escape him.

The two went running and flying over the ground, ducking under the board fence. Before they disappeared from sight behind a wooden feeder, Jonni saw the drake grab the duck's neck with his bill to force her to the ground. Jonni wasn't embarrassed by the ritual of animal breeding. On a ranch, procreation was necessary for livelihood, and accepted as the natural course of events in life—all life.

Gabe, who had observed the primitive courtship scene as well, turned to look at her. "You came home just in time for the mating season." The bold look in his eyes disturbed the normal rhythm of her pulse.

"It seems I did," Jonni agreed with a half smile, refusing to be self-conscious about the facts of life.

"I wonder," there was an undercurrent of intensity in his drawling voice, a darkening of his gaze, "whether Ted has ever done—this." He raised his arm, and before Jonni could take a step backward, his big hand covered the back of her neck. The warmth of his palm and the strength of his grip surprised her, and she was shocked by how good it felt.

"Or pulled you into his arms"—Gabe continued in the same intense tone—"like this." She didn't resist his encircling embrace; she didn't want to. But her head was tipped back to stare at him in mute astonishment. "Or kissed you . . ."

Despite the pause, he didn't add the words "like this" to the sentence. Instead his mouth covered her lips, claiming them in a hard kiss of possession. The suede material of his vest was sensually rough beneath the palms of her hands, like the soft brush of his mustache against her skin.

All sorts of reactions were being aroused by the driving power of his mouth, which demanded a response. His embrace lacked the practiced technique and expertise she had come to expect from Ted. Gabe's was simpler, more basic, awakening her desire in a way that Ted never, ever had.

The knowledge spread through her like a flame, heating her flesh wherever it was pressed against his masculine frame. Jonni trembled at the force of such a basic need, which could make her lips yield willingly to his compelling kiss when she would soon belong to another man.

The pressure of his mouth eased slowly, then it was taken away altogether as Gabe drew his head back. There was a troubled rhythm to his breaths, warm and caressing against her skin. Her eyes opened slowly, mirroring the shock of her discovery. Something hardened in his expression. His arms loosened their hold until her legs were no longer resting against the support of his hard thighs.

Bewildered by her reaction, Jonni raised her left hand to her lips as if by touching them she might discover the cause. His eyes narrowed at the gesture, his arms returning to his side.

"Why did you do that, Gabe?" She had experienced passion before, but this had gone beyond that to something more profound.

The sun touched her diamond and flashed a prism of light onto the shadowed features below the hat brim. Gabe looked grim.

"How the hell do I know?" he muttered. "What eats at me is I should have done it six years ago."

While Jonni was still puzzling over his cryptic response, Gabe pivoted and took long, swift strides to the parked truck. Her left hand reached out toward his departing figure, the words forming on her lips to call him back and explain it. Then she saw the engagement ring on her finger. Suddenly she didn't want to know if what she suspected he was saying was really true. That shaky feeling inside her made her afraid of his answer.

No, don't ask him to explain, she told herself as he gunned the motor of the pickup and reversed away from the pond. The wisest thing to do would be to forget about the kiss. She was engaged to Ted and there wouldn't be a repeat. But she wished she could quit shaking. Shoving her hands in her pockets, she decided to walk it off.

It was an hour later when she made her way back to the house. Ted was just coming down the stairs when she entered. The large grandfather clock in the foyer struck nine. One look told Jonni that Ted had showered as well as shaved. Dressed more casually this morning, he wore dark blue jeans that looked too new, a white turtleneck and a blue and gray tweed jacket with decorative leather patches at the elbows. Oh boy. Gabe was sure to comment on the country squire get-up.

"Hey there." She assumed a bright smile as she greeted him. "You're up early this morning." She repeated the phrase she herself had had addressed to her.

"Good morning," he returned, and bent to kiss her.

For some inexplicable reason, Jonni offered him her cheek. Ted didn't force a more intimate exchange. She wondered why she'd done it. Guilt, perhaps? Did she think Ted would be able to taste Gabe's kiss on her lips? Damn, she was supposed to forget about that. But Ted didn't seem aware that her behavior was out of the ordinary.

"After years of being lulled to sleep by the blare of taxi horns and the grinding of garbage trucks doing three a.m. runs, would you believe that the sound of a motor woke me up?" He smiled in wry amusement.

Jonni remembered Gabe's noisy, wheel-spinning departure in the pickup and tried to join in Ted's amusement at the irony of his statement.

"Who was it? Do you know?" he asked with absent interest.

"It was Gabe," she admitted. "He was on his way out to help move the cattle to another pasture."

"He was probably loud on purpose," Ted mused.

"If he was, I'm glad," Jonni teased. "It's time you were getting up. I hope you had a good night's sleep, though. Was the bed comfortable?"

He linked his hands behind her waist, drawing her hips against his. "I can think of ways it could have been more comfortable." He nuzzled her cheek. "But yes, I had a good night after I got used to the frogs croaking and the owls hooting. Mother Nature is very noisy," he concluded, taking a tiny nibble at her earlobe.

"You were listening to her night music." Jonni smiled. The sounds had been very soothing to her.

"It was monotonously loud. You should file a complaint and have her turn the volume down," Ted mocked, and Jonni laughed softly at his silly suggestion. "Don't you think she would listen?"

"No, I don't." She lifted her gaze to his face, amusement twinkling in her eyes.

His expression became serious. "Have I told you yet this morning that I love you, Jonni Starr?"

"No." She shook her head.

His mouth made the pledge as he covered her lips with a possessive kiss. Jonni responded to it and fought aside a comparison with Gabe's kiss. The result was as pleasant and satisfying as always. There was a curve to her mouth when they drew apart.

"Mmm, that was nice," she murmured.

"It merely whetted my appetite," he assured her.

"That's because you haven't had breakfast," Jonni teased.

His hands moved caressingly along her waist and hips. "I know what I'd like." His gaze roamed suggestively over her and stopped at a spot near her left shoulder. "What's this?" Ted plucked a piece of hay from the knitted weave of her sweater. "What have you been doing this morning? Rolling in the hay?"

"No," Jonni said with a self-conscious laugh. "I was at the barn, helping Gabe give the horses some hay."

"So that's what I smell."

"I was just coming in to wash," she assured him.

"You should change, too," Ted suggested, his gaze raking her figure. "What you're wearing doesn't do anything for you. Don't you have something cuter to put on?"

"Of course," Jonni admitted, and started to explain, then stopped. How cute did she have to be and why?

"Good," Ted interrupted. "I want you to look adorable for me."

Jonni hesitated for only an instant before nodding an agreement. No big deal. She had no reason not to indulge him a little if that was all he wanted. "Mom and Dad might still be in the kitchen. If not, the coffee is on the stove. Help yourself and I'll be down in a few minutes," she promised as she slipped out of his arms to climb the stairs.

In her bedroom she paused in front of the mirror. The jeans and sweater didn't look that bad on her. In fact, Jonni thought the denims showed her slim, leggy look, and the sweater rounded out nicely over her breasts to nip in at her waistline. But the clothes were a bit shabby and worn, which was probably what Ted objected to.

Stripping out of them, she chose a pair of pants with patch pockets and a different blouse that fit better. That was as adorable as she was going to get. This was a farm and he had two days to get used to that fact. After applying a touch of makeup, Jonni turned downstairs to join Ted and her parents.

The dishes from the evening meal had been washed and put away. Jonni sat in the living room feeling restless and on edge, as if the walls were closing on her. Caroline had just taken the coffee things back to the kitchen. Gabe had disappeared immediately after dinner with the excuse that there was paperwork to be done. The ranch manager wasn't so rough and tough that he couldn't keep two laptops going while he ran the spreadsheets for the farm, her father had told her proudly. He hadn't expected Ted to be impressed, but Jonni was. Right now she noticed the silence that had fallen between her fiancé and her father, the most important men in her life. Jonni slipped her hand into Ted's.

"Let's go out on the porch for a while," she suggested.

"Some fresh air sounds good," Ted agreed, but glanced to her father.

"You two go ahead." John waved a hand. "You don't need my permission."

Rising together, they walked to the front door. As Ted opened it, Jonni heard her mother return to the living room.

"Where did Jonni and Ted go?" she asked John.

"Outside."

"Oh, but I wanted to show Jonni . . ." her mother began in disgruntled protest.

"They want to be alone for a little while, Caroline," her father interrupted. "Or have you forgotten what it was like in be in love and engaged?"

Jonni didn't hear her mother's answer as Ted ushered her outside and closed the door. His arm curved around her waist and they strolled to the far end of the porch. The sun had gone down more than an hour earlier and the night was dark.

"I didn't realize the night could be so black," Ted commented.

"That's because you're used to streetlights and neon signs," Jonni told him.

Except for a quarter moon hanging in the sky, a light shining from the window of Gabe's quarters and the lights from the house, there wasn't any illumination, not even stars. Without their twinkling fires, the darkness seemed more intense.

An owl hooted in the trees. A chorus of frogs sang at the pond, a sound muted by the evening breeze whispering through the grass. From far off in the night, Jonni heard the bellowing of a bull.

"It's the mating season," she recalled, and a shiver danced over her skin.

Ted leaned his back against a supporting column of the porch roof. His arms circled around her to draw her shoulders against his chest. It was warm in his arms and she nestled closer, letting her head rest against his cheekbone. He crossed his arms in front of her stomach.

"That's a fine thing to say," he murmured near her ear, "when you know your parents are just inside the house." His hand slid over her blouse, cupping her breast.

Turning her face toward his mouth, Jonni smiled as he found the corner of her lips. She hadn't meant to sound provocative, but now his embrace was conjuring up memories that were more disturbing.

"Why are you smiling?" Ted asked, amused and curious.

"I was remembering other times when I was on this porch," she explained.

"In somebody else's arms?" he quizzed.

"Yes, until Daddy turned the porch light on." Her smile widened. "It was a very unsubtle hint from him that I'd been out here long enough and I should come in."

"I see."

"At least with you, he knows your intentions are

honorable." She turned in his arms, sliding her hands around his neck.

He kissed her once, twice, then drew back. "As much as I'm tempted to indulge in a front-porch necking scene, I don't feel like taking a cold shower later on," he said firmly.

With a sigh that bordered on disappointment at his control, Jonni half turned in his arms to rest a shoulder against his chest and cuddle into his tweed jacket for warmth. A frown knitted her forehead and she forced it away. She had been feigning passion and now she was irritated with Ted for not responding. What was the matter with her?

She tried changing the subject. "Mother asked me if we would like to go to church with them in the morning."

"I suppose it's expected?" His inflection made it a question.

"Yes."

"Then I'd be delighted to go," he said unenthusiastically.

"I'll tell her," she promised. After another few seconds had passed she said, "I thought I might go riding for a while tomorrow afternoon. Would you like to come along?"

"My love, you know I don't like horses," Ted reminded her. "Since I can't persuade you to stay away from them, don't try to persuade me to get on one."

"All right," she sighed.

"How on earth are you going to keep from being bored to death during these next two weeks?" he asked suddenly, sounding genuinely perplexed.

"There's nothing to do around here, and you're miles from civilization."

"Not quite." Jonni laughed at his words. "In case you haven't noticed, Ted Alexander Maltin the Third, that this ranch has indoor plumbing, the very latest kitchen equipment, satellite TV and radio, a pool table and billiard table, an extensive library, a garden to putter in, horses to ride and an endless array of breathtaking landscapes to view. Every type of amusement is right at hand. We don't have to go anywhere."

"I'll take Broadway and Carnegie Hall any day," Ted responded, unimpressed by her list.

"I would have added a swimming hole except the pond is too low." Jonni searched the cloudless night sky. "I hope it rains soon."

"My God!" He released a laughing breath. "Now you're beginning to sound like your father and Gabe at dinner tonight!"

"The lack of water is serious," Jonni insisted with a thread of impatience at his lack of understanding for the critical situation the range was in.

"I'm sure it is," he agreed in a placating tone. "But it hardly concerns us, does it?"

Jonni swallowed the sharp retort that trembled on her tongue. "No, I guess not," she agreed to avoid an argument, and sighed again.

"It's past your bedtime, isn't it?" Ted straightened from the post and shifted her out of his arms. "You'd better go in so you can get your beauty sleep."

She didn't feel tired, but she didn't feel like continuing this conversation, either. "It's been a long day," she offered by way of agreement. She took a step toward the door, then looked back over her shoulder at him. "Are you coming in?"

"Not right away."

"Good night, then."

"Good night," he replied.

The next morning Jonni was standing in church between Ted and Gabe, singing from the hymnal and listening to Ted's resonant baritone voice. It carried above the voices of the rest of the congregation. Only one voice competed with his natural volume, and it belonged to the stoop-shouldered woman in the row ahead of them. Unfortunately her wavering voice was way off-key. When she hit a sharply discordant note, Jonni saw Ted wince. Jonni tried hard not to smile.

When the last note of the organ had echoed through the rafters the congregation sat and turned to the pages of the responsive reading. Ted leaned sideways toward her.

"Someone should tell that poor woman she can't sing," he whispered in a judgmental tone.

"That woman happens to be my great-aunt Maude and she's practically stone deaf," Jonni whispered back. "She can hardly hear herself, let alone the organ."

Gabe's attention didn't waver from the book he held as he added his low comment to their conversation. "The Bible says to make a joyful noise unto the Lord. It doesn't say the noise has to be in tune."

Jonni thought his dry but forgiving remark was pretty funny, but Ted didn't. He glared across her at Gabe's bowed head as he studied the pages of the book. Jonni struggled to keep a straight face and finally succeeded. As the minister began the responsive reading she stole a glance at Gabe. A complacent gleam lighted his dark eyes but he continued to look to the front of the church at the pulpit.

Hatless in God's house, his dark hair sprang thickly in a careless, vital style. He wore a Western-cut suit of brown with a plain bronze tie. He looked comfortable and at ease. Jonni had difficulty assimilating the fact that he was the same man who had disturbed her with his kiss less than twenty-four hours ago. He certainly had been ignoring her since then. Not ignoring her, she corrected, but just treating her very casually.

His attention shifted and Gabe caught her staring at him. He lifted a dark eyebrow in a silent question, as if he had no idea what she might be thinking about. Jonni looked swiftly away, concentrating once more on the church service.

When it was over and the benediction said, the exodus from church began. Jonni knew practically everyone who had attended. Since she was a hometown girl who had become something of a celebrity, everyone wanted to speak to her. Her mother had already spread the word that she was engaged, so naturally everyone wanted to meet Ted, as well. They all seemed to cluster on the church lawn, and few cars left the lot. At some point Jonni became separated from Ted, and as she turned to see where he was, her mother came over to her.

"Your Aunt Maude is standing over by the steps. You'd better go over and say hello to her," she suggested.

"All right, Mother," Jonni agreed. "Have you seen Ted?"

"He's over there with your father and Jack Sloane."

Jonni looked in the direction her mother pointed. Ted looked up, saw her and shrugged in a helpless gesture, indicating he was trapped for a few polite minutes. She smiled and made her way through the crowd to the church steps where her elderly relative stood, leaning on her cane to catch her breath.

"Hello, Aunt Maude." Jonni greeted the woman in a loud voice as she stopped in front of her. Maude was in her eighties, gray hair thinning away from her wrinkled face. "Do you remember me?"

"What did you say?" Frowning, Maude Starr turned her head for Jonni to repeat what she asked in her good ear. "Speak up."

"I said"—Jonni leaned closer and spoke louder—"it's me, Jonni."

"Of course it's you," the woman snapped. "Do you think I'm blind?"

After six years, her great-aunt was still an irascible old grouch, Jonni discovered. She tried not to smile. "How are you?"

"What did you say?" Again her forehead acquired extra creases. "You'll have to speak up, girl. My hearing isn't very good."

"I said, how are you?" Jonni repeated.

"You don't have to shout! I'm fine, fine." A palsied hand shifted the cane to a more supportive position. "Sybil Crane told me you're getting married. Is that true?"

"Yes," Jonni admitted with an exaggerated bobbing of her head so the positive answer would be understood.

"Well, where is this young man of yours? Aren't you going to introduce me to him?" her aunt demanded in a querulous voice.

"He's standing over there." Jonni made the mistake of turning her head to point out Ted.

"What? How many times do I have to tell you to speak up?" A pair of sharp blue eyes sparkled with impatience.

Jonni breathed in to contain her exasperation over the conversation and maintained a pleasant expression. This time she didn't make the mistake of turning as she spoke. "He's right over there."

The woman's gaze followed her pointing arm, then snapped back to Jonni. "Why didn't you say you were marrying him?" she sniffed. "Did you think because my hearing is fading that my memory is, too? Gabe Stockman has been working at your father's ranch for a good many years now. Didn't you think I'd remember that?"

Gabe Stockman? Jonni's head swiveled to see Gabe walking toward them, directly in line with her pointing finger and blocking out Ted from view. "No, you don't understand, Aunt Maude." She hurried to correct the mistake. "I'm not engaged to him."

"Of course you've got engaged to him. Do you think I don't know what we're talking about? My mind hasn't wandered anywhere, although I'm beginning to worry about yours."

Aunt Maude jabbed a gnarled, arthritic finger at Jonni to emphasize her point. A flowered handkerchief, tucked under the expansion band of her wristwatch, fluttered below the finger.

"No, Aunt Maude, there's been a mistake," Jonni insisted, trying not to lose her patience.

"Nobody wants to make a mistake when they choose a man to marry," her aunt declared, catching only part of what was said. Jonni wanted to scream in frustration. How on earth was she going to make the woman understand? To make the situation worse, Gabe arrived to stand beside her. The older woman cast an approving glance at him before addressing Jonni. "You couldn't have picked a better man. Gabe here will make you a good husband."

Jonni didn't quite meet the questioning and amused look he sent her. "I've been talking myself hoarse trying to convince Aunt Maude that I was pointing to Ted as the man I was going to marry, not you," she explained, her voice pitched to a quiet level.

Maude Starr saw her lips moving and cupped a hand to her good ear. "What did you say? I can't hear you if you don't speak up." Her brow furrowed in a deep frown.

"I was . . ." Jonni began at a louder volume.

Gabe bent forward to shout in the woman's good ear. "She was talking to me, Maude. How are you today?"

"Fine, fine." A palsied hand waved aside the question. "That engagement ring you gave Jonni is too gaudy," she criticized. "It's in bad taste. You should take it back for something smaller."

"I'll think about that." He nodded as if taking the matter under consideration.

"Jonni is a good girl. You be sure and treat her right, Gabe Stockman."

Jonni was fuming at his failure to correct her aunt's

misconception. "Will you please explain to her?" she ordered through clenched teeth, her lips barely moving.

When Gabe glanced at her, there was a dangerous glint in his dark eyes, wicked and dancing. Her pulse fluttered. Again he bent closer to the old woman to speak loudly in her ear.

"You know what they say about breaking in a new horsc: a cowboy has to ride it hard and long in the beginning if he wants it to be worth a damn later on."

Her mouth opened, but Jonni didn't know whether to rage at him in angry frustration or simply hit him. Maude drew her head back, looking properly shocked by his innuendo, but it was Jonni she turned on, shaking her finger.

"You'd better teach him some manners," she informed Jonni in no uncertain terms. "In my day, a man didn't speak of such things in female company." With that, Maude moved away from them, tottering on her cane.

Recovering from her initial speechlessness, Jonni glared at Gabe and demanded, "Why did you do that?"

"I thought you needed rescuing," he answered evenly. The glint in his eyes was still there, but for the most part it was veiled.

"What I needed was for you to explain to Maude that you and I aren't getting married," she retorted.

"She would have asked endless questions and it would have taken the better part of the day to straighten her out," Gabe reasoned.

"So you let her go on thinking we're engaged," Jonni reminded him. "That wasn't right."

"Someone else will explain it to her," he said, completely untroubled.

That was probably true, but Jonni wasn't about to stop berating him. "And how could you make such an off-color remark to her? That was unforgivable! She's a spinster. You know she's never been married."

"Who knows? She might have some of the best dreams she's had in months," Gabe drawled, openly mocking Jonni's indignant air. "Besides, a person can't live to be her age without learning all there is to know about life. She pretended to be shocked for your benefit."

"You're impossible!" Jonni declared in an angry breath.

"So I've been told," he smiled.

She saw Ted approaching and hurried to meet him.

Chapter Six

After Sunday dinner Jonni went upstairs to her room and changed into her riding clothes. On her way down she met Ted coming up. They paused midway on the staircase.

"I'm going out riding for an hour or so," she told him. "Are you sure you wouldn't like to come along?" The question was asked more out of politeness than in the hope he might reconsider.

"No, thank you." Ted made the anticipated refusal. "I'm going upstairs to change. Afterward I intend to become entrenched in the newspaper."

"Ah, the newspaper, a touch of civilization in this wilderness," Jonni teased him.

"Precisely, my love." He kissed her lightly on the mouth. "Enjoy yourself."

"I will."

Jonni continued down the steps, then walked at an unhurried pace out the door and down the path toward the barn. It was another clear, sunny day, the temperature pleasantly cool, a good day for riding.

The tack room door stood open. Gabe was inside, removing the broken chin strap from a bridle.

He had changed out of his suit into a white shirt and a pair of mud-colored denims. He glanced up when Jonni entered then resumed his repair of the bridle.

"I'm going riding," Jonni announced. "Would you like to suggest a horse or should I take my choice?" She was curt, resentment still smoldering from the incident with her aunt at the church.

"A pleasure ride?" Gabe glanced up again see her affirmative nod. "Take Sancho, the zebra dun in the first stall. You can use the saddle and bridle there, on your left."

As Jonni reached for the bridle and saddle blanket, he added, "If your fiancé needs a gentle mount, you can saddle the claybank mare for him. She's as placid as they come."

"Ted isn't going riding." She slipped her arm through the bridle's headstall to drape it on her shoulder.

"I forgot. He's a city dude. He probably doesn't know how to ride, does he?" Gabe pitched the broken chin strap into the trash barrel. His action seemed to indicate he thought Ted deserved the same treatment.

"As a matter of fact, Ted can ride very well. He just doesn't like horses, nor does he enjoy riding them. So it isn't likely it would be something he'd do for pleasure."

As she issued the information, Jonni was tautly aware of his eyes on her, following her every movement.

"When does he ride, then?" he challenged in skepticism.

"One of his investors from Virginia does a lot of fox hunting. I know Ted has ridden with him on several occasions."

She gathered up the blanket and saddle pad. She felt on edge and blamed it on Gabe's inquisition, which seemed an attempt to find fault with Ted.

"In other words, he goes riding when there's money involved, but not for the pleasure of being with you." Gabe succeeded in coming up with a conclusion that made Ted look bad.

"I wouldn't want him doing it *just* for me," Jonni retorted.

There was a pause and Jonni thought she had finally silenced him. But she hadn't. "You're a morning person. Ted prefers the night. You like riding horses. He doesn't. Do the two of you have anything in common?" Gabe taunted.

Gripping the handhold behind the saddle horn, she lifted the saddle to the back of her shoulder. "Yes," she snapped out the answer. "We happen to love each other."

While she still had the last word, Jonni stalked out of the tack room. The dun gelding turned its head to look at her as she entered its stall. She slapped its flank to move it over. With an economy of motion, she set the saddle and blankets down and walked to its head to slip the bridle on over the horse's halter.

Although Jonni half expected it, Gabe didn't follow her out of the tack room to pursue the conversation. Once the horse was saddled, she led it out of the stall and out the side door. Looping the reins around its neck, she stepped into a stirrup and swung into the saddle. With a turn of the reins she pointed the zebra dun toward open land and touched her heels to its belly. Its first stride carried it into a canter.

Jonni's tension eased as she widened the distance to the barn. A mile from the headquarters of the ranch, she stroked the tan gray neck and slowed the gelding to a reaching trot. Tossing its black mane, the horse emitted a rolling snort. It was a contented, relaxed sound, which Jonni echoed with a sigh.

The land she rode through was wild and untamed. Its rocky, uneven terrain defied the rancher's attempts to subdue it, tolerating only the tenacious grasses, which drove hardy roots into the soil. The horizon was marked by jutting mesas and towering buttes. Their shapes had been created by wind and erosion carving into the red-stained sandstone and shale.

It was with regret that Jonni turned her mount toward the ranch before her hour was up. She would have ridden longer and farther if Ted hadn't been waiting at the house for her to return. But there would be other days during the next two weeks when she could ride and Ted would be in New York. There would be plenty of time to indulge in the luxury of riding without being confined by the boundaries of bridle paths in a city park.

Jonni reached the corral gate, opened it, rode through and maneuvered the dun horse into position so she could close it. One horse was loose inside the enclosure, a bay gelding. Gabe was standing beside it, cradling its front hoof in his hand. Although her antagonism had faded on the ride, Jonni tried to ignore his presence.

"Did you have a good ride?" His conversational tone kept her from succeeding.

"Yes, I enjoyed it." It was impossible to keep the genuine sincerity out of her voice. She felt refreshed and glowing, and looked it. Gabe patted the bay's shoulder and walked away from it. The gelding limped heavily toward the barn. "He's lame. What happened?"

"He fell on the ice this winter and lacerated a tendon in his front knee." Gabe didn't look back at the horse as he walked to where Jonni had halted her mount. "It healed stiffly. Looks like he'll always have a game leg."

A permanently crippled horse on a working ranch, and a gelding at that—Jonni knew that spelled bad news. "Will he have to be destroyed?"

"The verdict isn't in yet. He's one of the cow horses we have on the place. We probably won't decide anything for sure until the fall. It isn't that easy to replace a horse like Joker," Gabe told her.

"No, I know it isn't," she agreed quietly. A horse could make a cowboy's job easier or harder. And a really good horse could almost work by itself.

Gabe stopped beside her horse and combed a wayward chunk of black mane onto the proper side of the horse's neck. In doing so, his gaze strayed beyond Jonni in the direction of the house.

"Speaking of jokers, there's your lover boy on the porch."

"Gabe, will you stop?" Jonni sighed impatiently and turned in her saddle to wave. Ted wore charcoal gray slacks and an oyster-white sweater. It was a heavily ribbed knit, very rugged and manly. Ted raised an acknowledging hand in response.

Standing in the stirrups, Jonni cupped her hands to her mouth to call, "I'll be up shortly." Nodding that he'd heard her, Ted went back into the house.

"Have you ever seen him when he had a speck of dirt on him?" Gabe mused aloud, not really expecting an answer. "I can't help wondering if he sweats."

"You're just jealous," Jonni accused, but she was uncomfortably aware that she found a trace of humor in the question.

"Maybe I am." There was something remote about the good-natured smile he gave her. Swinging a foot out of the off stirrup, Jonni started to dismount, but Gabe's large hands slid around her slender waist and set her on the ground in front of him. His hands retained their easy hold.

"I expected you to go racing to the house to fall in Ted's arms, after being separated from him for more than an hour."

He was teasing her—in an old, familiar way that Jonni didn't find offensive. She was conscious of his hands on her waist. She could feel the outline of each finger through the material of her blouse as if he was touching her bare skin. His touch was warm and oddly stimulating. Her forearms were resting on his, her hands feeling the muscled flesh beneath his sleeves.

She laughed, trying to ignore how closely she stood to him. "I wouldn't throw myself in Ted's arms," she saidd. "Not when I'm smelling like a horse." Raising a hand, she sniffed at it and wrinkled her nose in distaste, laughing softly.

Gabe captured the same hand by the wrist and carried it so close to his face that Jonni could feel the tickling brush of his mustache against her fingers. Her breathing became shallow as she lifted her gaze to meet the growing darkness of his.

"You smell good to me," he said quietly. "Earthy and fresh like the land after a spring rain."

Jonni didn't draw her hand out of his grasp. She knew she should have. Her heartbeat began to quicken as his gaze slid to her mouth. He was going to kiss her, and she realized that she wanted him to. The pressure on her waist increased to draw her forward, but she was drifting that way, swept along by a powerful undercurrent she was powerless to resist.

There was no haste to achieve the union of their lips as their bodies slowly fitted together perfectly. His breath caressed her skin and Jonni inhaled the heady male aroma that belonged distinctly to him. When the kiss came, it was gentle and deep. It evoked a response from her that was more ravishing and seductive than hard passion. It was a bright, burning flame that curled all the way down to her toes.

His mouth moved over hers as though he worshipped the shape and taste of it. His hand encircled her throat to caress the sensitive skin of her neck and finally he curved his fingers into her hair as his kiss became hungry in its adoration. Her parted lips were giving him every invitation to satisfy his appetite. The world seemed to be dissolving into a mist from the heat between them.

The caress of his hand at the base of her spine was sensually erotic, pressing her hips to the unyielding hardness of him. Jonni needed no encouragement to arch closer to the sexual radiance of his embrace. His caress was like the language of desire, interpreting it to a degree she had never known before· His touch opened her heart to a piercing beauty that left Jonni shaken. She was trembling when his mouth trailed to her temple. The black mustache tangled with her windswept curls.

During the kiss she had fitted herself to him like a skintight glove. Now the first chilling winds of reality began to steal in. Lowering her head, Jonni stared at the buttons on his shirt and the shadow of chest hair beneath the white material. Her arms uncurled from around his neck to wedge a small space between their bodies. She suddenly realized why the perfection of their embrace had been wrong. The problem could be summed up in one word—Ted.

When she lifted her wary and bewildered gaze to his face, his dark eyes were waiting to meet it. They studied her expression intently, while his features betrayed nothing of his inner thoughts.

"Well?" Gabe prompted. He was aware of her emotional withdrawal, but was making no effort to reverse it.

"You'd better not do this anymore." It wasn't a warning, a statement or a plea, but a combination of all three.

There was a complacent twist to his mouth as he said, "You'd better not let me." The low drawl held the faintest hint of mockery. In the next second he let her go and turned to gather the trailing reins. "I'll take care of your horse for you."

Heat scorched her cheeks as Jonni watched him lead the dun gelding to the barn. She hadn't offered a word in her own defense because she knew Gabe was right. There had been no coercion in the embrace. She had been willing and eager for the kiss, a ready participant. And it had been enormously satisfying.

Now she had to go to the house, where Ted waited. The prospect didn't do much for her peace of mind. Try as she might, Jonni couldn't shrug off the kiss as innocent experimentation. In the first place Gabe wasn't the kind to experiment, and secondly, she was as guilty as he was for letting it happen.

Her homecoming was turning out to be nothing like she expected. In fact, her whole world seemed to be turning upside down. Jonni wasn't sure, yet, how she was going to put it right—the way it was before.

She had intended to tell Ted what had happened, to free her soul of the weight of guilt. When the opportunity presented itself she had a severe case of cold feet. She rationalized her silence with the consolation that it had been a last fling. Bachelors did it all the time before that fateful wedding day. And, since she didn't expect Ted to tell her all about his past affairs, there was no reason to speak to him of the indiscretions that happened before their marriage.

It all sounded oh-so-hip and cool, but her thoughts kept turning over and over to those few minutes in Gabe's arms.

Her uneasiness was intensified with each bounce of the pickup that rubbed her shoulder against Gabe's. The searing contact with his hard muscles was a physical reminder she didn't need. On a fairly smooth stretch of track, Jonni shifted to move closer to Ted.

Ten minutes earlier the chartered aircraft had buzzed the house before entering the pattern to land at the ranch airfield. Ted had finished his goodbyes to her parents. Gabe had already loaded the suitcases in the rear of the truck.

Against her better judgment, Jonni had ridden to the airstrip with them to say her final goodbye to Ted.

The close confines of the truck's interior and the overwhelming force of Gabe's presence, as well as the freshness of memory, had kept her silent for much of the ride. Ted noticed it, but he blamed it on his imminent departure. He wrapped an arm around her shoulders and kissed her hair.

"I'll call you every night," he assured her. "Early, I promise, so I won't keep you or your parents up."

"Good. I'll look forward to your phone calls." Jonni couldn't respond to his caress, not with Gabe sitting there. Her gaze strayed to Gabe's mustached profile. He was staring resolutely ahead, seemingly oblivious to both of them.

"I'm glad you're spending these two weeks here with your parents." Ted smiled against her hair. "There won't be anything else for you to do but miss me."

The truck spurted over the last hump, giving Jonni the impression that Gabe had stepped on the gas. But only the two of them were aware of what the potential for entertainment was. Ted was blissfully ignorant.

"And to start making plans for our wedding." Jonni didn't know why she added that. It had been meant for Gabe but just why she was determined to remind him of her engaged state, she couldn't say. For someone who claimed to be unavailable, she had certainly acted available to him.

The chartered plane had taxied to the metal shed and it sat waiting, its motors still running. From here Ted would fly to Kansas City to make his connections on a commercial airline to New York. Gabe stopped the truck on the clear side of the wing. He stayed in the driver's seat while Ted climbed out and reached back to help Jonni.

The roar of the plane's engines made conversation impossible. Turbulent currents generated by the propellers tumbled Jonni's ash blond hair around her head as Jonni walked with Ted to the rear of the truck for his luggage. Balancing the smaller suitcase under one arm and carrying the other in the same hand, Ted cupped the back of her head in his free hand and pulled her forward. He kissed her long and deep with sensual expertise. Striding toward the open door of the plane, he waved to her. Jonni saw his mouth form the word goodbye but she couldn't hear his voice above the noise of the engines.

Shortly after the door closed, the plane began taxiing toward the end of the grass runway. Jonni watched it from her position near the rear of the truck. With one hand, she tried to keep her hair from blowing in her face as the spinning wind from the propellers kicked up red dust.

As she watched the plane take off, she was haunted by the discovery that Ted's kiss had seemed all technique with no emotion. Or maybe she was the one with no emotion. Had it only been three days ago that she had arrived, so happy, so confident, so secure? The plane wagged its wings in final goodbye as it soared into the blue Kansas sky.

"A beautiful blonde stands forlornly near the

runway while the plane carrying her lover flies away. It's a very touching scene, but I think it's been done before," Gabe mocked. "You should be able to come up with something more original than that, Jonni."

Pivoting at the sound of his voice, Jonni saw him standing on the opposite side of the pickup. An arm rested nonchalantly against the cab as he gazed at her across the open sides of the truck. Her expression was wary and resentful. She held his gaze for a split second, but it was much too penetrating. Half turning, she broke the contact and walked toward the passenger door.

"Let's go back to the house," she said stiffly.

"That's exactly the destination I had in mind," Gabe replied in an ultra-dry voice and ducked his long frame inside the cab.

Jonni climbed in the passenger seat and slammed the door. The window was rolled down on her side and she hugged the door frame. The empty expanse of seat between them yawned an invitation to be filled.

She flicked a look at Gabe, who had made no attempt to start the engine. His black eyes were fixed on her, brilliant with ironic humor.

"Are you afraid of me?" he asked.

"Petrified." Her response was sarcastic, to hide the tremor of her nerves. "This truck won't go anywhere unless you start it."

"I wouldn't have guessed." He turned the key in the ignition and the motor rumbled into life. Jonni turned her gaze out her window. The plane was now just a dark speck in the sky.

"What's wrong, Jonni?" Gabe's voice was low and

dangerously intimate. "Are you beginning to have second thoughts?"

"Yes . . . I mean, no." In her haste to answer, she stumbled over her words. Gabe laughed as he shifted into first gear. "Would you like to tell me what's so damned funny?"

"You are." He slid a lazy, amused look her way and let it roam insolently over her face. "You didn't have enough guts to tell lover boy about our little interlude and now you're eaten up with guilt."

He just might be right. The way he was looking at her made her realize he was making love to her in his mind, and her senses were quivering in response. It was crazy! She jerked her gaze from his face.

"You don't know that," she insisted. "Maybe I told him."

"I know *you,* Jonni. Don't forget that," Gabe warned. "There were too many times in the past when you brought your confessions to me. I recognize that look of trouble all locked up inside."

"Nothing is troubling me," Jonni lied stubbornly and turned cool blue eyes toward him.

"Like hell," he jeered, then shrugged. "But have it your way. You always do, anyway." The last sentence was offered in a grudging tone.

They bumped over the track to the house. After they had gone several hundred yards in silence, Jonni gave in to a compelling demand to obtain explanations.

"Gabe, I want to ask you a question," she said.

"Shoot." His gaze didn't leave the road.

"Why did you kiss me?"

He reached up and adjusted the mirror in the top

center of the windshield, turning it so Jonni saw her reflection on its surface. "You're a beautiful woman, Jonni. Why wouldn't I want to kiss you?" Gabe answered with a question.

Releasing a quiet sigh, she turned to stare out the window. It wasn't a satisfactory answer, but maybe she had put the question to the wrong party. Maybe she should ask herself why she kissed him.

But she didn't. And she was relieved that Gabe didn't either.

Chapter Seven

Monday and Tuesday slipped by with relative ease. With the extensive holdings of the Starr Ranch, there were many demands to occupy Gabe's time from sunup to sundown. As long as she wasn't in his company, Jonni could almost make believe it had all been a bad dream, nothing to be concerned about. But whenever he was around and she caught him looking at her in a silently contemplating way, she was reminded that it had happened—and that it could happen again.

But those moments were more than amply compensated. There were Ted's nightly phone calls and the hours she spent visiting with her parents. They gossiped, discussed wedding plans, talked about the future, and became reacquainted. Jonni found herself slipping back into her old way of life on the ranch, and discovered it fit her comfortably.

Late Wednesday afternoon, Jonni was in the kitchen with her mother. The last-minute preparations for the evening meal were under way. John Starr was there, as well, sampling the fare and generally getting underfoot.

"This tomato sauce needs something, Caroline," he decided, taking another taste from the simmering pot. "Maybe a little onion salt or some garlic."

"Maybe it needs a few less cooks." She shooed him away from the stove. "If you'd get out of our way, John, we'd get a lot more accomplished. Gabe will be coming in and we won't have the food ready to be put on the table." The front door opened and closed. "There he is now."

As heavy footsteps approached the kitchen, Jonni mentally braced herself for Gabe's appearance. She barely glanced up when he entered the room, but her pulse hammered slightly louder in her ears. It was amazing how small and confined the kitchen seemed to become when he entered. Jonni felt almost claustrophobic. She shook dried parsley flakes onto the mound of mashed potatoes and concentrated on stirring them together.

"Dinner will be ready in a few minutes, Gabe," Caroline promised.

"No hurry. I still have to wash up."

"Would you like a beer, Gabe?" her father offered.

"A glass of cold water sounds better."

Gabe walked to the sink near the counter where Jonni was working and turned on the cold-water tap. The glasses were kept in the cupboard above her head. He let the water run as he opened the cupboard door and took a glass from the shelf. An electric awareness seemed to charge the air around her.

"How are you?" His drawling question sounded

like a caress, as if he was making love to her with his voice.

Her gaze was forced to him. Damn, why did he have to look at her like that? That lazy black intimacy of his eyes created havoc with her senses.

"Fine." Jonni tried to sound natural and not all tied in knots.

"If you keep stirring those potatoes, they're going to turn into a starch glue," Gabe warned in a tone heavily underlined with mockery. Then he turned to fill his glass with the running water.

Her hand stopped stirring the spoon around in the bowl. She moved away from the counter before she ruined the potatoes in her attempt to avoid Gabe.

"The potatoes are ready, Mother." She made her voice sound bright. "Shall I put them on the table?"

Before she had received an answer, there was a knock at the back door. Jonni was closest and she walked over to answer it, carrying the bowl of potatoes with her. One of the ranch hands, Duffy McNair, stood on the back stoop. In his forties, he'd worked at the ranch for the past fifteen years.

"Hello, Jonni." He courteously removed his sweat-stained Stetson. "I saw Gabe coming up the walk. Can I talk to—"

He didn't have the request finished before Gabe was standing behind her. "What is it, Duffy?"

"It's Lida, that chestnut mare with the four white feet. Bill found her about an hour ago. She's foalin' and been havin' a pretty hard time of it," he explained.

"Foaling?" Gabe repeated. "But she isn't due for almost another full month yet."

"I know." The cowboy shifted his position, fingering

his hat. "Bill mentioned last night that she looked as if she was ready, but I knew she wasn't due yet, so I never checked on her today." His head dipped down, revealing a balding patch on top of his head. He shuffled again uncomfortably. "It's all my fault. The mare's in a bad way down there. The foal's comin' the wrong way. Bill and me have tried to turn it—he's at the barn with her now. The truth is, Gabe, we might lose 'em both."

"Have you called the vet?" Gabe didn't bother to find out where the blame might lay.

"Yeah, I called him on the tack room phone." Duffy grimaced and lifted his shoulders in a hopeless shrug. "It's springtime, he's got a couple of emergency calls ahead of ours. He doesn't know when he can get out here. I think you'd better come take a look at the mare."

"You say the foal is coming the wrong way?" Gabe repeated.

"That's what it looks like." Duffy shrugged again as if he was no longer certain of anything.

Jonni nearly jumped when Gabe laid a hand on her shoulder. "You've helped me a couple of times when we've had a breech birth with cows. Do you want to come?"

"Yes." Her agreement was an automatic thing. A ranch depended on its animals. When something was wrong with one of them, all individuals were obligated to help. That was a lesson she had learned while growing up.

"What about you, John?" Gabe asked. "We might need your experience."

"I may have the experience, but I don't have your

instinct with animals, Gabe. I'll trust your judgment in any situation," her father conceded. "If you find you need me, I'll come."

Gabe took the bowl of potatoes from Jonni's hands and passed it to Caroline. Duffy was already starting down the steps.

"I'll keep dinner warm," Caroline Starr promised.

"You and Dad go ahead and eat," Jonni said as she walked out the door ahead of Gabe.

"And don't worry about keeping the food warm for us," he added. "Jonni and I don't mind eating cold food."

As the trio walked swiftly down the worn path to the barn Gabe's hand rested on the small of her back to usher her along. Jonni realized just what she'd let herself in for—possibly long hours of close association with a man it would be wisest to stay away from. She tried to forget about the male hand resting on the sensitive area of her back and to think only about the mare waiting for them at the barn.

"Damn, I'm sorry about this, Gabe." Duffy McNair apologized again, his hat firmly on his head again, concealing the bald spot.

"That mare has a history of easy foalings. You couldn't suspect that this time there would be complications or an early birth," Gabe insisted.

"At least she's in the barn," Jonni offered in consolation. "We could be walking out to the pasture."

"I knew you'd find a bright side to this." Gabe smiled down on her and her heart did a leaping somersault.

"Yeah, if the mare don't die," Duffy muttered under his breath, instantly sobering both of them.

Inside the barn, two drop cords ran parallel to an end stall where electric lanterns illuminated the wood-partitioned enclosure. Bill Higgins, the slim, bow-legged man Jonni had met briefly on the weekend, was inside with the mare. He was stripped to the waist, breathing heavily from exertion, sweat gathering in the hollows of his collarbones. When he saw Jonni accompanying Gabe and Duffy, he self-consciously reached for the shirt draped over the manger and hurriedly put it on.

"How is she?" Gabe paid little heed to the man as he knelt beside the mare lying quietly in the straw. Jonni stood beside him, ignoring Bill while he buttoned his shirt.

"She ain't good," Bill admitted. "Her breathing's too shallow, no steady pulse. I've been trying to turn that damn—darn foal, but the legs keep gettin' in the way and . . ." His voice trailed off lamely in defeat.

The chestnut mare was lathered from her labor, her shiny coat damp with sweat. She made a whickering moan and Gabe stroked her wet neck.

"Easy, girl," he crooned softly. Jonni saw the grimness in his eyes when Gabe glanced at Duffy standing just inside the stall door. "Get me some soap and fresh water, preferably warm." The mare made another low sound, plaintive and weak, which tore at Jonni's heart.

"Take it easy, girl," Gabe soothed. "We'll see what we can do about getting things straightened out. You just rest and save your strength for later on when we'll need it." He ran an exploring hand over the mare's extended belly then straightened.

"What do you think?" Jonni asked anxiously.

"I don't know yet." He shook his head in a troubled way.

Duffy returned with a bucket of water. "Lukewarm. It's the best I could do," he said.

Tossing his hat to Bill, Gabe began unbuttoning his shirt. There was a tightness in her throat as Jonni watched him shrug out of it and saw the overhead lights play across the rippling muscles in his back. His hard flesh was tanned a deep copper and rough, curling dark hairs covered his arms and part of his chest. Realizing how avidly she was staring, Jonni turned back to the mare and knelt beside her head to whisper calming sounds. She listened to the sound of splashing water as Gabe washed.

When he'd finished, he walked back to the mare to kneel in the straw. "Okay, little lady," he said to the mare. "I'm going to see if I can't help you a bit."

Jonni ran her hand slowly along the mare's neck and continued to talk to the horse in a low, soothing voice. The mare was now taking rasping short breaths, dangerously exhausted. Jonni cast anxious glances at the competent, thorough man working swiftly to do what he could for the mare.

"I'll be damned!" A sudden grin alleviated the stern concentration in his expression.

"What is it?" Jonni held her breath. Had he found what was wrong?

"No wonder you were having trouble, Bill," Gabe said, still wearing that smile that held more than hope. "You should have started counting legs. There are two foals here, both trying to get born at the same time. Now"—he grunted slightly as he strained—"if we can just convince them they have to come out one at a time, we'll be all right."

"Are they both alive?" A smile was starting to spread across Jonni's face as well. The birth of twin foals was an event.

"Alive and kicking." Beads of sweat were forming on his forehead, locks of black hair clinging to the moisture. "Both of them."

The heavy silence that had dominated the stall suddenly lifted. Glances were exchanged all the way around, bright, hopeful looks that lightened the atmosphere. Even Duffy's face, which had been gloomy with guilt, was now wreathed with a smile.

"Get me some rope, Duffy," Gabe ordered. "If I can get hold of the two legs of one foal, we'll try to hold back the one and make the way clear for the other."

Duffy was gone and back in quick time. They all watched as Gabe struggled and strained to achieve his goal. Sweat glistened on his skin, muscles flexing in undulating swells of power. Here was the combination Jonni had told Ted about, strength, skill and intelligence—brawn and brains.

"I've got it," he murmured, and relaxed for a minute to catch his breath. His gaze pierced Jonni. "Do you understand what I'm planning to do?"

"Yes, I think so," she nodded.

"Come and give me a hand, then," Gabe ordered. She moved to kneel beside him and help. "You take the rope and turn the backward foal around while I pull the other foal out," he instructed.

In unison, they worked in conjunction with the mare's weakening contractions. The strenuous task within close quarters involved physical contact. It was unavoidable. Yet Jonni was only conscious of the strength that flowed from his hard, warm body into hers.

When the tiny hooves and wet face of the first foal made their appearance, a low cheer was raised by Duffy and Bill. Large, luminous brown eyes blinked at Jonni, whose muscles were trembling from her effort. From somewhere in the depths of her reserve she found the strength for a weak laugh of joy. A few seconds later the foal was lying in the straw and Duffy was tenderly wiping it dry.

"One down. One more to go," Gabe declared tiredly, and smiled at Jonni. "I'll take over."

She scooted out of his way, weary but revived by a happiness she'd never know before. Leaning against the side of the stall, she watched the coming of the second foal. Without the obstacle of its twin, the birth was easy.

"A pair of fillies," Duffy announced, "as pretty as their mother."

"How's the mare?" Gabe asked, slowly pushing his tall frame upright.

"You just give her a few minutes and she'll be investigatin' those little girls of hers," Bill stated with a proud-papa look.

Jonni tore her gaze away from the delicate perfection of the foals to watch as Gabe walked to the bucket of water to rinse himself off. He'd saved the mare and her foals, but she knew no one would congratulate him for it—it was part of his job. But it contained its own built-in reward: those two tiny creatures in the stall, the beauty of birth.

There was no towel to dry on, so Gabe reached for

his shirt. He saw her looking at him and smiled. Tugging his shirt on over his wet skin, he made no attempt to button it. When he walked toward her Jonni rose guiltily to her feet. She hadn't exerted nearly as much effort, nor worked for the length of time that he had. She was sitting and he was standing, a circumstance Jonni immediately changed.

When Jonni stood up, the mare rolled upright to gather her legs under her. After one shaky attempt to rise, the chestnut mare succeeded in getting to her feet. Turning her head, she pricked her ears toward the foals and whickered softly.

A bit intimidated by their strange new world, the foals blinked at the sound. One curled back its lip and emitted a squeaky answer. The mare turned in the straw and lowered her head to investigate the pair.

"Sugar and spice and everything nice, that's what they're made of, Lida," Gabe told the mare. Whether he was aware of it or not, Jonni knew he had just named the foals.

"They're beautiful." Jonni made the obvious and unnecessary comment.

His arm moved behind her to cross diagonally from shoulder to waist, his hand cupping her hipbone. It was a silent communication of a shared experience and the wonder of it. Jonni automatically curved an arm behind his broader waist to complete the quiet linking together. It seemed a very natural thing.

"Look," Gabe instructed.

An awed and waiting silence stole through the four members of the audience. Straw rustled beneath miniature hooves as the foal with the spot of white on its forehead made its first attempt to stand on its toothpick legs. The mare nudged her encouragement after an initial collapse. The foal tried again. Its head made it top-heavy and its legs were too long, but it would grow into both in time.

With a precarious lunge the foal wobbled on all four feet. Immediately its little broom tail began swishing the air in a signal of victory. It was evidently the sign its twin had been waiting to see, because it then made its first attempt. The mare blew softly, communicating with her offspring in the low sounds coming from her throat.

A smile tugged at Jonni's mouth at the pathetically uncoordinated attempts by the twin foals to walk. Their spindly legs couldn't seem to decide which direction was their final destination. But there was a big lump in her throat, too, at the wondrous and age-old scene of mother and babies.

Instinct guided the foals to the mare's flank with a couple of helpful nudgings from her, their knowledge part of nature's marvel. They suckled hungrily, heads butting, legs wobbly, tails swishing.

"I guess this little family don't need us anymore," Duffy declared, and walked toward the door leading out of the stall into the barn's interior walkway.

"Yeah, we might as well be goin' to get our own supper," Bill agreed. "Here's your hat, Gabe." He handed him the hat. Respect and admiration gleamed in the look he gave Gabe.

Gabe took the hat and set it on the back of Jonni's head. "See you in the morning, boys."

"Good night," Jonni added, feeling intimately close to Gabe but not threatened.

"Good night."

Listening to the sounds of their footsteps fading into silence, Jonni made no move to leave the stall or the close, comfortable position beside Gabe. There was too much peace and contentment where she was for her to be anxious to leave it.

"Hungry?" His one-word question was spoken quietly.

"No." Jonni matched his tone, not wanting to break the spell. "I'd forgotten what it was like to watch something being born, to be a part of it."

"The miracle of life."

She nodded. "It's happening all the time. It's such a constant thing, yet it's always so new."

Jonni continued to watch the mare and her foals. "That's what makes having babies so wonderful."

"I suppose you plan to start a family immediately." An undercurrent of hard feelings threaded its way through his comment.

A sudden tension electrified her nerves. She felt instantly defensive against the hurt his words caused. She tried to laugh, but it was a brittle sound.

"Don't forget I have a career, Gabe," she reminded him with false brightness. "It's going to last for several more years yet. A model runs the risk of ruining her figure—and her future—if she gets pregnant."

"Wait too long and you'll be in your thirties."

"Lots of women have their first babies then." Jonni was well aware that fertility declined after 35, but she didn't mention it. It didn't seem like the time or the place to do anything but be happy and unconcerned.

"Hmm. How large a family would you like to have?"

Out of the corner of her eye, Jonni saw the downward

tilt of his chin as Gabe turned to study her. "Four, five, half a dozen," she wished aloud before cold reality made her add, "but I'll settle for one healthy baby."

"How many children does Ted want?" There was something in his voice that indicated Gabe knew he was asking a loaded question.

Her head jerked up. "Why do you always have to bring him up?" A mist of tears stung her eyes. Her gaze ricocheted from his narrowed look as she blinked away the moisture and struggled to maintain her poise.

"He doesn't particularly want any children, does he?" Gabe persisted, challenging her to answer his question.

She wouldn't admit that. "He'd like to have a son," she said. "Maybe I'll just have to keep trying until I get it right." Her attempt at humor failed miserably.

The invisible force of Gabe's anger seemed to fill the silence. "He'll grudgingly accept one child and you want a bunch. As incompatible as the two of you are, you're going to have a hellish marriage if you go through with it." His voice rumbled, low and almost ominous.

"They say opposites attract." Jonni knew it was a lame thing to say, but Gabe's take on it was pretty accurate. She kept trying to imagine Ted holding their child and kept having visions of the baby spitting up on his silk tie.

In a swift movement that expressed his not-so-hidden emotions, Gabe touched her shoulder and turned her to face him. "Jonni, you know better. Opposite personalities attract only when they complement each other. When the hell are you going to open your eyes?"

But she had opened them. And she was being consumed by the dangerous black fires burning in his look. Her defenses were being melted away by their overpowering heat. A savage despair seemed to flicker in his eyes.

"How could any man not want you to have his children?" Gabe demanded with harsh softness.

He pulled her inside the circle of his arms and crushed her to his chest. His chin rubbed against the side of her forehead as his hand, stroking the back of her hair, nestled her head in the hollow of his shoulder. His embrace offered comfort and support and Jonni was weak enough to need it, feeling pummeled and torn apart by emotions she couldn't understand.

"Break the engagement, Jonni, before it breaks you," he warned thickly.

"But I'm going to marry him," she protested in a pained whisper.

There was nothing to separate her from his bare chest. Unbuttoned, his shirt hung open. Beneath her hands his flesh was vital and firm; his chest hair was rough against her cheek. He smelled of soap and straw and, most of all, the vigorous male odor of himself. The hard feel of Gabe was a sensation she was becoming addicted to.

A work-callused hand roughly caressed her cheek as Gabe tipped her head up. His gaze skimmed over her face and lingered on her parted lips.

"How the hell do I get myself into these situations?" he muttered. "I've got to be the biggest damn fool ever born."

"No, I am," she corrected breathlessly.

In the next second his mouth was silencing her and dizzily sweeping her to a new emotional high. A wild kind of rapture raged in her breast. She felt it echoed by the thud of his heart beneath her hands. Her skin felt feverish wherever his caressing hands touched her. Desire became an aching torment that arched her soft curves to fit his unyielding male contours.

Forsaking her lips, his mouth moved to her neck. His strong white teeth nibbled at its sensitive cord. Jonni shuddered against him with the sweet intensity of longing and softly moaned his name.

"Damn it, Jonni, I'm too old for this," he groaned, rubbing his cheek against hers in agitation. "Kisses aren't enough to satisfy my sexual appetite anymore."

His hand covered her breast, demanding an intimacy and sending a shaft of dangerous pleasure into her being. "I want to make love to you. I want to feel you naked against me, Jonni. I want to satisfy you in every way, give you everything you want—"

"D-don't ask me, Gabe." A wave of panic washed over her, making her sway against him.

"What does that mean?" His hands dug into her flesh. "Am I supposed to take you without giving you a chance to say yes or no? Or is that a no?" He sounded cold with control.

Jonni had been uncertain of her meaning before, but his bold questions made it definite. "It's no." Shakily, she pulled out of his arms and turned away so her expression wouldn't reveal how easily her mind could be changed.

Gabe stood watching her for a tense moment, breathing hard. Swearing roughly, he reached down and picked up his hat, which had tumbled from her head. He dusted it against his leg to knock the straw off it, then pulled it low on his head. Out of the corner of her eye Jonni saw him start to button his shirt. His glittering eyes caught her look.

"If the sight of a man's chest bothers you, maybe you'd better not look," he suggested with hard cynicism and buttoned his shirt only halfway before tucking it into the waistband of his Levi's.

"You have every right to be angry," Jonni admitted. "It was my fault and I'm sorry."

"You're sorry?" Gabe repeated sardonically. "If you think I'm going to apologize, you're crazy as hell."

There was a flash of temper in her jeweled eyes. "Damn it, Gabe, I'm trying to—" What? She stopped, not knowing what she was trying to accomplish.

Gabe measured her with a look. "Yeah, maybe it's time you explained what you're trying to do—"

"Hello?" Her mother's voice dragged out the questioning call. "Gabe? Jonni? Are you still in here?"

Saved. Jonni was grateful for that. "Over by the lights, Mother," she answered.

Two sets of footsteps approached the stall. "Duffy just told us the mare's had twins," her father spoke up. "Caroline and I came down to see them."

Stopping outside the stall, the Starrs leaned against the sides of the manger to look at the newborn foals. Luckily, there wasn't much conversation required from either Jonni or Gabe as Caroline made exclaiming phrases over the new family.

Jonni was trapped by an unbearable tension; a brittle shell surrounded her. And Gabe, who rarely showed expression, looked more tight-lipped than usual.

"You two are probably starved by now," her mother declared, sighing as she pushed away from the manger wall. "I have a pot of soup warming on the stove and a plate of sandwiches on the table. You'd better come to the house and eat before you faint from hunger."

Jonni's gaze slid briefly to Gabe before she walked swiftly past him to the stall door. Her stomach was a churning mass of nerves. Food was the last thing she wanted, but she didn't want to go into a lengthy explanation of that fact to her parents.

"That sounds good, Mom," she lied.

"Aren't you coming, Gabe?" her father frowned as Gabe remained where he was.

"No." His answer was abrupt. "I'm tired. I've lost my appetite somewhere."

Her steps faltered, but Jonni resisted the impulse to glance at Gabe. She smiled at her parents and saw the funny look her father was giving her. "That's all the more food for me, isn't it?" she joked. She wanted to run out of the barn, but she restrained her pace to match her parents'. As she left with them, she felt Gabe's eyes on her back. Whatever he was thinking . . . she didn't want to know.

Chapter Eight

A few minutes past one on Friday afternoon, Jonni led the saddled dun gelding from the barn. The sun felt almost hot on her back and the air was deadly still. She swung into the saddle and turned the horse toward the corral gate. Gabe was on the other side of the enclosure, mounted on a big, muscled bay, its coat gleaming like polished mahogany. He had just started to ride out from the ranch yard, but at the sound of her creaking saddle leather he reined in the head-tossing bay horse to look back.

It was impossible for Jonni to alter her course. With squared shoulders, she rode to the corral gate and bent to unlatch it. Gabe watched, obviously waiting for her. Pushing the gate open, she rode the dun through the narrow gap, then reined it backward and to the side to close the gate, never hurrying in her motions.

"I just got done warning the boys, so I might as well tell you, too, if you see one of 'em breaking the rule." Gabe spoke when she had finished. "From now on, there'll be no smoking when we're out on the range. I know you don't smoke, but if you see someone who is, make damned sure they don't toss a lit butt away."

Jonni frowned and walked her horse toward his. "Why?" His warning wasn't an idle one. Something had prompted it.

"There was a grass fire near town this morning," he told her grimly. "Fortunately it was spotted right away and they were able to contain it."

"A grass fire, at this time of the year?" Her expression was incredulous. "My God, what's it going to be like in the summer?"

"Hell, if we don't get some rain." He reined the nervously eager bay toward the open land.

"Where are you going?" Jonni asked.

"I'm riding over to the Cimarron to check on the cattle." Gabe seemed to hesitate before he added, "You're welcome to come with me . . . if you want." His voice was indifferent.

"I might ride partway with you." She tried to match his tone.

One shoulder rose to indicate he couldn't care less and he sent the bay forward at a long, tireless trot. Jonni urged her mount into the same gait, feeling angered by his attitude instead of relieved.

Gabe took the lead and Jonni followed to one side, her horse's nose even with the cantle of his saddle. He paid no attention to her. On a level stretch, his horse broke into a ground-eating canter, and Jonni's horse was quick to follow.

The faster pace generated a breeze that evaporated the sweat on her neck and cooled her skin. Her long blond hair was tucked beneath the crown of her hat, a few wisps escaping to curl around her collar. She pulled the front brim lower on her forehead to shield her eyes from the glare of the sun.

Despite the lack of communication between them, Jonni found a certain companionship in riding over the red-tinted hills with Gabe. There was a destination ahead of her instead of an aimless wandering ride. With this inner satisfaction, she began enjoying the rugged vistas provided by the land they traveled through. If her gaze strayed more than once to the wide shoulders of the taciturn man riding with her, she told herself it was only natural.

As they neared the banks of the Cimarron River, Gabe slowed the tall bay horse to a walk. The dry, yellowing grass swished beneath their striding horses to accompany the creaking saddle leather and jangling bits. The stock cows were scattered over the land, some grazing, others chewing their cud. White-faced calves bawled for their mothers at the sight of the riders, but most lay sleeping in the sun.

They stopped at the edge of the riverbank. Below them the current was sluggish, the water rusty with the red earth of its riverbed. Jonni stared at it for several seconds.

"I don't ever remember seeing it that low before," she commented.

"I know," Gabe agreed tersely.

"What are you going to do?" She glanced at him.

He lifted his gaze, narrowing it at the southern sky. "Pray that those clouds aren't one of nature's practical jokes."

Jonni looked in surprise at the thunderheads building on the horizon. She hadn't noticed them before. "They came up fast. It might be a storm."

"Let's hope that's not an empty prophecy," he offered dryly. "It's hot. We'd better give the horses a breather."

By the time Jonni had dismounted Gabe was on the ground, loosening his saddle cinch. She did the same and the zebra dun emitted a rolling snort of pleasure. Gabe led his horse into the scanty shade of a tall cottonwood tree, its limbs just starting to bud with leaves.

Pulling on the reins, Jonni walked her horse over and tied it to a piece of heavy deadwood so it could graze. Gabe leaned against the tree, bending a knee to rest his heel against the trunk. He lifted a hand to his shirt pocket as if wanting a smoke, only to remember the restriction he had imposed and return his hand to his side.

"The cows look as if they're in good shape," Jonni observed. A meadowlark sang from off to her left.

Gabe didn't comment on her remark. Tipping his hat to the back of his head, he let his gaze run over her face, the slimness of her neck and the rise of her breasts, leaving her with the sensation that he had touched her.

"When you were growing up, what was your idea of marriage?"

The unexpectedness of his question made her stiffen. "I don't think I want to get into that kind of discussion with you," she said tensely.

"I didn't ask what your expectations are now," Gabe pointed out. "Only what they were when you were younger."

"I suppose I thought it would be like my parents' marriage," she answered to show she wasn't afraid, "with the wife cooking the meals, cleaning the house and working in the garden. Of course, my mother wanted more than that for me and so did my father."

"Like children?" Gabe prompted.

"Eventually. But they made sure I got through college and got started in a career. They always supported me. Anyway, yes, what about children?" Irritation flared that he should bring up that subject again.

He didn't pursue that particular topic. "Did you want to live in the city or the country?" he asked instead.

"In the country, of course," Jonni retorted, "like my parents. Where I could have horses and a place to ride. That's all I knew, so naturally it's what I expected."

"After spending the past six years in New York, you prefer a home in the city," Gabe concluded. "An apartment, I should say," he corrected.

"No, I don't necessarily prefer it." She felt the stirrings of unease. "I would like to have a house in the country, but with Ted's business interests, it's more convenient for us to live in the city."

"Whither thou goest, I will go," he mocked. "How noble of you to sacrifice!"

"Listen, if you're going to start in on this again, I'm—" Jonni began in agitation.

"Don't listen to me," Gabe interrupted. "Listen to what you're saying. You want a home in the country where you can get up with the sun, and children that you can tuck into their beds at night. Granted, your modeling career means you won't have to worry about money, but I still don't get why good old Ted is in charge of making all the decisions."

"He isn't," she hissed. "And he isn't old."

Gabe was relentless. "Seems to me he only wants the woman whose image is plastered on every magazine cover. Is that the kind of life you want?"

"I know what kind of life I'll have with Ted and I've accepted it." She began twisting the huge engagement ring on her finger, conscious of its heavy weight.

"Have you, Jonni?" Gabe asked in a low voice. "There's always going to be someone younger and prettier trying to shove you aside in that business. And one day they will. It all sounds kind of shallow to me."

"I can be happy with it," she insisted.

"Can you?" Gabe was skeptical.

"What do you care?" She flung him a shimmering blue glance, her voice rising sharply as her composure snapped, but she could no longer endure his baiting.

A deadly stillness settled over him. There was a cold and ruthless look in the gaze he leveled at her. His silence was more unnerving than any of his previous comments. It was a relief when he finally spoke. "I didn't deserve that remark."

Jonni averted her gaze before Gabe's sad look could get to her. "None of this is really any of your business," she said stiffly. "It's my life."

"And you're on the brink of making an unholy mess of it," Gabe informed her. "There were times when we could talk things out. You used to come to me for advice. Now you won't even listen to reason."

"It isn't the same anymore." She swung her gaze

back to look at him helplessly. "Things are different between us."

The sharp breath he exhaled emphasized that point. "At least you're intelligent enough to recognize that."

"This isn't fair." A tumultuous upheaval was going on inside her. Jonni hugged her arms around her stomach and stared at the ground, fixing her unseeing gaze on the blades of grass near the dead tree limb her horse was tied to. She'd never be able to recapture that supreme confidence and joy about her engagement she'd felt when she arrived. Gabe had created doubts where there had been none. "I almost wish I'd never come back," she said tightly.

"Believe me, Jonni, there have been times when I've wished you hadn't, too." His agreement was cool and sardonic, flicking her like a whip.

From the south came the rumble of distant thunder. Jonni lifted her gaze in its direction. The clouds had moved in to block out the sun and cast a solid shadow, over the terracotta buttes and mesas. Lightning splintered inside the billowing, gray-black clouds, electric and intense.

"Look at that. We're in for a storm."

Gabe had already pushed away from the tree to walk to his horse. "Good call. There are no bees around. The flies are sitting." He draped a stirrup over the saddle seat and began tugging at the cinch strap to tighten the saddle. "I haven't seen any birds in the sky for the past five minutes. We'd better head for the barn."

Feeling his calm urgency, Jonni hurriedly tightened the cinch on her own saddle. The subtle signs of nature he had observed made her aware that he had been cognizant of all that had happened around them. She, on the other hand, had been so wrapped up in their conversation that she wouldn't have noticed a thing until the threatening clouds swallowed the sun.

She glanced at the parched earth. "I hope we don't get caught in a downpour," she said. Gabe was already in the saddle and waiting when she mounted.

"I'm not worried about getting wet," he replied ominously, and dug a heel into the bay's flank to send it bounding forward into a canter.

Another rumble of thunder was muffled by the drumming of the horses' hooves as Jonni urged her horse into a fast canter after Gabe. They traveled swiftly, trying to outrun the clouds taking over the sky. The thunder rumbled closer, lightning flashing behind them.

They were halfway to the barn when the first fat raindrop struck Jonni. It was followed by a second and a third. Thunder boomed from the clouds and the rain splashed down. Her horse tugged nervously at the bit, trying to break into a gallop. She held it back, sparing a glance from the rough terrain to look at Gabe.

The much-needed rain had come. There was a rejoicing light in her eyes to match the smile on her lips, but there was no such answering expression on his face.

Her horse made a shying lunge sideways as lightning crashed nearby. Jonni felt the reverberation of the deafening thunder in the air. The wind came to whip the rain into sheets, soaking her clothes and plastering them against her skin.

One jagged flash of lightning was followed by

another and another until the air around her seemed charged with electricity. Danger heightened her senses as Jonni realized they were likely targets for the deadly bolts.

"We've going to have to take cover!" Gabe shouted above the thunder. It rumbled and vibrated the earth like a herd of stampeding cattle. "That way." He pointed to an outcropping of sandstone ahead of them.

At the base, the sandstone had been hollowed by the elements. Altering their course, they raced for the crude, cavelike shelter. The overhanging ledge that formed the rock roof was tall enough to enable them to ride under it, escaping the deluge of rain and splintering lightning.

The zebra dun snorted and danced nervously as Jonni dismounted. The recess carved into the sandstone formation wasn't very deep, but it was some twenty feet in length. There was room enough for the horses to stand side by side and be protected from the rain, except for what the wind drove in. Steam rose faintly from the heated flesh of the horses, wet from the downpour.

"Whew! That was some ride!" Jonni declared with a breathless laugh, revived and invigorated by the exhilarating flirtation with danger. "My clothes are soaked." She plucked the sodden material of her blouse and held it away from her rib case to show how wet she was.

Gabe looked. And in that brief, black glance, Jonni was made aware of the revealing way her blouse had molded itself to her breasts. The wet material was almost transparent. A scorching heat licked through her veins.

But there was no reference to her suggestive appearance when he spoke. "You look like a young girl with your hair tucked under your hat like that." He took the dun's reins from her hand and turned away. "There's a dry rock over there. You might as well sit where you can be out of the rain."

A chunk of flat sandstone rested near the recessed wall of the cliff. Jonni walked over to it, subdued, while Gabe tied the horses to a stubby bush. Removing her hat and sitting on the rock, she shook her hair free. It tumbled about her shoulders. Because it had been protected by the hat, her hair was only partially damp, its blond color darkened by the faint moisture. At a wicked crash of lightning she looked out.

"How long do you think the storm will last?" she asked as Gabe walked over to where she was seated.

"It's too violent to keep this up for long." Although there was room on the rock, he made no attempt to sit with her. Instead he towered beside her, intimidating her with his size. He reached into his shirt pocket and took out the cigarette makings from a small, waterproof pouch. He glanced down to see her watching him. "Do you remember how to roll a cigarette?" There was something gentle in his look, a remembrance of old times, more companionable occasions.

"Yes, I think so." She nodded, warmed by the memories of when Gabe had taught her how.

"Show me." He passed her the tobacco and a dry cigarette paper.

Smiling confidently, Jonni took the makings from him. Gabe crouched beside her, sitting off his heels and balancing effortlessly on the balls of his feet. She formed the thin paper into a trough and tapped a mound of tobacco into the center. With her fingertip she spread the shredded brown leaves along the paper trough.

"Am I doing it right?" She glanced brightly at Gabe as she lifted it to her mouth to lick the edge of the paper.

Before she could succeed, Gabe was reaching to take it from her. "You'd better let me do it." Part of the tobacco spilled as he took the paper from her hand.

Stunned by his abrupt behavior, Jonni frowned at him. "Why? What was I doing wrong?" She was sure she had been doing it correctly.

"Nothing." He licked the paper and rolled it around the tobacco. "I'd just forgotten what the sight of that pink tongue of yours could do to me."

Striking a match, he cupped the flame to the end of the cigarette between his lips. Jonni sat motionless, shaken by the sudden, disturbing intimacy of the conversation. A turbulent, elemental tension raced through her. It had no connection to the savage storm raging around them.

In agitation she rose to face the rain whipping into their crude shelter. She felt excited, confused and unnerved all at the same time. "Why did you have to say that?" she demanded of Gabe in a taut voice.

"It's the truth." Gabe straightened to stand at her shoulder. "Why shouldn't I have said it?"

"Because." She flung the weak, unsupportable reason at him.

He flicked the freshly lit cigarette into a puddle created by the storm. "Why does it bother you to know I'm aroused by you?"

When Jonni tried to avoid his intense regard, a finger turned her back to face him and remained beneath her chin. "It isn't just the pink tip of your tongue. I'm aroused by the way your breasts fill my hand, the way your hips fit perfectly against mine, and the sexy, animal sounds you make when I arouse you."

"I don't!" Jonni denied the last.

"You do," Gabe insisted and drew her into his arms to prove it.

Thunder rocked the ground beneath her feet but Jonni didn't know the difference between it and the tremors of desire that shuddered through her. The lightning paled in comparison to the golden flame his devastating kiss ignited.

Her fingers sought the silken smoothness of his wet hair, but his hat got in the way. Like a real cowboy, Gabe reached up and deftly tossed it to the rock wall. Then his hand was back on her spine, arching her into the ever tightening circle of his arms.

The wind whipped in stinging droplets of water to pelt her cheeks, but Jonni was oblivious to the storm. She was out of control, existing only because Gabe was holding her, kissing her, touching her, caressing her. Yet not even that was enough. She wanted more. A hungry, whimpering sound came from her throat.

Gabe pulled his mouth from her lips to drag it near her ear. "That's what I'm talking about," he whispered. "That wild little mating sound you made."

Turning and twisting, Jonni's lips sought to regain possession of his mouth, but he eluded her. "Yes," she moaned at last.

"Do you make sounds like that for him?" he growled against her throat.

"Gabe, please!" She didn't want to make comparisons, not at a time like this. Ted had been an expert in the art of love, but he'd never turned her on the way Gabe was doing.

Thoroughly frustrated, she forced her hands inside the collar of his shirt and dug her nails into the hard flesh of his shoulders, like a cat in heat. All she wanted was to satisfy her own needs and end the torment of his elusive mouth. She heard the sharp intake of his breath and felt the flinching of his muscles.

"Tell me, damn it!" He rapped the sensitive skin at the base of her neck in retaliation.

"It was never like this, Gabe," Jonni admitted in a breathless whisper. "Never."

He shuddered violently against her, as if some last barrier had finally been breached. Her admission was rewarded with a sensual kiss that made the previous moments seem less of a torment. Jonni responded to its blazing ardor with complete abandon. Gabe's hand forced aside the material of her blouse to seek the roundness of her breast.

Then he was dragging her to the ground as if caught in an undertow that not even he, with all his strength, could withstand. Jonni knew the glorious feeling—she was the subject of emotions too powerful to deny or resist.

The searing longings had her writhing and twisting beneath him as his mouth sought the dusty rose tip of her rain-moistened breast. Her fingers tugged his shirt open so she could feel the bareness of his fiery skin against her own. His mouth murmured her name over and over again as it moved against her throat, her ear, her cheek and finally her lips. His weight crushed her slim body onto the hard ground.

Lightning split open the sky in front of their rocky

shelter. The dun horse neighed in alarm and strained against the tied reins. Its rear hooves danced backward, black-striped legs bumping into the entwining pair on the ground. Reacting with animal-fast reflexes, Gabe rolled Jonni out of reach of the trampling hooves and continued the same fluid movement onto his feet.

"Easy, boy, easy." His husky voice attempted to quiet the horse. "Easy, now."

The gelding was on the verge of bolting. Jonni sat up, shifting out of its possible path and drawing the front of her blouse closed. Gabe laid a hand on the tan rump and walked slowly to the horse's head. It rolled its eyes and snorted, but didn't elude the hand that reached for the reins. The ends were still tied to the branch, broken from the bush.

While Gabe remained there to quiet the horse, Jonni shakily began to button her blouse and tuck it securely inside her jeans.

Staring at that virile figure of manhood, she knew she wished the interruption had happened much later, after the ache inside had been fully satisfied. And she was shattered by how willing she was to cast aside the laws of morality and fidelity she had been raised to respect. It simply wasn't possible to be in love with two men. Yet there she was, engaged to one man and eager to make love to another.

She rose to stand on weak legs, and the movement attracted Gabe's attention. Absently patting the horse's neck, he retied the reins and walked back to her. His hands moved to hold and caress the soft flesh of her arms. The smoldering light in his eyes told her he wanted to take up where they left off, and the temptation was sweet agony. Her hands rested naturally on his waist, but she didn't sway into his arms.

"I'm engaged." Troubled confusion and want shimmered in her eyes.

His dark gaze lost its lazy, seductive quality and widened with mockery. "Are you reminding me of that? Or yourself?"

Jonni winced. He'd struck a vulnerable nerve. Her gaze dropped to the tantalizing hollow at the base of his throat. She studied the sinewy cords in his neck. "There are so many things . . ." she began, and wearily shook her head. "I'm finding it all difficult to understand."

His grip tightened to demand her undivided attention. "I love you, Jonni." A muscle twitched in his jaw. "What's so difficult to understand about that?"

"No." She shook her head, not wanting to believe him, wary because she knew how much more complicated it would all become if he was telling the truth.

"Yes." The laughing sound he made lacked humor. "I love you. I've been in love with you for years. Half the time I've been like a rutting stag without a doe. And the other half . . . the rest of the time, it's been pure hell."

The shock of his confession whitened her face. "I don't believe you. Not all this time."

"From almost the moment I set eyes on you," Gabe told her, his jaw hardening. "You were fourteen and your boyish figure was just beginning to fill out. But you were beautiful even then. I tried to convince myself it was your beauty that fascinated me, but within a matter of months I knew it went a hell of a lot deeper than that."

"No." Jonni pulled out of his hold, rejecting everything he said. "It isn't true. You never so much as hinted to me, not even that time when I—"

"When you developed a crush on me," Gabe interrupted to complete her sentence. "You'd barely turned fifteen then, Jonni, and I was twenty-eight. Believe me, I was tempted to make the most of your adoration, but I couldn't trust myself to be satisfied with the innocent affection you wanted to give. So I kept you at a safe distance, even if it meant I had to be outright rude to you sometimes. I just prayed that I could arouse it again when you matured into a woman."

In a gesture of agitation Jonni combed her fingers through her hair. Gabe had always been skilled at hiding his thoughts, she knew that, but she was frightened by what he was revealing.

"In the meantime," Gabe continued, his narrowed eyes watching her changing expression, "I had to listen to all your talk about your dates, how many times your boyfriends kissed you and whether they were any good at it or not. Your teenage love life nearly drove me insane with jealousy."

"Why?" She turned on him, half-convinced but still doubting. "Why didn't you ever indicate that you were interested in me? Not in the beginning, but later on, when I was older."

"I did. When you were seventeen, I decided I'd waited long enough. I went to your father and told him—"

"You went to my father!" The ground seemed to rock beneath her feet. "He knew all this?"

"Yes," Gabe admitted evenly, "I told him I was in love with you and that I wanted to start asking you out, if he had no objections."

Had her father kept Gabe from coming forward, she wondered. "Did he?"

"John had his doubts. I was a good deal older than you, and considerably more experienced. But he respected me for coming to him first before I made a move on you. He gave me his permission."

Jonni was thoroughly confused. "Then why didn't you ever ask me out?"

"I did."

"When?" she challenged.

"You'd just had an argument with that Jefferson boy who played football," Gabe began.

The memory came flooding back. "And you said you'd take me to the dance that Friday if I wanted to go," Jonni remembered, her eyes widening in astonishment.

"As I recall, you turned me down flat, insisting that you weren't *that* desperate." His eyes were cold as they remembered the exact words of her rejection.

"I . . . I thought you were joking," she said defensively, "that you were just offering to take me because you felt sorry for me. I never dreamed—"

"No, you never did," he agreed flatly. "So I decided to wait a little longer until you finally looked at me and saw a man instead of a convenient shoulder to pour your troubles on. Unfortunately you got that crazy notion in your head to become a model and you took off for New York."

"I never could understand why you were so opposed to my going," she said in a marveling voice of discovery. After all this time, it finally made sense. "You kept insisting I'd hate New York and I'd never succeed."

"And the more I kept telling you that, the more determined you became to prove I was wrong. Every time we got into an argument over your leaving, I knew I was driving you into going, but I was too damned much in love with you to keep my mouth shut." There was a haunting agony to his tightly clipped admission.

"I never guessed, Gabe," Jonni murmured.

"No, I know you didn't. Which meant I still had a chance. I kept waiting for you to come home. I don't know how many times, maybe hundreds, over the past years that I made up my mind that I was going to fly there and bring you back, but I never did. I told myself that if you were the woman for me, you'd come back. I even made a try at forgetting you." His mouth quirked in cynicism. "Seemed like every time I got into town and picked up a magazine, I saw your face staring back at me."

"I did come back, though." She had the feeling she was seeing Gabe for the first time for who he really was: a man with deep, abiding emotions, strong and unshakable, a rock in a windswept desert.

"Yes, you came back. When I saw you step out of that plane, I didn't know if I was dreaming or whether it was really you. I'd been waiting for so long I thought my mind had snapped."

"But when I kissed you hello, you nearly broke my ribs pushing me away," Jonni accused, finding his actions that day at odds with his confession.

"Pushing you away?" He laughed at that. "It was all

I could do to keep from crushing you in my arms and never letting you go!" His expression sobered. "Then you introduced lover boy as your fiancé. I've never come any closer to killing a man in my life." He grasped her shoulders tightly. "You aren't going to marry him, Jonni."

Under the spell of his touch, Jonni believed he was probably right. But so many of the things she had believed had turned out to be so wrong. Maybe this crazy wildfire Gabe had kindled would burn itself out and there would only be cold ashes left. This past week had made chaos of her life.

"I'm too confused to be certain about anything." All her insecurities played across her expression, tousled ash blond hair sweeping her shoulders with the bewildered shake of her head.

"I love you. You can be sure about that." He lowered his dark head and took her mouth, kissing it deeply. Jonni was again swept breathlessly into the emotional current of his passion, which carried a pledge of eternity. When the pressure of his lips became seductive, she struggled against his persuasive force. Gabe let her escape his kiss, but not his arms. "All I want you to do is love me just a little."

"I need time to think," she protested, and fought the impulse to admit she already cared for him too deeply for her peace of mind.

His jaw was clenched as he suppressed the surge of impatience that flashed in his eyes. It was as if he knew how easily he could physically arouse an answer that would be more satisfactory to him.

"How long?" he demanded.

"Not . . . long," Jonni promised. She wanted to

make her decision when she was free from the unsettling influence of his touch. And she needed to reevaluate her feelings for Ted.

"It had better not be." Gabe released her and took a step away. He seemed to need the distance between them as much as she did. "I don't know how much more of this I can stand." He pivoted toward the horses. "The lightning has moved on. I think we can risk riding back to the barn."

"All right." Jonni silently agreed that there was greater danger in remaining where they were.

Bending, Gabe picked up her hat as well as his own and handed it to her. She took it and swept her hair on top of her head, pulling the hat over it. While she tucked a few wayward strands under the crown, Gabe untied the horses and turned them outward. He held the dun's bridle while she mounted and then passed her the reins. Jonni waited under the protective overhang as he swung into his saddle.

The rain was still coming down steadily but the wind had died and the lightning flashes were a considerable distance away. The thunder was a gentle roar. The horses moved reluctantly at their riders' bidding into the rain, their hooves clip-clopping on the wet ground.

Chapter Nine

The barn door stood open. Ducking her head, Jonni rode the gelding inside out of the rain. Gabe had paused to close the corral gate and was only a few feet behind her. Water dripped from the crease of her hat brim as she dismounted, her toes squishing in wet socks, her leather boots saturated inside and out.

"I'll take care of the horses." Leading his horse, Gabe reached for her reins. "You'd better go and change into some dry clothes." His gaze didn't quite meet hers.

"Gabe?" There was something she wanted to ask him. Or tell him. Jonni wasn't sure which. She just knew she didn't want to leave him yet.

He turned back to her, and something written in her expression snapped the thin thread of his control. With a stifled groan he caught her in his arms. It must have been what she wanted because she immediately wound her hands behind his neck and met the downward descent of his mouth halfway.

The heat of his body warmed her rain-chilled flesh,

which shivered beneath her wet clothes. His deep, incredibly sexy kiss swelled her heart to the bursting point. The thought of never feeling this mindless joy again made her cling to him. If this was love, she didn't want to lose it.

"So this is what's been going on while I've been gone!" A voice as sharp and cutting as a broadax sliced them apart.

Jonni looked in disbelief at the man standing just inside the doorway, his legs spread slightly apart, his hands clenched into fists at his sides. Her pulse drummed an alarm, its message beating wildly in her throat.

"Ted!" The shock of identification was in her voice. Her gaze moved to Gabe, who had pivoted at Ted's cold challenge. He stood half a step in front of her, partially shielding her. The wet shirt, plastered to his skin, revealed tautly coiled muscles ready to spring.

"If you remember my name, maybe you also remember that I'm your fiancé," Ted said in cold, sarcastic condemnation.

"What are you doing here?" Jonni breathed the question, her feet rooted to the barn floor. Despite her kiss-dazed senses, she was beginning to realize the potential danger in the situation.

"Surely it's obvious. I came here to be with you for the weekend." Ted's eyes never stayed on her long. They kept flicking to Gabe, aware of where the opposition stood and of the threat he represented.

"Why didn't you let me know you were coming?" she demanded in agitation. If she'd had any advance warning at all of Ted's arrival, the atmosphere wouldn't be crackling with such violent undercurrents.

"I wanted to surprise you. Some surprise!" he jeered. "I flew in ahead of the storm, only to discover you'd gone riding. Or at least that was what your father said. He failed to mention that you'd gone riding with *him.*"

"Dad didn't know that," Jonni protested, not wanting Ted to think her father had any knowledge of the change in her relationship to Gabe.

"I was riding out to check the cattle," Gabe said in an emotionless voice that made Jonni's blood run cold. "At the last minute Jonni decided to ride along with me."

"And to think that while I've been pacing the floor, half out of my mind with worry over you out there in that storm, you were with him!" Ted had begun to tremble visibly with jealous anger.

"We would have been back sooner, but when the storm came up we had to take shelter," Jonni explained. Considering Ted's present state, she had the feeling she was wasting her breath, but she had to make some attempt to keep this scene from erupting into something really ugly.

"That must have been cozy," he taunted.

"Nothing happened." Jonni knew how close that statement was to an outright lie, and her complexion crimsoned at Ted's skeptical glance. Almost immediately it swept to include Gabe.

"I had a feeling all along about you, Stockman," Ted accused him, his lip curling in a sneer.

"Isn't that a coincidence?" There was something reckless and dangerous in Gabe's coolly amused response, all pretense of politeness discarded. "I had the exact same feeling about you."

Her heart hammered wildly. She was being left out of the conversation, ignored. The two men were now regarding each other with open challenge, their eyes locked in combat, each trying to stare the other down.

"I've always suspected the code of the West was just a myth—the honest, hardworking cowboy with all his supposed righteous morality for another man's property." Ted was blatantly contemptuous. "You're nothing but a thief, trying to take something that doesn't belong to you."

"I'm not the thief." Cold steel ran through Gabe's voice. "Jonni was wearing my brand long before she ever met you."

A chill of inevitability shivered through her veins. The encounter was about to spin out of control. Jonni was powerless to slow the momentum that was racing to a final confrontation. There seemed nothing she could say to prevent it.

Ted laughed, an icy sound. "I'll bet you'd like to believe that. You probably had it all worked out, didn't you, Stockman? If you could marry the rancher's daughter, you could get your hands on the whole operation. You wouldn't be just the hired hand anymore."

Jonni stopped breathing. That remark was a direct insult, a slap at Gabe's pride. A deadly stillness enveloped Gabe. She was reminded of a cougar, poised to leap on its prey. Any hope that there was something she could say or do to stop this vanished.

When Gabe finally spoke, it was with a calmness that said he found a certain satisfaction in the situation. "I sincerely hope you're prepared to provide proof of that, Maltin, because I'll enjoy making you take it back if you can't."

Ted hesitated for only an instant. "You're damned right I'm prepared." He started forward, shrugging out of his suit jacket as he walked toward Gabe.

"No! Stop this!" Jonni grabbed at Gabe's elbow in a desperate appeal.

His eyes never left Ted as he removed her hand from his arm and pushed her to one side. "Stay out of the way, Jonni," he told her. "This is going to be a pleasure."

Jonni retreated until she came up against the rough lumber of the barn wall. Her hands were behind her, palms pressed against the wood, indifferent to the splinters as she watched the scene unfolding before her eyes.

With rare disregard for the care of his clothes, Ted tossed his suit jacket toward the corner of the barn and began tugging the knot of his silk tie loose. Never once did he slow the deliberate strides that carried him toward Gabe.

"I thought you were full of it the first time I met you." With the tie thrown aside, Ted unfastened his collar button, and two more. "I wished then that I'd rammed my fist down your throat. I should have. This time I will, you can count on it."

Gabe never said a word. He just waited for Ted to walk up to him. At the last minute he ducked under Ted's swing, the blow glancing off his shoulder, and hooked a fist into Ted's midsection. Ted grunted and blocked the following right to his jaw.

Paralyzed by the action, Jonni couldn't look away. Ted was no match for Gabe—she knew it. Gabe had the weight advantage, was stronger and had a longer reach. It was all stupid and senseless, but she seemed to be the only one who realized that.

Jonni winced when Ted staggered under Gabe's fist and came back for more. An overhand punch snapped Gabe's head back and Jonni saw blood trickling from the corner of his mouth. Ted had drawn first blood, but that didn't mean he'd win the fight.

After an exchange of more smashing blows, Ted was knocked to the ground. Jonni watched him rise. There was a gash across his cheekbone and a thin trail of red from his nose. She wanted to scream at him to quit, to give up before he was badly hurt, but she knew Ted wouldn't hear her—and if he did, he wouldn't listen.

Halfway to his feet, he lunged at Gabe. Gabe sidestepped the first blow, which carried the full force of Ted's weight behind it, and rocked under the second before landing a punch of his own. Both men had begun to breathe heavily, grunting with each swing. The brawling sounds had the stabled horses whickering nervously and shifting in their stalls, adding to the noise.

A right from Gabe sent Ted sprawling on the floor near the opposite wall. As Ted staggered to his feet he grabbed a pitchfork propped against the wall. Jonni's gaze widened in horror.

"Gabe! Look out!" She shouted the warning.

Even as she called out, Ted was swinging the pitchfork like a baseball bat, apparently unaware of the lethal, pointed prongs weighting the end. Gabe's raised forearm warded off the blow, then twisted to grab hold of the weapon. While Ted fought to keep possession of the pitchfork, he left himself open for Gabe's right cross. It knocked him backward onto the floor, tearing the wooden handle from his grip.

Gabe turned and speared the pitchfork into a small mound of hay in the corner. Cold anger darkened his expression as his attention returned to the half-conscious man in the blood-splattered and dirty silk shirt. Ted was trying to rise. Gabe reached down to grab him by the front of his shirt and haul him to his feet. The savage intent written on his face ended Jonni's silent role as spectator.

"No. No!" In a frightened rage, she flung herself at the arm Gabe had cocked to swing. "You're going to kill him! Stop it!" She beat at him, aware that her blows barely registered with him. "Stop it, you big brute!" she screamed at him. "Can't you see he's hurt? Leave him alone!"

"I'm finished with him." Breathing heavily from the brawl, Gabe let him go.

Ted swayed and would have fallen if Jonni hadn't rushed to his side to support him, taking his weight. Ted made a weak attempt to push her aside without success. Her hand lightly and soothingly stroked his jaw as she turned his head to look at her. His eyes were glazed over, betraying his barely conscious condition.

"It's over, Ted," she whispered to him, an ache in her voice. His handsome, chiseled face was bloodied and bruised and no trace of his cocky self-confidence remained. "You're hurt. You can't fight anymore." He stopped resisting and leaned heavily on her. He was beaten and knew it. Her flashing eyes turned on Gabe in accusation. "Just what did you prove?" she challenged, almost choking on the sob that rose in her throat.

There was a dangerous narrowing of Gabe's black eyes. The back of his hand was pressed to his mouth, half covering his mustache. When his hand came away there was a smear of blood on his skin, but Gabe hadn't taken the abuse Ted had received.

"That he sweats and bleeds just like the rest of us," Gabe answered, and reached to pick up his hat from the barn floor.

"You're nothing but a brute and a bully!" Her voice quivered. "You knew you could beat him. You knew you were stronger and faster, but you just had to let him provoke you into fighting. Ted wasn't any match for you, and you knew it. You challenged him!"

"He didn't have to take me up on it."

"You know he did," Jonni accused.

"Skip the instant replay and get the first-aid kit. Lover boy needs a little patching up," Gabe suggested dryly. He hesitated a fraction of a second, his hands on his hips, then he added, "I'll help you get him to the house."

"No!" Jonni rejected his offer of assistance with an angry toss of her head. "I don't need your help, and Ted wouldn't thank you for it. You've done enough damage without humiliating him still more by dragging him to the house for Mom and Dad to see."

"Jonni, I—" Whatever Gabe had been on the verge of saying, he clamped his mouth shut on it, a jaw-tensing hardness in his expression.

When he failed to make a retort to which she could answer back, tears welled in her eyes. A puzzled anger and hurt made her throat ache, and she lashed out at him in frustration. "I don't understand you . . . I don't understand either of you! It was senseless and stupid to fight. What kind of satisfaction could you get out of hitting each other?"

"It was strictly a personal satisfaction," Gabe answered grimly. "You see, Jonni, we didn't have anything to lose. One of us had already lost you before the fight ever started." Flat, expressionless black eyes made a slow sweep of her. "I don't see why you're so upset. Women get a kick out of men fighting over them."

"It's revolting to see anyone getting beaten up," Jonni said in a flash of anger.

Ted lurched against her and her arms tightened to steady him. "My legs don't want to stand up," he murmured in a dazed voice.

Her heart contracted at the sight of the bruised and swelling face reeling close to hers. "Ssh—oh, honey!" She soothed him with her voice, treating him like an injured and confused child. "I'll help you."

With a gesture of weariness Gabe pulled his hat low on his forehead and turned away. "Take him up to the house before he bleeds all over you."

Jonni glared at the callously indifferent man walking to collect the saddled horses. His total lack of sympathy for his defeated opponent angered her, but Gabe wasn't paying any heed to her.

"Come, on, Ted." She shifted her attention to the wobbling man leaning against her. Draping his arm over her shoulder, she turned him toward the barn door. "Let's go to the house and treat those cuts and bruises on your face."

Ted tried to make his legs obey, but his staggering

walk relied heavily on Jonni for both support and direction. The ground, muddy from the heavy rain and continued drizzle, didn't provide solid footing for either of them. Jonni slipped and slid, half carrying Ted. The sprinkling rain ran down her hair and into her eyes, hampering her vision and making the short journey even more difficult. By the time she reached the front porch of the house she was panting from the exertion.

"We're almost there," she promised Ted, and gathered herself for the effort of pushing the door open and maintaining her balance at the same time. Turning the knob, she kicked the door open with the toe of her boot. She was trying to maneuver Ted across the threshold when her father appeared in the foyer. Bewildered astonishment opened his mouth and drew a frown on his forehead.

Jonni didn't have time for explanations at the moment. "Help me get him inside, Dad!" The strain of her burden echoed in the gasping request for assistance.

But John was already hurrying forward to steer Ted into the house and add the support of his arms. One took at the battered face and he shouted, "Caroline!" Then his gaze slashed questioningly to Jonni. "What happened? He looks as if he ran into a brick wall."

"It was Gabe," she said stiffly.

An eyebrow arched. "That's the same thing," her father muttered, almost to himself. "Let's take him into the kitchen," he directed.

"Good heavens, John, what's the panic?" her mother inquired in a laughing voice as she rounded the doorway of the dining room, wiping her hands on her apron. She didn't require an answer when she saw

Ted. Having been a nurse before she married, she was instantly all crisp efficiency and bustling concern. "I'll get some warm water and the first-aid kit. Bring him to the kitchen."

Together Jonni and her father took him to the kitchen. Ted walked slowly and a basin of warm water was already on the table, along with clean towels and an antiseptic, when they got there. The first-aid kit was opened and Caroline Starr was removing the items she felt she might need.

When they had him seated in a chair, Caroline handed Jonni a small bottle with its cap removed. "Here, give him a good whiff of this ammonia. That should bring him around."

Jonni held the bottle to his nose. When Ted gasped and started coughing, she took it away. "Enough," he insisted in a more lucid voice.

Moving Jonni aside, her mother took over, wiping the blood from his face and checking the seriousness of his cuts. She asked Ted a list of clinical questions about his vision, his hearing, any dizziness or nausea. Jonni stood beside his chair and watched, exhausted and shivering in her rain-soaked clothes. Her father pressed a cup of steaming coffee into her numb hands.

"He's all right," he said. "You go change out of those wet clothes before you come down with pneumonia. Your mother will see to him."

After a second's hesitation, Jonni submitted to the commanding tone of his voice. She walked out of the room to the stairway to the second floor and her bedroom, nursing the strong, sweet coffee. As she started up the stairs, her father caught up with her.

"What does Gabe look like?" he asked, partly from concern and partly from curiosity.

"What do you think?" Bitterness crept into her voice. "He's hardly got a mark on him." The fight's outcome had been predictable and it still irritated Jonni that Gabe had found it necessary to prove it.

In her bedroom Jonni finished her coffee while the bathtub was filling with hot water. After the bath she toweled her hair damp-dry and changed into a sweater and dry jeans. Half an hour from the time she had left the kitchen, she was walking back downstairs.

Ted was in the living room. A thin strip of bandage covered the cut above his eye. A larger one was on his cheek, but it didn't totally conceal the purpling bruise surrounding the gash. An ice bag was alternately being applied to his cheek and to his split and swollen lip. Jonni paused at the doorway, then walked in.

"How do you feel?" she asked with quiet concern, aware of how he looked.

"The way any man feels when he's on the losing end of a fight," Ted answered testily. "Like a jackass."

"You shouldn't. It was wrong of Gabe to fight you when he knew he could win," Jonni insisted.

"Look at this." He tipped his head back and carefully parted his lips. "One of his punches chipped my front tooth." There was a gap in the row of even white teeth.

"I'm sorry, Ted." Jonni wasn't sure why she was apologizing.

"I'm glad I have a good dentist." He grimaced and pressed the ice bag to his lip. "I'm just sorry I ever picked a fight with him."

"So am I." She stood close to his chair, too ill at ease and upset to sit down.

He caught at her left hand, looking up at her with a warm light in his brown eyes. A smile was too painful for his injured mouth. "At least I have the consolation that his victory was a hollow one. You're here with me."

Jonni wasn't certain it meant anything so she kept silent. His fingers twisted the diamond ring she wore, unnecessarily reminding her that she was engaged to him. He pulled her down to sit on the arm of his chair.

"I suspected all along that Stockman couldn't be trusted. I had a feeling he'd try to make mischief, but it didn't do him any good." Ted was placing all the blame on Gabe and treating Jonni as an innocent participant, which she knew she hadn't been.

"Ted—" Her attempt to correct that misconception was interrupted.

"You don't have to worry about him anymore," he assured her. "I've made arrangements for the chartered plane to pick us up at nine in the morning, and I confirmed our reservations on a New York flight. I've talked to your parents. They understand that it's best, under the circumstances, for you to cut your vacation short."

He was taking it for granted that she wanted to go with him. Since Jonni wasn't sure whether she wanted to or not, she said nothing. There would be time enough to make up her mind between now and tomorrow morning. Ted seemed unperturbed by her silence as he affectionately squeezed her hand.

"Babe, would you mind going into the kitchen, and

seeing if your mother can fix me something to drink, preferably with a straw?" he asked.

"Of course not," she answered, and straightened from the chair, slipping her hand from his light hold.

As she walked to the kitchen Jonni was aware that his touch had done nothing for her. His caress had not sparked a savagely sweet rush of emotions. There had been no odd tremor of excitement.

Her mother was at the kitchen sink peeling potatoes when Jonni walked in. Caroline glanced up, her look faintly anxious. "Ted told us you were leaving in the morning."

"Yes, I know." For the time being, Jonni didn't contradict the statement. "He'd like something to drink. Would you take it into the living room for him?" She continued through the kitchen and paused at the back door where a yellow rain slicker was hanging from a hook.

"Where are you going, Jonni?" A knife and a half-peeled potato were set on the porcelain drain board of the sink.

"I want to see Gabe."

"Is that wise, dear?" Caroline frowned.

"I hope so." Jonni sighed and fastened the last of the snaps before stepping outside into the drizzling rain.

Pulling the vinyl hood over her head, she started off across the path straight for Gabe's living quarters in the renovated bunkhouse. She stopped at the door, fighting the twisting uncertainties in her stomach, and knocked twice, loudly.

"Come in." His voice was muffled by the thickness of the door.

The interior of the bunkhouse was austere. A small kitchenette was on one side, birch cabinets built around the stove, sink and refrigerator. A small wooden table with two chairs stood next to another wall. With the exception of a floor lamp beside a leather recliner, the rest of the space was taken up by a desk and several filing cabinets. A short hallway ended in a closed door. Another door in the hallway stood open. Light streamed out and Jonni heard the sound of running water. She walked toward it, pushing the rain hood back.

Naked from the waist up, Gabe was standing in front of the sink in the bathroom. He didn't turn around when she appeared in the doorway, but glanced into the mirror above the sink where her reflection joined his. Without speaking, he finished rinsing the washcloth, then dabbed it at the cut at the corner of his mouth, wincing slightly. His knuckles were swollen and faintly discolored. On the back of his left hand there was a gash that looked sore and angry.

There was a closed expression on his face. "Did he live?" he asked dryly.

His baiting tone made Jonni snap, "No thanks to you!" The sight of him bare to the waist was making her uneasy. "You broke off part of his front tooth," she said accusingly.

"Really?" Gabe flexed his injured hand as if realizing the source of the wound.

This wasn't the conversation she wanted to have with him at all. She took a calming breath and tried to start again. "Ted is sorry he fought with you."

"He probably is," he agreed smoothly, and reached for a towel to dry his hands. "And by the way, if it crossed your mind that I might ever raise my hand to you—well, I wouldn't. I can see how a woman might think that, but I'm not a fighting man as a rule. I just wanted to let that prick know where I stood, that was all."

There was too much complacency in his response and her temper flared. "You could apologize, too." The blame was just as much his.

Gabe turned around to face her, completely controlled and impassive. "I've never walked up to anybody with my hat in my hand, and I'm not going to start now." A clean shirt was hanging on the doorknob. Picking it up, he slipped a bronze arm in one long sleeve and shrugged into the other. His gaze lightly skimmed her tense face.

She tried to goad some reaction out of him, unable to tell what he was thinking or feeling and needing to know. "Ted is leaving for New York in the morning. He expects me to go with him."

Gabe buttoned his shirt. "Naturally he wants you to go with him. Since you're still wearing his ring, he obviously still considers you his fiancé."

Frustration welled at his noncommittal response. "Don't you care whether I'm leaving with him or not?" Jonni demanded in a faintly desperate voice.

"You know were I stand. The next decision is yours. Either you stay or you go." Gabe tucked his shirt in his pants as if they were discussing some trivial subject instead of their future.

His indifference hurt. She wanted to be told more than just that she knew where he stood. She wanted Gabe to say he loved her and wanted her to stay. She wanted to be persuaded. She wanted him to sweep away any resistance with a blazingly passionate embrace.

"What if I told you I was going?" Jonni challenged.

"Are you?" There wasn't even a flicker of emotion in his steady gaze.

"Yes!" she declared out of sheer contrariness.

"Then there isn't anything more to be said, is there?" A pair of impersonal hands moved her out of the doorway so he could walk past.

Shocked by his calm acceptance of her supposed decision, Jonni could only watch as Gabe walked to his desk. He sat down in a creaking swivel chair and opened a laptop. From a sheaf of notes he began typing down figures in a spreadsheet.

Feeling lost and forlorn, Jonni pulled the yellow hood over her head and walked numbly to the door. Her hand closed over the cold metal of the doorknob.

"Goodbye, Jonni," Gabe said with an air of finality.

"Goodbye."

With a muffled cry like a wounded animal, she jerked open the door and fled into the gray drizzle.

The next morning Jonni stood at the bedroom window overlooking the front of the house. Her clothes were all packed in the suitcases standing at the door waiting to be carried downstairs. It was half-past eight and the chartered plane was due at nine. She'd heard Ted go down fifteen minutes ago but still she waited, nibbling at her forefinger.

At the sound of a motor, her hand came away from her mouth and Jonni brightened anxiously. The pickup truck rolled up to the sidewalk leading to the front door of the house. The driver got out and her heart sank. It was Duffy McNair who would drive them to the airfield, not Gabe. Her last hope faded.

She walked to the hall door, picked up the two lightest suitcases and proceeded down the stairs. Duffy was standing with her father in the entryway. Their voices hushed when she approached.

"Let me take those for you, Jonni." Duffy stepped forward.

"I'll carry these," she insisted. "There are two more, heavier ones, upstairs in my room. I'll let you bring those." She tried to sound light and uncaring, but her voice just sounded weird.

"Be glad to." He began mounting the stairs on bowed legs.

"They're sitting right by the door," she called after him, then turned to her father. "Where's Ted?"

"He took his bags out to the truck. Let me carry one of those for you," he offered.

"No. You aren't supposed to be carrying heavy things," Jonni refused.

"Don't be pampering me," John Starr reproved. "My heart isn't in such bad shape that I can't carry a few tubes of lipstick." With that, he took the cosmetic case from her hand and opened the door. Ted was standing by the truck, along with her mother. Jonni paused at the porch steps while her father closed the front door.

"Where's Gabe?" she asked, trying not to sound too interested as her gaze scanned the ranch buildings "I thought he'd be here this morning to see us off."

"He went to a livestock auction today." John's sidelong look was narrowed and sharply questioning. "I thought you'd said your goodbyes yesterday. Didn't you?"

"We did." Her voice wavered. With gritty determination, Jonni steadied it. "Yes, we did."

A quarter of an hour early, the plane was circling the field to land as Duffy came out of the house with the rest of Jonni's luggage. In a numbed state, Jonni submitted to her mother's hugs, kisses and tears and her father's fierce hug and gruff wish for a safe trip.

Their farewells to Ted were more restrained and less emotional. He looked worse that morning. His bruises had colored into vivid purples and yellows. One quarter of his lip was half again as large as the rest of his mouth. The chipped front tooth added to his battered appearance.

Duffy was careful to avoid looking at Ted when he slid behind the wheel. Jonni suspected Duffy found the sight of that bruised face amusing, but she was too wrapped up in her own misery to care about any slight, implied or otherwise, to Ted.

The ride to the airfield had always seemed such a long one, but this time it was incredibly short. Much too soon, her luggage was being stowed in the baggage compartment of the twin-engine aircraft, its motors idling in readiness for flight. Before she climbed aboard Jonni took one last look, hoping against hope that Gabe would suddenly arrive. When she hesitated, Ted hustled her inside.

Automatically she buckled her seat belt while staring out the window at the hangar. The plane began taxiing and she continued to watch, a tightness closing her throat. At the end of the runway the plane made its roll down the grass strip and lifted off. A few minutes later she saw her parents standing in front of the house and waving at the plane banking northeast.

Ted leaned over. “I know you’ll miss them, but they’ll be coming to New York in less than a month’s time to help you get ready for the wedding.” His hand covered the balled fist in her lap. “We’ll be married soon, honey. The next time we come back here for a visit, you’ll be my wife. And you won’t have to worry about that Gabe Stockman ever bothering you again.”

“Shut up, Ted.” Jonni turned her head and stared out the window, letting the first teardrop fall.

Chapter Ten

The music was loud. It had to be in order to be heard above the noise of an apartment full of people, all laughing and talking at the same time. A portable bar, borrowed from a neighbor, was the center of attention, drawing nearly as big a crowd as the buffet table loaded with snacks and goodies. Streamers draped the ceiling, their festive colors reminding more than one guest of a high school prom. A huge sign hung across one wall; emblazoned on it were the words We'll Miss You, Vickie.

"Excuse me." Jonni inched her way through the crowd around the buffet and added two more platters of finger sandwiches to the assortment of hors d'oeuvres.

"Hey!" As she turned away, someone grabbed her left hand. "What happened to that rock you were wearing? That thing was dazzling. Don't tell me you lost it." Laughing, Dale Barlow, a photographer Jonni had worked with often, wouldn't let go of her hand.

"I returned it." She shrugged diffidently and tried to withdraw her hand from the clasp of his fingers.

She didn't want to remember how difficult it had been to convince Ted she didn't want to marry him.

"Hey, gang!" Dale held her hand aloft. "We may be losing Vickie to the lure of smoggy California, but her roommate, the beautiful Jonni Starr, is footloose and fancy-free again. She's ditched her tycoon, Ted Terrific!"

Jonni winced at the description of her. She wasn't footloose and fancy-free, not by any means. She was too poignantly aware of the mistake she'd made by leaving the ranch instead of staying with Gabe, but her stubbornness had gotten in the way. She wanted to go back, but she needed more courage—more courage and less pride.

"Enough, Dale." She removed her hand from his amidst the cheers that followed his announcement. "You're interfering with the hostess while she's on duty."

"Very well. More champagne and caviar, my good woman," he requested in a falsely deep voice before breaking into laughter.

Presented with the opportunity, Jonni slipped away into the relative quiet of the compact kitchen. She was relieved to be in charge of the farewell party for her roommate. It meant she was occupied with an endless array of things to keep the party running smoothly and didn't have to pretend to be enjoying the festive occasion.

The doorbell rang as she was opening the refrigerator door. Jonni had discovered early on in the evening that her ears seemed to be the only ones attuned to the sound. She removed the shrink-wrapped tray of biscuit wafers topped with caviar and set it on the counter. Smoothing a hand over the front of her long black pinafore gown, she walked back into the crowded living room.

"Jonni! I haven't had a chance to talk to you all evening!" Within seconds of entering the room, Jonni was cornered by a former model friend turned actress. "Don't you have a drink?" The girl turned to the man beside her. "Bob, get Jonni a drink."

"Don't bother, Bob," Jonni refused, and backed toward the door.

"Where are you going?" The girl frowned. "We haven't had a good gossip in ages."

"Later, maybe," Jonni stalled her with a wave, and motioned toward the apartment door. "The doorbell is ringing. Late arrival, I guess."

"It's ringing? How can you tell with all this racket?" The girl laughed.

An answer wasn't required as Jonni smiled and continued on her way to the door. Its buzzing ring came again, insistent in its tone. Jonni schooled her expression into a welcoming smile and opened the door.

Her heart did a somersault and she just stood there, trying to catch her breath. Gabe stood outside—at least it looked like Gabe, unless she was hallucinating. His broad-shouldered frame was clothed in a tailored dark blue suit with a striped tie of blue, gray and gold to blend with the pearl-gray shirt he wore.

The clothes didn't seem to belong to the jeans-clad Western man she knew, but the sun-hardened features looked the same. The neatly trimmed brush of black mustache was there, and the black hair was in its natural casually rakish style, which some men paid the earth to achieve. The bold blackness of his eyes could belong to no one else. Yet Jonni was afraid her own eyes were deceiving her. It had only been two weeks since she'd seen him. How could he have changed so much?

"Gabe?" she questioned hesitantly, half-afraid she would blink and he'd disappear.

"Hello, Jonni." The vibrant, caressing pitch of his voice flowed warmly over her. His gaze strayed behind her to the noisy party. "You've having a party."

"Yes." She was dazed with joy, mesmerized by the sight of him standing there at her door. "It's a farewell party for my roommate. She's moving to California."

"I wish her well. May I come in?" he asked with faint mockery.

A wave of self-consciousness made her blush. She wanted to fling herself into his arms and shut out the party but the moment had passed when she could do that. She opened the door wider and stepped aside.

"Of course, Gabe. You'll have to forgive my manners," she apologized with a nervous laugh. "When I answered the door the last thing I expected was to see you there."

"I wanted to surprise you," Gabe admitted, hardly taking his eyes off her.

"You succeeded. It was the best surprise I've ever had." She remembered how he had said that he once intended to come to New York to bring her home. That had to be why he was here now. It had to be! And her heart soared at the heady implications of that. The shimmer of untold happiness was in her returning look.

Gabe moved closer until there was barely the width of a hand between them. His hands rested in light possession on the curve of her slender waist. They stood in the midst of the party, but Jonni didn't notice anyone but him.

"Your father mentioned that you'd broken your engagement to Ted," he said.

"Yes." Jonni nodded once. "I did. I didn't love him." How could she, when she had fallen with love with Gabe? She would have told Gabe that, but a guest intruded into their intimate conversation . . . a female guest.

"Leave it to you, Jonni, to snare the handsomest hunk of man at the party," the woman chided. She turned to Gabe, her red mouth curving into an alluring smile. "I'm Cynthia Sloane."

"It's a pleasure, Miss Sloane." Gabe nodded politely to the woman and slid an arm around Jonni's waist to draw her to his side.

"Aren't you going to introduce him to me, Jonni?" the woman prompted.

"This is Gabe Stockman. He's"—Jonni was unsure how to identify him—"the general manager of my father's ranch and other, um, holdings." Jonni managed a somewhat incoherent introduction.

"Gabe." The brunette repeated the name, rolling it over as if tasting it. "Is that short for Gabriel—as in Gabriel, come blow my horn?" she asked with deliberate suggestiveness.

"No, it's Gabe, short for Gable as in Clark," Gabe stated in a tone that wasn't amused. "You'll have to excuse us, Miss Sloane. I have some family business to discuss with Jonni."

"Oh. Lucky Jonni," the woman replied with a pout of envy before she moved away.

Jonni did feel lucky—extraordinarily so. And proud, too. Cynthia had made her aware of the admiring looks Gabe was receiving from the other, less bold female guests at the party. She'd never seen him in a group before. All the other men paled in comparison, lacking that inborn air of command.

"Is there someplace we can talk where we won't be interrupted?" Gabe asked, bending his head to speak low in her ear. "I'd suggest the dance floor, but"—Jonni giggled, because his mustache tickled—"what I had in mind was slow dancing where you just sway to the music. It won't work with what's playing now."

"Hardly," Jonni agreed. The pounding of drums vibrated through the room like the magnified sound of a heartbeat. Her own pulse was matching the song's tempo. "We could try the kitchen," she suggested.

"Lead the way." Gabe's hand remained on the curve of her waist as Jonni moved ahead of him through the crowd. Once they were inside the kitchen the closed door muffled most of the loud party sounds. "Aren't you worried that one of the neighbors will complain about the noise?"

"It's all taken care of." Jonni smiled mischievously. "I invited all the neighbors to the party. If they're making the noise, they can't very well complain about it."

"That's smart." He chuckled.

"Yes." Her smile faded into wonderment as she surveyed Gabe anew. He looked so self-assured and relaxed in the clothes that seemed so out of character. "I've never seen you dressed like that before. You look different. Natural, but . . ." Jonni couldn't explain it.

"When in Rome." Gabe shrugged away the rest of the cliché.

It was Jonni who was unsure. She glanced around the kitchen, feeling a little confined by the smallness of the room—but liking the privacy. "Would you like something to drink?" She assumed her role as hostess since she wasn't sure what other one to play. "The refrigerator is stocked with just about everything."

"I'm thirsty." He drew her toward him, his gaze shifting to her moist lips. "Like a man in the desert sun."

With a moan of surrender Jonni met his descending mouth. Her arms wound around his neck while his encircling arms crushed her against his length. She loved it—absolutely loved it. If he wanted to take her right here, she would be tempted to let him, but—

"Jonni!" The kitchen door opened and a blonde came bouncing in. "Oops! Sorry," she apologized as the pair broke apart.

Flushed and glowing, Jonni ran a self-conscious hand along her neck. "Was there something you wanted, Babs?"

"Mac is almost out of ice at the bar. He sent me out here to get some. You just tell me where to find it and you two can go back to doing your thing," the girl assured them with a knowing look.

The embrace had been too torrid for Jonni to resume it in front of someone else, even if that someone else did look the other way. Besides, she felt an odd shyness about behaving so boldly with Gabe. Being with him robbed her of her poise. She slipped the rest of the way out of his arms. Her gaze skittered away from the glittering amusement she saw in his dark eyes.

"The bags of ice are in the coolers." Jonni walked to the insulated ice chests sitting on the floor near the table. "I'll help you. How many do you need?"

"I'd better take three." Long, blond hair swung forward as the girl bent over while Jonni started dragging the bags of ice from the cooler. Babs nearly dropped the third one Jonni handed her, but rescued it at the last instant.

"Can you handle all that?" Jonni frowned.

"Sure," the girl insisted, and winked, "Have fun, you two!"

It wasn't that easy to walk back to Gabe after the woman had left. He was standing by the counter where she'd left the plate of caviar hors d'oeuvres. He had sampled one and was staring at the bite-size piece still left in his hand.

"What is this?" He flashed her a wary look.

"Caviar."

"Huh. So that's what caviar tastes like." A raised eyebrow indicated that he had expected something better. "You might have warned me that fish eggs are salty."

"The next time I will," she promised, relaxing slightly at the banter. "Caviar is an acquired taste, I think, like snails. Vickie, my roommate, loves caviar. I prefer peanut butter on my crackers."

"I'll remember that," said Gabe in a voice that made her heart completely skip a beat. But he didn't pursue that happy implication. Instead he walked toward the refrigerator. "I think I'll take you up on that offer of a drink."

"Help yourself," Jonni said, even though he was already doing so.

Holding the refrigerator door open, he held up a bottle of Perrier. "What's this?"

"Water," she told him.

"Imported from France?" He frowned with skeptical amusement.

"It's very popular," Jonni grinned. "It's usually served with a twist."

"And that's all?" he mocked, and twisted off the cap.

"That's all."

"It's water all right," Gabe said after taking a swallow. "Sour-tasting water. Wait 'til I tell the boys in the bunkhouse I was brave enough to down some Perrier and caviar, though."

"That's real uptown," she laughed, then found herself wondering. "When did you get here? Why didn't you let me know you were coming?"

"I wanted to surprise you." Gabe answered the last question first. "My plane arrived three days ago."

She shot him an astonished look, suddenly confused. "I hope you don't expect me to believe that you've been lost for three days, because you never get lost. Where have you been? Why haven't you come to see me before now?" To think he had been in New York three whole days, and she hadn't known. It was something Jonni didn't understand.

"No, I haven't been lost." He studied the bottle for a moment before lifting his black gaze to her. "I've been touring New York, visiting all the places you mentioned in your letters home—Wall Street, the Statue of Liberty, Times Square, Central Park. I've been to a couple of Broadway shows, a concert at Carnegie Hall, the museums, eaten at the best restaurants."

"And?" Jonni prompted when he paused.

"And I've come to the conclusion that it's a great place to visit." Gabe set the bottle on the counter. There was something final about the gesture.

"But you wouldn't want to live here," Jonni finished the common ending to his statement. "No, I don't think you would, either."

"I need space around me," said Gabe, and she could almost see his broad shoulders trying to make room in the small kitchen. "I need room to breathe. I want dirt beneath my boots, red Kansas dirt, not concrete. I don't belong here, Jonni. It's as simple as that."

"I know what you mean." There was an air of serenity about her expression. It was the same discovery she had made since returning to New York. This wasn't the place she wanted to live for the rest of her life, and not just because Gabe wasn't here. She started to tell him that. "I—"

"Hey, Jonni, there you are!" The kitchen door burst open and a couple hurried in. The man was short and fairly stout. The girl with him was beanpole-tall and coltishly attractive. She was the one doing the talking. "We've been looking all over for you. Come on!"

The urgency in her demand moved Jonni toward them. "What's wrong? Has something happened?"

"Nothing's wrong," the girl sighed with exasperation. "Vickie is getting ready to open her presents and she won't do it until you're there. So come on."

Jonni glanced helplessly at Gabe. "I'm the one who's giving the party for her. I should be there," she offered in defense of the request. "Are you coming in, too?"

"No, you go ahead," he suggested with a nod, indicating that it was all right with him. "It's where you belong."

Unwilling but feeling obligated by the friendship with her roommate, Jonni allowed herself to be marched into the living room by the oddly matched pair. She was immediately pushed into the center of the party to join in the fun of watching her roommate open presents that were sometimes outrageous, sometimes practical and often imaginative.

Nearly an hour had passed before Jonni could steal away and return to the kitchen. She stopped abruptly inside the empty room. Thinking it was possible that Gabe might have joined the party after all, she went back inside the living room and searched through the crowd of people.

There wasn't any sign of Gabe. A wave of desolation washed over her. She pressed a hand to her mouth to hold back the sob of panic and scanned the happy throng. There wasn't anyone that she could even mistake for Gabe.

"Hey, Jonni, what's wrong?" Babs, the girl who had come into the kitchen for the ice, was frowning at her with concern. "Don't you feel well?"

"It's Gabe, the man who was in the kitchen with me," Jonni explained, trying to keep her voice calm. "Have you seen him?"

"No."

"I can't believe he'd leave without telling me," Jonni protested.

"When did you see him last?" Babs asked.

"In the kitchen. I came out here when Vickie was about to open her presents. I went back in after she was done and he wasn't there." Jonni's voice broke slightly on the last word.

"Did he say he'd wait for you? Or tell you anything?" the other woman quizzed.

"No, he just said for me to go ahead and join the party," Jonni recalled. "He said it was where I belonged."

"Meaning what?" Babs smiled wryly. "That you

didn't belong with him? That's a strange thing to say."

"He didn't mean that." Jonni started to shake her head to say that the idea was foolish, then a frightening thought struck her. "Did he? Just few minutes before that we were talking about New York and he said he didn't belong here. Babs, he *has* left," Jonni said. "He's left to go home, home to Kansas."

"Jonni, I'm sorry," the girl sympathized, and laid a consoling arm on Jonni's shoulders. But Jonni had already come to a decision and was moving away. "Hey, where are you going?"

"Give my apologies to everyone at the party. I'm going to be busy packing," Jonni told her. "I'm going home, too."

By the time she had packed what she would need Jonni had missed the last plane for Kansas City that night. The next day's planes were all booked. Two days had gone by before she finally got a flight and made the connection to the charter company. Below her now were the red hills of the Starr Ranch.

Jonni leaned forward to tap the pilot on the shoulder. "Buzz the house."

He banked the plane toward the ranch buildings. "This run is becoming a regular thing for us," he shouted back to her. "Maybe the company should start a commuter airline service!"

"This is my last trip here," she told him. "I'm coming to a full stop this time."

The plane flew low over the buildings. The horses in the corral shied and bolted in circles around the enclosure. As the plane climbed up to landing pattern altitude, Jonni saw a familiar figure step out of the barn. A smile began lighting her face.

When the plane turned on its final approach, the pickup truck was racing and bouncing over the rutted track to the airfield. Jonni's heart was thumping so loudly she could hear it above the drone of the motors. The wheels touched down and she was home.

She was sitting on the edge of her seat as the plane taxied to the metal hangar. Gabe was standing beside the pickup, waiting. There were tears of unabashed happiness in Jonni's eyes. She could barely see to climb out of the aircraft. The pilot helped her to the ground.

Gabe continued to stand there. He didn't come forward to meet her. Jonni took the first hesitant step toward him, then another and another. Then she heard his voice, his rich, vibrant voice say, "It's about time you came home."

Jonni broke into a run, flinging herself into his arms to be lifted high in the air while Gabe kissed her and whirled her around in boundless joy.

"You're back where you belong, girl," he said huskily.

"I know. With you. For the rest of my life."

"Our life. You ready for it?" He kissed her again, until she was breathless.

"Yes. Oh, yes," was her answer.